The Salamander Stone

Endorsements

"In Heidi Nickerson's *The Salamander Stone*, every monster once had a heart. Teenage self-discovery has life-or-death consequences in this action-packed story of magic, mystery, heartbreak, and friendship."

—**Marta Acosta**, Award-winning author of Marvel's *She-Hulk Diaries* and *Dark Companion*

"If you've ever felt like an unspeakable monster in a sea of regular folks, then this book is made for you. If you've never felt that way? Okay, we all know you're lying. Fast, funny, and weird in the best way, *The Salamander Stone* has the extremely messed up teen angst you're looking for."

—**Travis Baldree**, author of *Legends & Lattes*

"A rich and packed story in which the supernatural aspects blend with the unnerving reality of our world to perfection. It cleverly uses fantasy to expose the absurd flaws of humanity and I'm here for it."

—**Lumaga**, Creator of the Webtoon Original *Four Leaf*

THE SALAMANDER STONE

(Beowulf Brigade Series)

HEIDI A NICKERSON

WITH ILLUSTRATIONS BY Io NOMYCIN

M·J

NEW YORK

LONDON • NASHVILLE • MELBOURNE • VANCOUVER

THE SALAMANDER STONE

Published in New York, New York, by Morgan James Publishing. Morgan James is a trademark of Morgan James, LLC. www.MorganJamesPublishing.com

Proudly distributed by Ingram Publisher Services.

ISBN 9781631959967 paperback
ISBN 9781631959974 ebook
Library of Congress Control Number: 2022943428

Cover and Interior Design by:
Chris Treccani
www.3dogcreative.net

Disclaimer/Author's Note

This book includes myths and folklore from a variety of sources (primarily European) that feature shapeshifting and transformation. I am a particular fan of foxes and enjoy stories of the Japanese Kitsune and the Korean Kumiho (or Gumiho)—foxes/fox spirits with magical abilities. For a story set in modern-day North America, I wanted to feature the variety of foxes that are native to the United States in order to direct the reader's attention to predator control programs of the 1930's that nearly killed off all swift foxes, as well as fur farming practices that still exist today.

I do not own these myths, and I recognize that borrowing stories from other people groups can cause harm even with the best of intentions. I hope that my writing represents these stories with respect, honor, and complexity.

Also, this story discusses mental illness, told specifically through the lens of my own understanding (and my personal struggles). I do not claim to speak for anyone else who struggles with depression, anxiety, or any other mental battle. I only strive to share what I've experienced, with the hope of connecting with others.

Finally, this story shows a mild amount of violence and gore (both against humans and animals) for the purpose of encouraging empathy between all living things.

For my grandparents, who taught the importance of sharing stories over a large slice of pie.

"In off the moors, down through the mist bands
God-cursed Grendel came greedily loping.
The bane of the race of men roamed forth,
hunting for a prey"

—*Beowulf,* Seamus Heaney (trans.)

"I look down, down, into bottomless blackness, feeling the dark power moving in me like an ocean current, some monster inside me, deep sea wonder, dread night monarch astir in his cave, moving me slowly to my voluntary tumble into death."

—*Grendel,* John Gardner

"I knew the apathetic, cold look I needed to wear on my face to survive.
. . . The day I finally left [home] was at the end of fall. I had been watching the sky for months. . . . Funny thing is, I had been packing since I was fourteen."

—*Cyndi Lauper: A Memoir,* Cyndi Lauper

Chapter One

Ellie

When I was nine months old, my mother left me in a booth at Denny's.

Grandpa picked me up an hour later, of course. Says he found me sitting with a waitress behind the counter, happy as a clam while the nice lady fed me mashed potatoes and peas. He made excuses to the police officer filing a report, trying to convince him that it wasn't necessary. My mother was just being forgetful that day.

"You know how new parents are," he'd said. "She's probably just overtired."

Then Grandpa packed me up in the car and drove home, fully expecting my mother to be there when he pulled in.

She wasn't.

She didn't come back for thirty-nine days.

Nobody knows where she was or why she left; all they know is that she was gone for over a month, and the first thing she did after driving back into town was park at that same Denny's and run in, demanding to know where I was.

When the waitstaff refused to tell her, she threw a chair through a plate-glass window.

Initially, this incident only appeared on a few local news stations. It wasn't until a bigger newspaper picked up the story with the headline, "New Hampshire Woman Orders a Baby at Local Denny's: Breaks Window After Trying the Chicken-Fried Steak," that the story went viral. It gained national attention overnight, and waves of people online began calling for my mother's head on a Grand Slam Platter.

The public outcry for retribution was heard and swiftly granted. Not wanting the bad press, our local police force strong-armed their way into my grandparents' home to find Roen Adair, my mother, shriveled up in the corner, clearly suffering from a psychotic break. The courts declared her mentally unfit, and she was hauled away to the looney bin.

I was too young to remember any of this happening at the time, so I only know what I've been told. It was my grandmother who finally whispered the truth:

"Something's been wrong with your mama since the day you were born. Sick in the head, like she caught a disease when you came out because you just cried and cried and cried."

My mother told the courts that it was my fault she left, that I was born wrong, with something insidious in my bones waiting to burst forth and destroy.

She couldn't sit around and watch it happen. That's why she ran off. That's what the stenographer recorded from her testimony, anyway.

Now she's locked high in a tower, high on her meds, floating around in her head so that she can forget the ugliness she created. The rotten fruit she bore that dropped too soon and too soundly.

She's been refusing visitors at the mental health facility ever since my sixteenth birthday. That's the reason Grandpa gave when he stopped visiting her last month, anyway.

"They won't let anyone in to see her. Sorry, Ellie."

Ellie. Short for Elijah.

Seriously, it's on my birth certificate. She and my father liked the name Elijah for a boy, so when my father died just months before I was born, no one could convince my mother to name me anything else.

"I'll try calling her tomorrow," Grandpa said. "Maybe things will be different in a few weeks."

The details surrounding my father's death still gnaw at me, no matter how much court-ordered counseling I'm forced to attend. His body was never found; all that was left at the scene of the crash was his car, twisted around a tree on the side of a highway. And yet, after only a few weeks of labeling him as a missing person, the local police closed my father's case due to a lack of new leads, and he was marked legally dead.

And the world moved on.

"He's gone, kid." Grandpa would say, "That's all that matters. Waiting for a missing person to come home . . . that stuff will ruin your life."

I've never wanted to stop looking into my father's disappearance, but when there's no new information, it's hard to keep searching. Sixteen silent years and all that remains of my broken family is my grandfather: a man who does his best, who raised me for ten years with my grandmother's help, and another six alone, after she passed.

Grandpa and I get along well enough. I just wish I wasn't such a discarded leftover for him to have to worry about.

"Can I get a scoop of almond chocolate coconut ripple?"

I glance up from beneath my visor to find a pair of girls standing outside of the takeaway window. The one who spoke first teeters back and forth on her toes while reading the menu.

Before I can grab a pen, she continues, "In a cup. And a scoop of toffee crunch?"

I finally locate a nearby pad and write down her order. "Anything else?"

The first girl nudges her friend, who hasn't looked up from her phone since they arrived. "Hey, what do you want?"

The second girl glances at me, then up at the menu without reading. She asks, "What's good here?"

Fighting back annoyance, I recite my corporate training in an even tone:

"Here at Howard's Frozen Treats, we have ice cream, sherbet, sorbet, and Italian ice. You can have it scooped into a cone or in a cup."

I purposely omit that we can also make milkshakes or sundaes, since I've already cleaned and restocked half of the store in an effort to leave early, and the milkshake machine is a pain to clean.

But it doesn't matter what I say—she's not listening. Instead, she takes my reply as a cue to finally read the menu. As if I, an employee of this fine establishment, am not a trustworthy source of ice cream knowledge.

She finally settles on something and asks, "Can I get a milkshake with any ice cream flavor? What about key lime pie?"

Sighing, I scoop the ice cream without making too much of a mess and hand it through the takeout window.

The girls scamper to a bench to discuss whoever's been texting them about a party happening later tonight, and I shuffle back to the milkshake machine, glaring at its existence.

Cyndi emerges from the breakroom, smelling like clove cigarettes.

"Heya champ, working hard or hardly working?" she says, opening a nearby freezer and dipping a plastic spoon into an ice cream bucket inside. She takes a bite.

"It's confirmed. Black raspberry is the greatest flavor of all time."

She takes another bite and points the spoon at me. "Wait, I already cleaned the milkshake machine. Did somebody just order one?"

"Yup," I say, rinsing off the machine's parts.

"But it's two minutes 'til closing."

"Yup," I repeat and unplug the machine. "But now I'm all done, so let's turn off the sign, split the tips, and go home."

Bear, our shift supervisor, steps out from the back with a freshly counted cash drawer. His starched polo shirt and pleated khakis are essential for his costume of authority—something that would be more effective if he weren't only seventeen.

"The drawer looks good for this register." He says, oblivious to Cyndi's recent smoke break. "I'll count the other one now."

His gaze goes to the order window. "Wait. Have either of you helped that guy?"

Cyndi and I turn suddenly to see the dark shadow of a man looming at the order window.

The stranger's sudden appearance causes Cyndi to drop her spoon, which falls in a quiet plop at our feet. Her remaining dollop of ice cream puddles onto the tile floor.

I look to her, and then to Bear, before slowly walking up to the counter. "Um, sir, we're right about to close."

When I reach the window, I notice the man's features and freeze. Dark stringy hair hangs over his eyes, which he pushes back with a hand containing long, splintered fingernails. His pale complexion is colored with bruises and scratches that extend down his neck. He appears to be no older than thirty, but if I didn't know any better . . .

"Please." He murmurs before reaching into his wallet and handing me a card. "I just need a quart of your sorbet."

The card he hands to me is a New Hampshire state driver's license. It reports that he's blood type V, approved to receive blood for dietary reasons.

Vampire.

Before I answer him, I step away from the window, grab a taster spoon, and scoop out some of our Impossiblood™ sorbet. It's a newer product we offer that contains hema, a blood substitute for vampires attempting to follow more sustainable and ethical diets.

"Would you like to try some first?" I offer.

This sort of visit has become increasingly normal for us. Our store is one of the few in the area to actively support vampires since the CIA exposed that vampire cult in Arizona a few years back. The news story ran for weeks until vampire communities across the globe "stepped into the sun," hoping to cooperate with their countries' governments and avoid unnecessary bloodshed. Cultural tensions have been high ever since, but with labs working on vegan alternatives to human blood, it's been easier for vampires to adjust their diets.

Our store's decision to offer the Impossiblood™ sorbet wasn't meant as a sign of vampire support as much as it was about making more money. Howard's is part of a national chain of ice cream stands, and our CEO didn't want to miss the opportunity to be one of the first shops to offer a product that vampires could eat without having to hunt animals or humans.

Vampires have been the least of our town's concerns lately, anyway. About a year ago, a massive meteor shower colored the landscape of the planet, with meteorites the size of small cars landing all over the world. New Hampshire had a few nasty ones hit the side of Mount Washington, which destroyed dozens of trees and walking trails.

The arrival of space rocks was unexpected, but news outlets moved on from the story quickly enough—at least until the flies, hornets, and locusts started growing in size, causing problems with crops and livestock. Soon after, the occasional reports of animal attacks would get attention, with mountain lions, bears, and alligators being seen more frequently in neighborhoods and shopping malls.

Those occurrences were strange, but not impossible.

What was impossible, but most certainly happened, was when a manticore appeared in Times Square and ate a group of seventh-graders on a field trip.

Experts called it a Supernatural Tectonic Disruption, theorizing that the meteorites impacted Earth's evolutionary cycle enough to create an excess of beasts and mythological creatures running amok in everyday society.

The world has a few hotspots of activity on this front, with repeated stories of the Loch Ness monster attacking boats in Scotland, packs of werewolves hunting near Canadian campsites, and possible dragon sightings coming in from just about everywhere. But with even the smallest towns across America reporting beast attacks, the government has been on high alert, trying to inform citizens of the best tactics to use when facing these new threats to their way of life.

Vampires, looking for a way to strengthen peace between themselves and humans, have offered to lend a hand wherever they can. It doesn't benefit anyone for human life to be lost so swiftly, so humans and vampires have formed a hesitant alliance—to better protect their neighborhoods.

The dark-haired gentleman in front of me nods in gratitude as he takes the taster spoon from my hand. Upon taking a bite of Impossiblood™ sorbet, he instantly relaxes, and the color returns to his face. I give him a cup of sorbet to eat while I pack his quart.

Most people are scrambling to survive, with cities being declared outright war zones and suburban families hiding indoors as much as possible, clutching their kitchen knives. But for those of us out in the middle of nowhere, we can't live frozen in fear. We have to adapt, or else we die—that's what Grandpa keeps saying, anyway.

"Everyone's gone soft, and no one remembers how to think without their phones. What happens when those phones stop getting service? What happens when you look up 'how to kill a man-eating centaur' and there's zero search results? As for me, I'll just keep buying firearms with silver bullets and sharpening my throwing axes. Which reminds me. We need to visit the smith in town and get you some real monster-hunting gear."

I hand the gentleman vampire his sorbet of genetically modified blood, but just as he's about to pay, he pauses.

"Do you hear that?"

I strain my ear to listen, and sure enough, there's rustling in the bushes behind him.

He freezes. Bear, Cyndi, and I do the same.

The two girls on the bench keep chattering away, oblivious.

"There'll be a bonfire in the woods after the game tonight," the first one mentions between bites of ice cream. "Nadia's boyfriend stole some beer from his dad's fridge, so it might get pretty wild."

The bush is shaking now.

The second girl scoffs, "Honestly, I don't get the appeal of beer. It tastes like pee and has a ton of calories." She sips her key lime pie milkshake, unaware of the rustling bush to her right. "I'll probably just smoke someone's vape and chill."

A flame salamander, about as tall as a horse, suddenly slithers out from the bushes. The creature is made of stone and magma and flame, with glowing eyes and a thumping, threatening tail, heavy enough to flatten a car.

The two girls immediately pull their feet up onto the bench and grab hold of each other, terrified. To their credit, they don't scream. Rather, they hold their breath until one of them can't take it any longer and begins to sob.

I don't blame her. There's nowhere to run.

The salamander slinks toward them, hissing and crackling with each step. Noxious, sulfuric smoke billows from its mouth, a warning of the flames to come.

I remove a frequent customer punch card from below the counter and show it to the vampire, who's motionless in the window, holding his sorbet.

"Here." I shove the card into his palm. "If you can save their lives, your next three quarts are free."

He looks back only for a moment. "And you'll replace this one."

I roll my eyes, frustrated. "Yes, sure, whatever. Just do something!"

Without another word, the vampire opens his quart of sorbet and launches it at the salamander. It crumples on impact, spilling its contents across the animal's shoulder.

The salamander wails as sorbet sizzles and melts into its skin; its red-hot scales cool to black beneath the layer of frozen blood substitute.

Then, with the monster distracted, our friendly neighborhood vampire rushes to the girls, collects them in his arms like dolls, and proceeds to race across the parking lot.

As he runs away, I can hear the vampire yell, "I'll be back for my sorbet once you've taken care of that thing!"

I sigh and try to keep a watchful eye on the flame salamander while glancing back at Cyndi and Bear. "What do you think we should do?"

Cyndi shrugs. "Run?"

"We can't do that!" Bear whines. "The owners just promoted me to shift manager! If I let the store burn down, they'll demote me for sure!"

Cyndi throws her arms up in mock horror, "Oh no! Not your extra two dollars an hour!"

Still fighting to regain its faculties, the salamander spins around in a circle and sets a bench on fire.

"Okay, no time to argue," I yell, "Cyndi, call the fire department. Bear, can you take all the empty buckets from the back and fill them with ice from the machine? If we can throw enough ice on the monster, maybe it'll run away."

While they get to work, I run to the utility closet, grab the hose we use for watering plants, and race back outside to find the water spigot. I screw the hose in place and turn the handle before returning to the storefront.

My head tells me to get back inside, to help Bear and Cyndi fill the buckets with ice, or at the very least to tell them my idea and wait for their input. But the sound of the salamander's violent destruction is compelling me to action. It demands that I ignore logic's nagging voice while it lists the many reasons I shouldn't do what I'm about to do.

I peek around the corner, hose sprayer in hand.

The salamander has paused in its fiery destruction long enough to eat our "flavor of the week" display. The sign has always bothered me, as it's cut in the shape of a little boy with chocolate ice cream covering his mouth and chin, proclaiming, "Yum! Today I'll have (the flavor of the week)!" with an expression of terrifying, unblinking glee. At least, that was the cardboard boy's expression, until the salamander removed its head.

Can't say it's not an improvement.

While the salamander takes a bite of the sign's torso, I crouch behind it with the hose. I can't get too close, in case it starts to charge, but if I'm too far away then the water won't properly douse it.

If I can just get a little closer . . .

My foot hits a branch, previously attached to the now smoking hedge. The dry, crispy twig lets out a loud crunch.

At the sound, the flame salamander swings to face me. It chomps down on the cardboard remnants in its mouth and bares its teeth, just ten feet away. Flames dance atop its forked tongue.

This is it. If I don't do it now, I'll quite literally be toast.

I squeeze the sprayer as hard as I can, aiming right between the salamander's eyes, and hear a click. Then nothing.

Shaking the sprayer, I see it's locked in the "OFF" position.

"Why does that button even exist?!"

There's no time to fix it. I glance up with seconds to dodge the fireball hurtling toward me.

Tossing the hose aside, I jump to the left and stumble into the bushes.

The salamander follows, fast and violent and determined to chase me down.

I try to push up from the ground, to run away, but staring down the fire-breathing beast has turned my legs into useless, numb appendages.

I look at the storefront just in time to see Cyndi through the takeout window, phone to her ear, mouth agape.

It's been fun, I guess.

The salamander corners me and opens its large jaws before letting out a bellowing, earth-shifting roar. The heat emanating from its mouth blisters my cheeks.

I squint back into the hot coals of its eyes, uncomfortably warm but otherwise unafraid.

If I die here, will anyone notice?

Will anyone miss me?

Will anyone care?

Then I let out a roar of my own, louder and more guttural than expected.

To my surprise, the salamander stops and closes its mouth.

It stares back at me, motionless.

Before I can react, Bear and Cyndi rush in from my right, each carrying a five-gallon "Safe-T-Ice" bucket. They empty the translucent blue buckets of ice—ergonomically designed for easy pouring from any height—onto the overgrown lizard.

The salamander screeches in freezing, icy pain and sloughs off a section of scales before slithering into a nearby sewer drain.

"Are you okay?" Cyndi grabs my shoulders, shaking me back into focus.

It takes a few seconds for my eyes to shift away from the blurry, red-hot outline of the salamander, or where the salamander just stood. "Yeah. I think so, anyway."

She playfully knocks off my visor. "What were you thinking? Trying to take on that thing by yourself? With the hose?!"

"I just thought . . . "

Bear claps a hand on my shoulder. "I'm glad you're not hurt. Let's clean up what we can and give animal control a call before we leave. The fire department said they'd be here in a few minutes."

I nod, rubbing my eyes in disbelief. I'm not sure what possessed me to take on the beast alone, but the impulse struck with no time for me to think it through.

Cyndi and Bear walk back inside, leaving me alone on the patio. I watch as moths and other bugs hover around our ever-glowing neon sign, occasionally ramming their bodies into the neat lettering of "Howard's Frozen Treats."

Behind me, the wind gently whistles through the trees, knocking a few leaves into my hair. I pull them out and remember my visor, pushed off by Cyndi, now sitting on the concrete next to the pile of shed salamander skin.

I take a few cautious steps forward, worried that disrupting the molten scales might inspire the salamander to return, and lift the brim of my visor. Something glows beneath it.

A reddish-yellow ember, similar in size and shape to a quarter, but not as thin, lies on the ground at my feet. It looks red-hot, but I press a finger to its surface anyway.

To my surprise, it's smooth and cool.

I gather the stone in my hand just in time to see the reddish light fade to matte black, not unlike how the salamander's magma-coated scales cooled against the ice. It remains black as I turn it over in my hand a few times.

Curious, I readjust my visor, turn back to the ice cream shop, and slide the mysterious stone into my pocket.

Chapter Two

Ellie

"Bear's parents just called—he needs to pick up his brother from that bonfire thing tonight. Let's crash it with him after this."

By "this," Cyndi means answering questions from the police, fire department, and animal control while trying to close up the store and field phone calls from the store branch owners.

Bear is still in the back room with the fire chief, reviewing the damage report they suggest we send to the insurance company. It's unclear if the branch owners filed for supernatural creature coverage and what that would even cover, but the salamander only left minor damage to the front siding, hedges, and a few benches, so Howard's Frozen Treats should be able to reopen in a few days.

Great. Just in time for my next shift.

I rinse off the last ice cream scoop and place it on the drying rack.

"A bonfire in the woods? Really? You haven't played with enough fire today?"

Cyndi laughs and throws a towel at me before she grabs her backpack.

"You can bring the hose if you want, Smokey the Bear, but I'm changing out of this uniform before we leave. I brought some extra clothes in case you need something."

I scoff. "What, you don't think our peers will appreciate my khakis and visor?"

"I mean, you can wear that, but you'll look like a turd sandwich if you do."

"Good point. What do you have in there?"

She opens her bag to reveal some t-shirts, flannels, and a plastic baggie with different options for her 00-gauge ear piercings. I recognize a Dashboard Confessional band tee amongst her offerings.

"Wait a minute." I furrow my brow in annoyance. "This is my shirt!"

I take back my t-shirt and grab an additional flannel.

"Now you're not getting this back for a month. Let's see how you like it."

"Fine, fine." Cyndi pulls out an orange striped tee and a green neon windbreaker. "You can keep that one if you want."

She digs into the bottom of her backpack to pull out a pair of bright pink Doc Martens, "The better to fight the patriarchy with," as well as a pair of black jeans. Cyndi's always reveled in loud, graphic patterns and even louder accessories, as anyone could see from her bright red-orange hair and sharp, painted nails.

My color palette is more muted than Cyndi's, but I don't mind. I'm most comfortable in darker neutrals like black, blue, and dark green. That's why I dyed my boring brown hair black last month when Grandpa wasn't home.

Once the officials drive away and Bear says we're ready to close up, Cyndi and I take turns getting dressed. I finish first, walking out of the restroom as I tuck the oversized band tee into the jeans I brought from home. I don't have shoes to change into, but I doubt the slip-on sneakers from my uniform will offend a group of tipsy high schoolers in the woods.

While Cyndi gets changed, I stand near the door, wondering if I should wear the flannel over my t-shirt or tied around my waist. I notice Bear checking his phone every few seconds.

"You two are taking forever," he says, grabbing a shirt from his bag. "If I don't get home before midnight, my parents will kill me."

I roll my eyes. "Bear, do you ever do anything you want to do?"

He thinks for a minute. "Sometimes, when I'm supposed to be studying physics, I study calculus instead."

"You're building a robot in your garage, aren't you?"

"What? Listen, turn around so that I can change my shirt."

I turn toward the front of the store, dimly lit by the blue glow of the industrial freezers. Beyond the takeout window, I see our friendly vampire chatting happily with the two girls from earlier. One of them laughs along to whatever joke the vampire might have remembered from the 1800s while her friend, the one who previously ordered the milkshake, walks up to the window.

Milkshake girl notices my change of attire, "Oh, sorry, are you closed?"

I nod. "Yep. We're closed. Sorry."

She glances behind her. "Oh. Vlad just mentioned that you might have something for him to take home."

"Right. Give me a second." I walk over to the freezer holding the vampire's quarts of Impossiblood™ sorbet and place them into a to-go bag.

Upon returning to the window, I notice a faint red stain on the girl's collar. The whites of her eyes are red and irritated.

I hand her the bag of sorbet through the takeout window.

"Are you and your friend . . . okay?" I ask, wanting to intervene despite my normal role as "aloof teenager number 4."

She nods enthusiastically. "Yes! And thank you for asking Vlad to save us when you did. If he hadn't grabbed us . . . Well, I don't know what would have happened."

Despite my attempt to listen to the girl's story, I can't help moving my eyes from her dilated pupils to the red mark on her collar, growing in size.

"That's great, " I say, grabbing a napkin. "Here. You're bleeding."

"Huh? Oh that." She takes the napkin from me and rushes to apply it to her neck, embarrassed.

"Thanks. Yeah, after he saved us, Vlad mentioned how hungry he was—he's a vegetarian and all. I guess no grocery stores around here have food for him. How sad is that?"

I purse my lips. "Uh-huh."

"So, he asked if we wouldn't mind donating some blood. I'm surprised! It didn't hurt one bit!"

I offer a noncommittal nod and bite down on the words bubbling up in my chest. I want to warn her, to launch into an after-school special about how being polite to someone is not the same as inviting them into your life, and how consent isn't possible with a vampire, since vampires can easily manipulate their prey.

Because that's all humans are anymore: vulnerable, scurrying prey obsessed with keeping themselves busy until something larger and more powerful eats them for lunch.

But I'm not stupid enough to bring that up with a vampire in earshot. Drawing attention to those issues might make things more dangerous for the girls and myself, and I'm too drained to fight off another threat tonight.

Instead, I ask, "Are you two going home after this?"

The girl cocks her head at me in confusion. "Um . . . maybe. Why?"

"I overheard your friend chatting about the bonfire earlier. It looks like my coworker is driving over there now, too, so if you need a ride . . . "

At that, she perked up. "Oh, right! We have a car, so don't worry about us. Hey Sara!" She yells over her shoulder, "We should probably head over to the bonfire now!"

We both look to see Vlad whispering something in Sara's ear, while Sara poorly suppresses a giggle.

The girl in front of me laughs. "We'll figure it out. Thanks for the ice cream!"

"No . . . problem," I say, but the nameless girl is already bouncing away. Hopefully, she and her friend return home safe tonight, instead of becoming another face on the news. I sigh and lower the shade, locking eyes with Vlad before the three of them fade from view. Sure, his wave goodbye is friendly enough, but something in his expression makes me wonder if we shouldn't follow them out of here.

I shake my head. It's none of my business what happens to them. I can only control what I do, not what anyone else does.

I just hate feeling so powerless.

At that moment, the stone in my pocket grows warm, nearly burning a hole in my jeans.

"Ah!" I yell, tossing the scalding rock out of my pocket and into a nearby hand towel, damp from the night's cleaning. I inspect my hand, and, after finding no lasting burns, return to the towel on the counter.

The stone is still glowing red, and while the towel beneath it doesn't catch flame, it's smoking from the residual heat.

I give the burning ember a tentative poke, and just as before—I can't feel the heat it's giving off. But when I lift the stone and place it into my palm, it's left a burn mark on the wet hand towel.

Balancing the red stone between my thumb and forefinger, I take a deep breath. On my exhale, the stone's light fades, returning it to a matte black once more.

I consider throwing the stone back into the bushes. Sure, it's a cool souvenir, but it's not worth setting my pants on fire.

"Ellie? Where'd you go?" Cyndi asks from the back room.

Rather than discarding it, I shove the stone back into my pocket and resolve to look into it when I get home. It's probably just a piece of broken salamander scale, but the stone's ability to grow hot and cold is too weird to ignore.

I return to the back room to find Bear wearing a robotics club t-shirt tucked into his work khakis. When I look back at Cyndi, pulling her hair into a spiky ponytail, she chuckles. "I know, right? He might as well buy the cell phone holster already."

Bear looks annoyed, "What? It's the only clean shirt in my bag. Anyway, I'm not going there to party. I'm picking up my little brother and then we're leaving. And if you try to keep me there for longer, you'll have to find your own way home."

Cyndi waves a hand at him dismissively. "Yeah, yeah, okay. Worse comes to worst, Ellie's gramps can pick us up, right?"

I try to imagine a world in which Grandpa won't scold me for partying in the middle of the woods. We'd definitely get an earful about it, but as a last resort, it's not the worst idea.

"Yeah, he's an option."

"Great. Now I know we need to leave, but Ellie, you've got to add some eyeliner to your look. After all, if you're not wearing dark eyeliner, how will anyone know you're depressed?"

She isn't wrong.

Ten minutes later, the three of us pack into Bear's pickup truck. Cyndi bickers with Bear while we get on the road, complaining that he promised to let her drive, no matter how much he explains that he never made any such promise—especially when she doesn't have a license yet.

Cyndi crosses her arms and pouts. "As if a plastic form of ID can accurately measure my driving skills."

"The driving tests required to get a license are literally designed to measure your proficiency behind the wheel."

"Oh, whatever. If those tests are how you learned to drive, then I don't want to take them. Stopping at every stop sign, going slowly on backroads—you drive like an old lady! Why can't you just drive faster?"

"Because we're driving on backroads, and there are always deer out here."

"C'mon. Live a little!"

"I drive this way so that I may continue living, thank you."

I laugh to myself and look out the window while they continue tossing barbs at one another. Bear is a senior at our school, and it doesn't matter if he's studying, entering chess tournaments, or scooping ice cream, he's always been a high achiever. When you compare his work ethic to that of Cyndi and me—two sophomores constantly ditching class to go kick rocks down the road—then it's easy to see we don't have much in common with him.

And yet, after the last three months of working together, he and Cyndi have formed an unlikely friendship, with each one pressuring the other to broaden their horizons and see life beyond their immediate goals. Cyndi's always trying to push Bear's buttons, but he usually gets the better of her, reminding her that trolling comments sections online instead of doing her assigned reading isn't adding to her knowledge banks, but depleting them.

I think he spooked her the other day, going on about how knowledge can disappear with disuse after she couldn't answer a basic American history question. Later that day, I caught her peeking into her history textbook when he wasn't in the room.

Bear and I haven't worked much together without Cyndi present, so he and I aren't as close. I'm not sure if we'd get along as well without Cyndi there as our friendship liaison. After all, watching Bear use downtime at work to get ahead on school assignments always makes me uncomfortable.

I've never cared that much about anything before.

I used to enjoy going to concerts, drawing, and reading comic books—back before the monster attacks started. Now, I'm too worried about surviving to plan for much else.

As for Cyndi, she doesn't seem to care what she's doing, so long as she's having a good time. She's pretty happy with how things are these days, as if the ever-changing threats to our existence are just new anecdotes for her to share rather than something to keep her up at night.

She's always acted as if the time we waste is a renewable resource, and whenever I ask her about her plans after high school, she just shrugs.

"I'd like to stay young like this for a hundred years at least," she told me once. "That way, even if things around me change, I'll still be the same. At least until it feels like time to grow up."

That's another thing: she's always so cryptic. I've never met her family, and she often talks about them in the past tense. I've asked to visit her house a few times, and sometimes she'll agree to it, but something always comes up the day before I'm meant to stop by.

"We're monster-proofing the house this week. This time, with more bear traps!"

"The cellar is flooded with sentient algae again. It's going to take weeks to get it all out."

"Everyone has the flu."

I never push the issue because there's a good chance her home life isn't ideal. Her parents don't seem to care what she does, if they're around at all, and it's not my place to criticize her situation—not with my family as messed up as it is.

I know all too well what it's like to have personal family details exposed to the prying eyes of outsiders, people with nothing better to do than to discuss how they would have handled my issues differently.

As far as I'm concerned, Cyndi can keep her secrets until she's ready to share them.

Bear pulls off to the side of the road and parks the truck. It takes a minute for my eyes to adjust once we get out, but when they do, I'm able to see well enough without a flashlight.

Stars litter the sky in dazzling clusters. Twigs and leaves crunch beneath my sneakers. And the chorus to an overplayed pop song echoes from a Bluetooth speaker, increasing in volume as we walk toward the bonfire, the sole source of light for miles.

To my surprise, there are about forty people here. I imagined those attending a party in the woods to be a handful of burnouts or loners, or, well, people like Cyndi and me. Seeing several Varsity football players and cheerleaders, some still in their uniforms from the night's game, tells me that this gathering is intended for celebration—not oblivion.

We near the stockpile of beverages and Cyndi grabs two wine coolers, offering one to me. When I shake my head, she laughs and pockets the second one for later.

I search for nonalcoholic drink options along the more neglected side of the beer pyramid and discover three dented cans of diet Pepsi and an untouched six-pack of Fresca.

Sighing, I pick up a can of "grapefruit-flavored citrus soft drink" and look to Bear, who's too busy scanning the crowd to even notice the drinks.

"Bear?" I ask, "what do you want?"

He shakes his head. "What? Oh, nothing. I can't see my brother anywhere. I'm going to take a lap around. Can you two stay put while I look?"

But he's gone before I can answer, and when I glance over my shoulder for Cyndi, I see she's already mixed into the crowd around the keg, cheering on a poor freshman from the JV team while he fails miserably at a keg stand.

I take a sip of my Fresca, grimace at the taste, and decide to navigate through the crowd while Bear finds his brother. I didn't want to come, but Cyndi's always got me going along with her ideas. Even if those ideas put her in the center of the action while I sit and watch from the fringes.

After spotting an empty log to sit on, I set down my soda can and stare into the bonfire. Aside from the couple furiously making out to my right, I'm alone.

I scan the crowd for anything of interest, but other than the general rowdiness spreading amongst my peers, there's nothing out of the ordinary. A troop of girls records videos of one another while they practice the latest dance trend. A few athletes stand in a circle, passing around a joint and talking about their Fantasy Football drafts. Smaller pockets of people play drinking games like, "Never Have I Ever," or "I Bet I Can Shotgun This Beer Faster Than You."

As I casually people-watch, my eyes wander to the edge of the clearing. We're surrounded by massive pine trees, and if it wasn't for the headlights of passing cars, I wouldn't be able to tell where we came in. It's hard not to feel like this party has made us easy pickings for nearby threats, attracting them with the firelight and noise of our frivolity.

I guess that's the point of partying in the woods, though. It demands that we raise a fist to fear, telling any potential threats that we won't stop living just because there are new, untested terrors waiting for us. Rather, the new terrors make any moments of joy feel like acts of rebellion.

Though whether or not friendship and inebriation are adequate shields against monsters remains to be seen.

Speaking of which . . .

My gaze flickers from the partygoers to the dark woods just beyond, catching glimpse of a pair of lights, nestled in the underbrush.

No, not lights.

Are those . . . eyes?

They blink at me.

But there's no need to panic. It's probably a deer or a raccoon. Or a rabbit.

The glowing eyes rise, revealing the head and shoulders of the creature to be more than five feet tall.

Okay, so not a rabbit.

I look around warily. With the music this loud, raising my voice won't reach many ears, and announcing a monster attack before I know what it is will cause chaos.

I'll have to wait until it's out in the open. That way everyone can see what we're dealing with before they start to panic.

The creature steps closer, still hidden in shadow. If I tune out the din of the party and my violent heartbeats, I can hear the sound of breaking branches.

The beast's lack of concern for making noise confirms my fears that it's a predator—one that's larger and more confident than it should be, with glowing, unwavering eyes. It stalks closer and closer before emerging from the trees and revealing itself to be a teenage boy.

Well, the description still fits.

The wild teenager enters the clearing with nonchalance, dressed in black pants and a dark purple hoodie beneath a leather jacket. Dirty blond hair hangs over his ears with an off-center part, though whether his haircut is intended to mimic a K-Pop idol or a nineties teen heartthrob is unclear. There's eyeliner smudged on his lower lash line, and when he lifts a hand to push the hair from his eyes, I notice black nail polish on his short fingernails.

He's gorgeous.

His eyes settle on me and I look away, realizing that I'd mistaken the fire's reflection on the whites of his eyes as an unnatural glow, not unlike the fire salamander from before.

I'm too tired to be this paranoid. Maybe it's time for me to go home.

But the dark and distant boy continues walking forward, nodding to the greetings of passing classmates, until he stops a few feet in front of me.

An embarrassed flush spreads across my face while my brain misfires with fear and confusion and panic. Only now, instead of fearing for my life, I'm afraid to speak, in case I say the wrong thing.

"Yes?" The mystery in front of me has a soft and welcoming voice.

I glance up cautiously, and upon seeing his warm smile and honey-colored eyes, two sensations hit me at once: a spike of nervous energy and a sudden, inexplicable feeling of dread.

"Did you need something?" he asks.

I furrow my brow as I process the question, only to realize that I've been wordlessly staring at him for the last ten seconds.

"I, uh. What?" I point, trying to remember what I'd just seen. "No. Um, sorry. I just saw you. Over there. In the woods?"

The mysterious boy laughs and grabs a nearby lawn chair, pulling it up next to the fire. He sticks out a hand.

"I'm Wade. What's your name?"

I shake his hand and do my best to avoid his gaze. Yes, he's attractive, but he's also a stranger, and I don't normally spend my time talking to people I don't know. No matter how pretty they are.

"My name's Ellie," I say. "Do you go to Errolton High?"

Wade nods. "I'm a junior, though the word 'go' implies that I'm in class when I'm supposed to be, so . . . " he shrugs, mimicking my earlier tone, "I guess?"

"Oh, you skip class too?" I ask without thinking. "Cool. Rad. Same here." I mime a pair of finger guns and pretend to shoot him. Because that's what people do when they flirt, right?

No, Ellie. Just, no.

I shake my head in embarrassment and try to steer the conversation away from my awkwardness. "Anyway, I'm a sophomore."

"Nice. So, how does it feel, jeopardizing your future for a few spare hours of freedom?"

"I mean, we're usually skipping class to eat fast food and hide under the bleachers, so it feels okay, I guess."

"We?" Wade tilts his head to the side, curiously.

I try to ignore the reflection of firelight in his eyes.

"Oh, just me and my friend Cyndi. Skipping is usually her idea." I glance around the party, hoping to point her out, but no luck. "You might have seen her earlier. Bright orange hair, bright green jacket, bright extroverted personality?"

"Ah. Haven't met anyone like that, but I'm sure she's easy to spot in a crowd." He leans in close to whisper, "You don't seem the partying type, though. What brings you to the middle of the woods so late at night?"

I raise my can of lukewarm soda as a barrier between us.

"The drinks, obviously. What about you?"

He nods to the Bluetooth speaker. "The songs are too good."

"Oh?" The final verse of a pop hit fades out, only to be replaced by the tell-tale twang of a country song—a ballad about the singer's car radiator. "You don't seem like the type to enjoy . . . whatever this is."

"What gave you that idea?" Wade laughs. "You're right though. I'm here to meet up with some friends. They invited me out." He points to a smaller group of football players and upperclassmen I don't recognize.

"Ah, so you know people?" I pretend to be impressed.

"I guess. But I don't normally come to their parties."

"Why not?"

Letting out a weary sigh, Wade says, "It's just all the same. People get drunk or high and then someone makes a fool out of themselves, or the cops get called, or someone fools around with someone else, and then everyone talks about it the next day like it's this big thing when it's not."

"So then, why did you show up tonight?"

He scratches underneath his chin for a moment. "Honestly? I was bored at home. And I guess I was hoping that tonight would be different, and I'd meet someone cool."

Wade flashes me a smile.

"Well, I can't promise that I'll live up to those expectations." I laugh more from awkwardness than humor. "It's strange, though. Errolton is a pretty small school, so I'm surprised I never . . . noticed you before."

"I could say the same about you," he replies, still smiling. "Maybe this will help you to recognize me."

Wade reaches into his pocket to pull out his cell phone. He turns it on, opens up his photos, and scrolls until he finds what he's looking for.

"Here we go. This is from last year."

As I lean in, I see a photo of the school marching band from the previous year's homecoming game. Wade's in the full uniform, with a fluffy military hat, fringe hanging from his jacket sleeves, shiny black shoes, and a silver trumpet in hand.

I look over the photo in disbelief. "You were in marching band?"

He laughs dismissively. “Yeah. But only until last year. Then I pulled the plug on everything—grades, clubs, all of it. All that pedantic achieving was what my parents wanted, not me.”

“Pedantic, huh?” I raise an eyebrow at his three-dollar vocabulary word. “Well then, what do you want?”

Wade doesn’t reply at first, unsure of how to answer the question.

After a beat, he says, “I guess, I’m still figuring it out. But I know that I won’t find it competing for first chair.” He pushes back a lock of messy hair and settles into his cool-guy persona. “Everyone in band takes it so seriously, and I was never going to study music in college, so what’s the point?”

I nod in agreement. “Electives shouldn’t be a big deal, but they are for some reason. Am I not allowed to study art just because I like to draw? If someone doesn’t want to go to college, does that mean they have to take a class in welding or cosmetology? It’s stupid.”

Rolling my eyes, I continue. “I swear, if my guidance counselor lectures me one more time about how, ‘The choices I make today will impact my future,’ and, ‘Not making a choice is making a choice,’ then I might just get my GED and graduate early.”

Wade chuckles. “That’s not a bad plan. You could always join a club, just to shut her up.”

I turn to him. Somehow, we’re sitting much closer than before.

“Oh? Like what?” I ask.

“Well, I heard that there’s a ‘monster-hunters club’ forming, which should be recognized by the school this month. It’s their way of legitimizing the group in camo shooting off their guns in the parking lot after school, but with how good your grandfather is at tracking and hunting, I bet you could . . . ”

He stops himself, but it’s too late. He’s already shown his hand.

“I never said anything about my grandfather,” I say through clenched teeth.

Wade glances to his left, sees no exit available, and sighs.

"No, you didn't."

"So, you already knew who I was when you came over here?"

He meets my eyes warily. "Yes, I did."

I stand up, glaring at him.

"What is this really about? Did you come over here just to bother the loner so that you could tell your crappy friends how weird I am? Or is this for some stupid bet, like you wanted to see what it'll take to piss me off?"

I can hear my voice rising. I can't help it.

The couple to my right, as well as a few others within earshot, stop what they're doing to eavesdrop.

"Well, mission accomplished, Jerkwad. Hope it was fun. Now, go away."

It's always been like this. To other people, my life is just a freaky circus act to watch and chat about when there's nothing good on TV.

"Hey," Wade says, reaching up to me.

He looks apologetic, for a turd sandwich.

"Sit down, please? Give me a chance to explain."

"Why should I?"

"Because I didn't come over here for any of those reasons. Please?"

He pats my previous seat with the expression of a sad puppy dog.

I sit, begrudgingly, and stare at my sneakers. Where's Cyndi when I need her?

Wade begins with an apology. "I'm sorry I didn't say anything before. I just didn't want to make things awkward. Sure, everyone in town knows about your family. The news story about your mom is one of the biggest things to happen around here, at least until the Super-Mart was built."

He's right, of course. My mother's court case and institutionalization made national headlines back when I was still a baby. It took years for things to legally resolve, and I was almost placed in witness protection during that time due to all the reporters hounding me for an interview.

Thankfully, Grandpa scared them off, shooting beanbags and airsoft pellets at them whenever they came by.

Grandma was still alive, then. I have vague memories of the two of us on Saturday mornings, eating freshly baked blueberry muffins topped with cold butter from the fridge while we watched Grandpa shoot people from the porch.

"Ellie, dear, don't go outside." Grandma would say. "When your grandad gets into one of his moods, he's liable to miss. Best just let him shoot the mailbox a few times before the sheriff comes 'round again."

"Anyway," Wade continues, unaware of my mental detour, "I didn't think bringing up what I knew within the first few minutes of meeting you would go so well. And, well," he gestures to me. "I wasn't wrong."

I toss him a look of annoyance. Sure, his face is symmetrical and his eyeliner is the right level of smudged, and of course his eyes sparkle like the moon, but that doesn't mean he's allowed to get smart with me this soon after meeting.

"I guess I'm not that great at pretending I don't know something." Wade clicks his tongue, thinking. "I'm sorry it had to come up at all. You seemed interested in getting to know me, and I didn't want something as stupid as town gossip to get in the way of, well, talking to you."

I cross my arms and search for deceit in his expression. When I detect none, I exhale.

"I'll believe you for now. But that doesn't mean I trust you."

"Fair enough," Wade replies with evident relief, then reaches into his pocket and pulls out a vape pen. "Wanna strengthen our alliance with a puff on the peace pipe?"

I raise an eyebrow. "Don't you have to be eighteen to buy one of those?"

"Do you always follow the rules?" He holds out the pen to me with a curious smirk.

Rolling my eyes, I reply, "I've smoked before, thank you very much."

It's not a complete lie. Cyndi had me try a cigarette months ago, after calling me a weenie for never smoking before. But when "one puff" made me cough until I got a headache, we agreed that nicotine and peer pressure were bad for our friendship.

"It's just not my style." I finish.

"Neither is drinking, I've gathered." He gestures to the can of Fresca placed at my feet. "But that's not a bad thing. It just means you're saving your brain cells for later."

He shrugs and lifts the vape pen to his lips. As he inhales, I can't help noticing the neat line of his jaw and the small dimple on his chin.

Wade then pulls the pen away and makes a weird shape with his tongue, expelling rings of vapor from his mouth. He looks back at me with a twinkle of childlike mischief in his eyes.

"Eh? Eh? C'mon. That was cool."

I laugh lightly.

"Yes, yes. You're very cool."

We sit in silence for a bit, letting the noise of the party fill the space between us. I absentmindedly reach into my pocket and close my hand around the stone—my souvenir from the salamander attack—and stare into the bonfire. The flames' soft blue edges curl around the logs as they splinter and pop in the heat.

Suddenly, a sharp spike of heat climbs up my arm and into my chest. My forearm starts to perspire in my sleeve as the stone burns into the flesh of my palm.

Am I about to set my arm on fire?

On instinct, I drop the stone in my pocket and pull my hand out.

The stone instantly cools.

I open and close my hand in disbelief. There's a red welt forming in the center of my palm.

Great job, Ellie. First, you talk to strangers, and now you're being careless with a potentially magical object that may or may not be able to set things on fire. Nice.

"That looks like it hurts."

Wade peers over my shoulder at the red mark on my hand.

"Are you okay?" he asks.

The act of turning to look at him does two things. First, it brings our faces inches from one other, which raises my heart rate and ties my stomach in knots.

I've never been this close to a boy before.

And second, it distracts me from the welt on my hand for a few seconds. By the time I look back at the mark, it's reduced in size and color. I continue watching as it transitions from a light pink circle to a faint white outline, to nothing at all.

As if it never happened in the first place.

My eyes widen as I turn my hand over, confused.

I look back at Wade, apologetically. "I guess I'm . . . fine?"

Before he can reply, Wade is interrupted by the sound of snapping tree branches and the scattered echoes of clattering hooves. I hear a few voices yelling in the distance.

"That way!"

"Hiya!"

"Be sure to surround them!"

The unexpected shouts cause partygoers across the clearing to pause, mid-swig of beer. Smaller groups huddle in the center, hoping to find a defensible position.

Hidden amongst the trees, a scattered pack of hounds howls together to alert their masters—likely the Beowulf Brigade, our town's local monster-hunting militia—of our location.

Ah yes. I'd forgotten there was a hunt tonight.

The first horse to jump out from the trees is a dark, imposing animal, with bone-crushing hooves and a wild mane. The man riding it is an imposing force all his own; with a black and gray speckled beard, a rifle strapped across his chest, and a large double-edged axe hanging dangerously from his saddle, Peter Karlsen, my grandfather, is not a man to be trifled with.

At least, not during a hunting party. At home, it's pretty easy to hide the remote from him.

"Party's over, you vagrants!" Grandpa bellows over the remaining murmur of fearful adolescents. "Go home before you get eaten by something!"

Other riders fall in behind him, seated on horses varying in color and size. They circle the clearing to round up as many trashed jocks and student council members as they can find, pushing them out of the woods and back toward the road.

A woman wearing silver-laced chainmail and camo military fatigues shouts to another man on horseback:

"Form a group on the far west side of the clearing. No, not over there, Jones, you dingus. The other west."

Her dark, textured curls are braided back into a low bun to keep them away from her eyes. She knocks a stray twig from her shoulder, and, seeing her subordinate walk in the opposite direction as everyone else, lets out an exasperated sigh. "Jones, I swear. Just follow the person in front of you."

Then she blows a whistle from the chain around her neck, instructing the pack of dogs to charge in from the woods and aid with the herding efforts.

A basset hound trudges up to me, barking happily.

"Hey Scout!" I reach out to pet him, and the dog pauses, unsure of whether he should receive a pat on the head or continue doing his job. Another blast of the whistle reminds Scout of his duty, and he barks again, headbutting me.

"Okay, okay." Standing up, I pour the remaining dregs of my soda onto the bonfire. "I guess it's time to go."

Wade nods, slowly walking toward the exit. "Too bad. But, hey," he turns back to me for a moment, apparently unsure of his next move, "I was thinking of asking you for your number. To continue our talk?"

I ignore the dancing puppies in my head and provide him with a counteroffer. "What if we both make a concerted effort to improve our attendance at school, and I promise to look for you in the hallways?"

Wade rolls his eyes. "I could also just look you up online and pester you that way."

"You could try." I start walking again, and he follows. "But I don't have any social media accounts."

He raises an eyebrow, "Really?"

"Yeah." I nod. "I've never had one. It's the only way to prevent harassment online, what with my very public family history."

"Ah. Right." He pauses thoughtfully. "I forgot that people can be actual garbage."

"Yep."

We stop walking once we approach the crowd of people waiting to leave. Wade speaks up again.

"Well, fair enough. I'll keep an eye out for you. And maybe one day you'll trust me enough to let me send you cat emojis." He leans into me for a moment, speaking in a lower tone. "I certainly hope that day comes soon, Ellie."

Shaking off the wave of nerves inspired by Wade's proximity—and the way he says my name—I spot Cyndi running up to me with an open beer in her hand. Bear rides on her back, the latter clearly distressed at the situation.

"Put me down!" Bear yells while they run together. "I did not agree to be carried!"

Cyndi drops him unceremoniously at my feet and curtsies to me.

"A delivery for you, ma'am. One curmudgeonly shift manager caught red-handed."

I nod. "I see. The dangerous sort."

Still sitting on the ground, Bear yells up at us. "What crime have I committed?"

"Having zero fun at a social event." Cyndi finishes her beer and tosses the empty bottle into the woods with a grin. "Though I could charge you with that same crime, ma'am, unless . . . " She looks past me and notices Wade, watching us with an amused expression on his face. "Unless you were able to find some fun of your own when I wasn't looking?"

Bear's eyes follow Cyndi's, but upon seeing my companion, his expression is mixed with relief and irritation. "Wade?"

Wade offers him a hand up. "Get off the ground, Ted."

Cyndi and I watch the exchange between the two of them, and our eyes widen. We nearly scream in unison.

"Ted? As in, Teddy?!"

Bear glares at Wade, then us. "If you two must know, my middle name is Theodore, hence the nickname 'Ted.' My parents are . . . " he sighs, "hilarious. Anyway, Cyndi, Ellie, this is my brother, Wade. Wade, these are two of my coworkers. Now, can we all get out of here before I'm grounded for eternity?"

"Too late for that, I'm afraid."

The four of us turn to see my grandfather, high atop his horse, glowering at me.

"Ellie, how did I know I'd find you here?"

"Because you're aware of my flare for self-destruction?"

"Indeed." His gaze shifts to Cyndi. "Miss Renard, did I just see you throw a beer bottle into the woods?"

Cyndi hops from one foot to another. "No, sir. Not me." She looks down at her shoes, hoping to direct his wrath elsewhere.

"Hm." My grandfather grunts. "Must have been the other girl with bright orange hair, then."

When she doesn't respond, Grandpa scratches at his beard and looks us over before gruffly asking, "I suppose I should just let it slide that you two snuck off after work to party in the woods, then? As if that would have been allowed even if our town wasn't in a red zone?"

I don't remember there being enough recent attacks to upgrade Errolton from a yellow zone to a red one, but then I guess Grandpa would know the situation better than anyone. The Beowulf Brigade keeps a thorough database about this sort of thing. They cross-reference newly reported monster attacks, missing persons, and supernatural animal sightings each week, to get an accurate picture of threats as they appear. They also send out a cute newsletter once a month.

I notice Grandpa's wrist twitching in irritation. It hovers over his axe, wanting to enact some violent outburst that will scare us into doing the right thing next time.

Instead, he waves over the lady in chainmail. She nods to him and continues surveying the chaos of vacating high-schoolers as she and her horse trot over.

Once she's within earshot, Grandpa gestures to us.

"Adams, this is my granddaughter and her . . . friends, I suppose." Then he looks back at us. "Ellie, Cyndi, teenagers-I-don't-care-to-learn-the-names-of, this is Colonel Simone Adams. She'll be making sure you get home safely and that your parents are aware of how you spent your evening."

With one blow of her whistle, Colonel Adams has every dog in the clearing stopped at attention. The colonel inspects us with an inquisitive eye. I can see her jotting down notes about each of us and filing them away in her mind for later, in case she needs to reference an obscure detail at a moment's notice.

A long, dark scar runs down one of her cheeks, framed by the gray wisps that weave in and out of her black curly hair. Her expression is reserved, but not unkind.

"Oh, no need for all the formalities, Pete," she says to my grandfather. "I am retired, after all."

"Nevertheless." Grandpa leans down to make eye contact with Bear, Cyndi, and Wade in turn. "You three will show the colonel respect as she escorts you home, or she'll file a report for underage drinking, or breaking curfew, or whatever she finds most convenient to charge you with. And if I find out that this sort of thing happens again, especially around my granddaughter, your punishment will be more severe. Understood?"

They nod. Wade glances at me, an amused expression lurking behind his mask of guilt.

Bear raises his hand, tentatively. "Sir? Permission to speak?"

"Denied. Cyndi, you'll be dropped off at home last. The colonel needs help putting the dogs back into their kennels tonight."

Under her breath, Cyndi murmurs, "I hate kennel duty."

"What was that?" my grandfather bellows.

"Nothing, sir."

"Good." Grandpa pats the back of his horse. "Get on, Ellie. Say goodbye to your friends. You're grounded for eternity."

"Super." I turn to Cyndi, Wade, and Bear. "Sorry about all this. See you at school tomorrow?"

The three of them nod tentatively.

"I'll text you pictures of Scout eating snacks later," Cyndi whispers. "For a dog, he's not so bad."

"Agreed," I say before walking over to Declan, my grandfather's dark courser, and patting the horse.

"Hey, Dec. I hope the old man's not pushing you too hard."

Then I slip my foot into the saddle's stirrup and climb up behind Grandpa, who presses the horse into a run without another word.

And as we ride off into the dark trees, I catch the glow of distant campfires and finally lower my guard.

We'll be home soon—sheltered from what goes bump in the night.

Chapter Three

Ellie

Are you trying to get yourself killed?!"

Despite the ride back being relatively silent, I knew to expect a lecture within seconds of the front door closing.

I toss my backpack into the coat closet and sit on the bottom stair to take off my sneakers, coated in mud. Grandpa follows me inside, weighed down by his hunting gear and his fury.

"I heard about what happened at the ice cream shop, by the way. So, you decided to take on a fire salamander on your own, without waiting for animal control or anyone to help you? Are you out of your mind?" He carefully hangs his axe on the hooks by the door and removes his jacket before repeating his earlier question: "Honestly. Are you trying to get yourself killed?"

I don't look up. Meeting his eyes would mean that I want to defend my choices, which I don't.

I could argue that I wasn't making any real decisions tonight, that I was just going along with what everyone else was doing, but that's not much of an excuse. No, it's better to put on a face of contrition and deal with the consequences as they come.

Grandpa furiously kicks off his boots and walks into our small kitchen with faded laminate countertops and crooked cabinets. His cabin has a rustic charm, with drafty, rattling windows and floors that squeak with every step. He opens the fridge, grabs a beer, and plops into a chair at the kitchen table. After opening the bottle and taking a long swig from it, he sighs.

"I know you're smart enough not to be drinking with your underage friends, but Cyndi doesn't know better, and even being there will get you in trouble. You know that, right?"

I nod, staring at cracks in the floorboards.

Grandpa rubs his eyes, clearly exhausted. Up on the horse, decked out in his hunting gear and best withering stare, my grandfather seems like an otherworldly force that can take on any fanged beast he comes across. But up close, his pronounced wrinkles and stiff joints are an uncomfortable reminder that he can't do this forever.

He's tired, and rightfully so. Our town would be in much worse shape if he didn't push for the Beowulf Brigade to get full support from the local government. And while some townspeople don't love the new curfews or the patrols limiting citizen freedoms, most are willing to adjust their schedules to ensure a renewed sense of security and control.

But it's a full-time job, and for a man who was ready to enter retirement before all this happened, hunting with the brigade is taking its toll. Though something tells me that he'd rather spend his later years hunting monsters than sitting quietly on the porch, whittling.

Grandpa takes another drink and stares at me, carefully choosing his words.

"I think I give you a lot of freedom, Ellie. You're more often not in class than you are, but you're smart. You read a ton and you usually stay out of trouble, so I don't press you about things like attendance or who you spend your time with.

"But not calling me about the salamander attack? Sneaking off after work to go party in the woods? Getting an F on your latest biology test?

And before you say anything, Miss Raposa already emailed me about it. She said you need to stay after for tutoring."

I glare at the floorboards, wondering what kind of revenge I should enact on the busybody Catherine Raposa for being a snitch. Miss Raposa is my biology teacher, which is my first class of the day, so she's lucky to see me once a week. I have nothing against her personally, but getting breakfast in town with Cyndi is way better than sitting in our assigned seats, listening to her yammer on about her time at whatever university she just graduated from. She claims to be nearly thirty, but the woman looks like she's barely eighteen, and manages the classroom about as well as a teenager would.

The class is full of rowdy, older students, with Miss Raposa spending more time asking everyone to quiet down than covering any legitimate material. It's too noisy in there for me to want to attend every morning, when I could be off spending my time as I please. I figured I'd pass the class so long as I came in on test days and turned in the occasional homework assignment, but when the newest test covered nothing from the textbook, despite being a chapter test, I knew she was just trying to punish me for skipping class.

Grandpa tugs on his beard. "Ellie, is this about your mom not letting you visit last month?"

I grit my teeth at the mention of my mother.

"Why should I care about visiting her? She doesn't want me there, and I don't want to be there."

"Listen, I know your mother, and she—"

I stand up and meet Grandpa's eyes, finally.

"Do you know her? The woman who was doggedly determined to give me a stupid boy's name but couldn't commit to abandoning me? Mothers are supposed to make lunches and kiss skinned knees but mine just sits there, staring at the wall while you read to her from the newspaper. She barely acknowledges me when we visit—if she recognizes me at all. And the few times she does look at me, you know what I see in her eyes?"

Before he can respond, before I realize what I'm doing, I walk over to the closet and retrieve my backpack.

"Fear, Grandpa. She's afraid of me." I feel the hot sting of tears forming at the corners of my eyes. "What did I ever do to her? I never asked to be born."

I shake my head, refusing to cry. "I'm so sick of waiting around for her to decide if I'm worth her time. I'm not going back to see her anymore. And if you try to make me, then I'll just run away now and save you the trouble of finding me somewhere else to live."

I open the front door and look out into the night.

A fox screams in the distance.

"Now, now," he says, walking over to me, "None of that. Where would you go, anyway?"

I hesitate in the doorway, the chilly air biting at my bare feet.

"Probably nowhere without shoes," I murmur.

Grandpa rests a hand on my shoulder. "C'mon. Put your bag down and sit at the table. We both need dinner."

"Promise me," I say.

"Promise what?"

"Promise me I don't have to go back there. That I don't have to see her again if I don't want to."

He sighs, then turns back to the kitchen. "You visiting her once a month has been more helpful than you realize. She has these moments of lucid conversation, where it almost seems like she's back." He pauses, mournfully. "And they're more frequent when you come with me than when I'm alone. But, if it's that painful, then okay. I won't force you."

I nod and close the front door, putting my bag down next to it. "Is it okay if I skip dinner? I ate earlier."

"You don't have to eat, but just sit with me. I'll even make some hot cocoa if it'll help you feel better. But we have some things to talk about."

Reluctantly, I sit and check my phone while he heats up a frozen dinner. Cyndi's sent me a photo of herself and the hunting dogs, pinching her nose at their smell. Behind her, I see the rough outline of Scout, my grandfather's basset hound, chewing on Cyndi's pant leg. Her text reads:

Tell your grandpa that kennel duty sucks.

When Grandpa joins me at the table, he hands me a mug of hot water with lumps of instant cocoa floating on top. I give him a sideways look.

"What?" Grandpa takes a bite of instant mashed potatoes. "I said I'd make it for you. I didn't promise it'd be good."

I roll my eyes and stand up to find a spoon while he continues. "Have you heard about our town being classified as a red zone again?"

I shake my head.

"You haven't heard anything from school?" He stabs at some green beans when I don't reply. "Maybe they'll make an announcement next week. They were supposed to hand out pamphlets at least, explaining new restrictions with transportation and after-school activities."

"What's going on?" I ask while stirring the floating chunks of cocoa powder.

"Some girls have gone missing."

I stop mid-stir. "Seriously?"

Grandpa nods. "It's not just girls, but most of the missing persons reported this month have been high school girls. They're supposed to cancel all after-school programs starting next week, and while the buses are still running now, parents will be encouraged to drive students to school until further notice."

"So, wait." I sit back down at the table. "Anyone I know?"

He nods again. "Mr. Clark, the owner of Farrowfield Farms. Not him, but both of his daughters. Going on two weeks now."

"No way." I hold my mug tightly, trying to fight the unsteady feeling in my stomach.

"It's not just him. Your principal just lost her daughter, too. Only a few days ago. The girl was supposed to be at a friend's house, but it turns out she lied to go see her boyfriend. Only, she never showed up."

"No. Way." I repeat, worried. The two girls, ordering ice cream just hours before, flash before my eyes. "Earlier, at the store, there was a vampire. Maybe he . . . "

My grandfather raises a hand at my comment. "We've already spoken to Lord Vance. He's having his weekly book club with the region's most powerful vamps, but so far he hasn't heard anything."

"And you trust him?" I scoff. "No offense, but a preference for young girls doesn't strike me as the behavior of your average mountain lion attack. "

"Vance has demonstrated his trustworthiness over the last few months, working with my team to track down some rogue vampires," Grandpa speaks between bites. "New Hampshire doesn't have the same kinds of issues with vampires that they did in Texas and Arizona. Most folks around here just want to survive the winter, not enslave the neighborhood."

He goes on. "Anyway, I'm not telling you this because I want you to start interrogating locals. I'm trying to impress upon you that things are bad right now. And you," Grandpa points his fork at me, "are a teenage girl, by the way. So, no more skipping classes and no more going out into the woods with friends. I don't have time to drive you to school, so you'll go everywhere with Cyndi from now on. In fact, I might have her start staying in the spare room until all this is over."

"Really?" I'm surprised. This is not how I expected my grounding to go.

Grandpa sighs again. "Cyndi means well, and I'm glad you have friends. Just try to reign in her more creative ideas. Otherwise, you'll really be on lockdown." He swallows the piece of Salisbury steak he's been working on and asks, "But can you stay away from those boys until this is all over?"

I laugh at his look of concern. "Sorry, Grandpa. For a minute there it sounded like you were worried about Bear luring us into the woods and chopping us up. The only thing he's capable of dissecting is a frog for the science fair."

"Even so. What about that other one? With the dark clothes and the . . . " He trails off, pointing to his eye.

"Eyeliner? Are you talking about Wade?"

My grandfather nods. "Whoever. Back in my day, if you dressed like that, you were either on drugs or in a cult. So which one is he into?"

"Neither, as far as I can tell," I mutter. Aside from the vape, my statement is mostly true. "But if you're that worried, I'll stay away from them for now."

"Good. Because there's evidence of victims being kidnapped and groomed in these missing persons cases, so I'd rather you not spend time with anyone you don't know well. Or even someone you do know well but who could put you into a compromising situation. Not just a boy: an adult, a teacher, anyone. Just stay away from everyone. At least until we figure this out."

"Okay, okay. Fair enough." I grin, excited to avoid being grounded. "Can I call Cyndi and let her know?"

"Sure. But before you do that, I have one more thing for you."

Grandpa pushes away from the table to get his saddlebag and unzips it. After rooting around inside for a bit, he pulls out a sheathed hunting knife, which he offers to me. "Here. This is for you."

I pull the knife from its leather sheath to inspect it. The steel blade is about six inches long, with a dark wood handle that fits comfortably in my hand. In the center of the blade, there's an inscription that reads: "Ellie Shea Adair." My name.

I look up at Grandpa, astonished. "What is this?

"This, first and foremost, is not a toy. It's a gift, for your protection. Under normal circumstances, you'd only really need this for hunting, but since you can't go to work without a salamander dragon attacking, I want you to carry it with you everywhere."

"Even to school?" I raise my eyebrows.

"Even to school. Don't use it unless absolutely necessary, because you'll get in trouble for having it on you. But I don't want you to be caught off guard if someone—or something—comes after you."

I turn the knife over in my palm, getting used to the weight of it. "It looks too nice to use," I say.

Grandpa puffs up with pride. "Yeah, It's a pretty one. Had it specially made. No need to thank me," he laughs. "I'll need to show you the proper way to skin and clean an animal at some point, when things calm down. Oh, and if it gets dull, you can sharpen it. I think I have a whetstone in the garage."

He putters out the side door to dig through his mountain of tools and supplies in the garage, while I study the knife. I run my thumb over the blade's inscription and hope to never need it, but can't help smiling.

With this, maybe I won't be so powerless.

Back in my room, I arrange my new treasures on the nightstand. My knife sits comfortably in its sheath by the window while I root around in my pocket to find the salamander stone, or volcanic rock, or whatever it is that I recovered from the ice cream shop. Placing the stone beside my new knife, I return to the other pocket and find the metal tab from my earlier Fresca can, wedged into the lip of my phone case. I dislodge the tab from the case and lay in bed, exhausted.

Spinning the metal soda tab between two fingers, I think back to my conversation with Wade around the bonfire.

Wade was certainly interesting to talk to. I wouldn't have minded talking for a bit longer, but maybe the hunting party showed up at the right time. I'd met the guy mere minutes before, and it didn't take long for him to break through my barriers. That, in addition to the new disappearances happening at school, means that the smart thing to do would be to keep away from him.

But then, he's Bear's brother. How bad could he be?

As if my thoughts summoned him, my phone buzzes to show a new text from an unfamiliar number. It reads:

We never finished our earlier conversation

Puzzled at the sender's identity, but not completely in the dark, I reply with a gif of the caterpillar from Alice in Wonderland. Atop his mushroom throne, the caterpillar sprays smoke in Alice's face, asking, "Who are you?"

A response comes in a few seconds later. A skull emoji, followed by:

It's Wade. Bear gave me your number

Immediately, I get another text. This one's from Bear.

Hi. Sorry about my brother. He was determined in getting your number from me, so I gave it to him, but if that's a violation of your privacy I'll make him leave you alone.

I reply to Bear first.

No worries. Are you free to help me with Biology this weekend? There's a test coming up and if I fail it, I might not pass this semester

Bear replies with a "Sure, when and where?" and we make a quick plan to meet on Saturday morning at the town library.

I switch back to the other text, which, so far, I've left without a reply. Wade seeking out my number breaks the rules we previously agreed upon, but does that matter? Doesn't this extra step in my direction prove that he's interested?

I tug my bottom lip in concentration, unsure of my next move. Texting someone cute is new territory for me, and it's a surprisingly stressful task.

Aside from going to school or work, or talking with Grandpa or Cyndi, I spend most of my time alone in my room, listening to music. I commiserate with brooding lyricists who slice the twisted words from their heads into song.

I never know how to express my jumbled feelings—those that fester and bite at me with no way out. Instead, I turn up the volume on songs that describe how I feel better than I can ever put into words, as if the songwriter and I are in the same room, sharing the same space.

Too often, songs like that are my lifeline back to feeling okay. They help me feel less alone in a world full of people who, for the most part, don't care what happens to me.

While I fiddle with the tab of the soda can, trying to determine if I should text Wade back or push him away, I get a new text message. This one's from Cyndi.

Finally heading to bed. Those dogs smell horrible.

I check the clock and see that it's nearly one in the morning. Sheesh. We should all should be asleep.

I text her back:

I bet you could have avoided kennel duty if you hadn't thrown that bottle into the woods

Cyndi: *Yeah, but where's the fun in that? [sparkle emoji] [juice box emoji] Oh who was that guy from earlier? Teddy said it was his brother?*

I chuckle. Bear Theodore Drummond. Ted. Teddy.

Cyndi's never going to let it go.

Yeah. His name is Wade. He just texted me.

Cyndi replies with a surprised emoji. *You gave him your number??*

No. He got it from Bear. Not sure how I feel about it

She sends me a photo of a cat in a taco costume.

Yes. I reply. *Exactly like that.*

Tacocat understands your confusion. Like, is she a taco, or a cat, or a palindrome? The world is not ready for the reign of Tacocat.

I roll my eyes.

You're so dumb. Can you meet me at my house before school tomorrow? I have a lot to tell you.

Sure. Where do you want to go to breakfast?

We can't do breakfast for a while. I need to pass Biology.

Cyndi replies with another cat image, though this one is surrounded by rainbows while it gives me the middle finger.

Boring. But fine. See you at 6!

Laughing, I place the soda tab next to the other items I've collected. I need to tell Cyndi about the stone, and the disappearances, and I guess about Wade, too.

It's so much easier to have a conversation when I'm not worrying about what the other person thinks of me. Of course, I want to warmly react to Wade's advances. I'd like to lower the drawbridge and grant him access to the inner courtyard of my thoughts. But can I, when my instincts are shouting that I should be up on the castle walls, arming archers for battle?

He seems determined to disarm me.

Sighing, I close my phone and plug it in. I'll decide about replying to Wade once I talk to Cyndi tomorrow morning.

I turn out the light.

Chapter Four

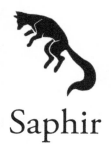

Saphir

There is blood in my mouth.

I don't mind the taste, though the feathers collecting under my tongue aren't ideal. It would be fine if not for the occasional quill stabbing the inside of my cheek.

Running in the dark while carrying a kill is tiresome.

I take a deep breath in through my nose, careful not to drop the dead barn owl between my teeth. I would have eaten the owl already if DeLucia hadn't specifically asked me to bring it.

My paw brushes against an upturned root as I speed up, chasing the smoke of ritual incense that guides me through the trees.

I hope I'm not late. If that barguest arrives before I do, I will never hear the end of it.

I leap over a felled tree and into the clearing, apparently the first to arrive. In the center, a pile of coals glows from the extinguished fire, still warm despite the night's harsh wind.

Hours earlier, these woods were crawling with humans celebrating with intoxicants and initiating clumsy mating rituals. Yet all that remains of the night's earlier frivolity is an occasional beer bottle, crumpled can, and rolling plastic cup.

Slowing my steps, I approach a soda can covered in ants. I lean down to sniff.

Sure enough—the familiar scent of human pheromones. My mouth salivates at the smell, a reminder of how little I've eaten this past week. It takes my remaining willpower not to devour the owl in my mouth.

Instead, I take hesitant steps toward the coals.

They should be here by now.

Once I'm within two feet of the firepit, I pass through an invisible barrier and recognize Marquess DeLucia, alone behind the veil. His ceremonial robe of dark green velvet is embroidered with an intricate vine of red and black thorns that climbs up his sleeves and across the brow of his hood, signifying his rank.

Relieved to locate the correct summoning circle, I toss my owl atop the burning coals between us and begin to shift.

Shapeshifting, like all important skills, requires practice and attention to detail. Thankfully it's been years since I first gained my abilities, so I barely notice the way my spine stretches and reorients to accommodate the bipedal form. My limbs lengthen with muscle memory as the last patch of fur recedes and I complete my transformation from gray fox to human.

The wind bites at my now hairless body, reminding me of the foreign self-awareness that occurs with human nudity—especially when others are nearby—and I shiver, growing cold. Only my chin and throat are warm, coated in the owl's blood.

Marquess DeLucia grimaces at my bloody appearance. He hands me a basic black robe and switches his gaze to the body of the owl, slowly charring on one side.

"You've got some . . . entrails . . . on your shoulder," he says with a sneer.

I glace at my right shoulder. Sure enough, there's a bit of dried intestine stuck to my skin.

"Do we need this for later?" I ask the marquess.

He shakes his head.

I toss it into my mouth raw. "Thanks. Best thing I've had all week."

DeLucia looks like he's going to vomit.

"Get your robe on, Saphir. We've got work to do."

Pulling the black robe over my head, I spot the fire salamander, Mishal, skulking into the clearing. He raises his head in search of cooking meat and slithers toward us, his flaming tail thumping audibly as it scorches the ground with each step.

Flame salamanders usually have no sense of stealth, but this one is excessively noisy. He thinks that leaving a path of destruction wherever he goes is a sign of confidence, but it's silly for him to assume he has no natural threats in these woods. If anything, he's just made himself easier to track.

The salamander enters the barrier encircling us, pauses to survey the scene—now visible to him—and cracks his neck to one side. Unlike my seamless transformation, his shift is jagged and imprecise. Perhaps that's the price of being comprised of magma, but something tells me his technique has more to do with temperament than biology.

After all, if Mishal can bludgeon his way through a task, he will.

When the salamander finally stands on two legs, his eyes are the same round, glowing orbs from his previous form, and the hair growing from his head cracks off in chunks of volcanic stone.

He won't pass for human like that, but it's not an unsuccessful transformation. At least his limbs are in the proper order this time.

As he approaches, I gesture to my eyes and cough. "Mishal. Your eyes."

"Hmm?" A moth flutters over to our circle, catching his attention. On instinct, he extends his flame tongue, snaps the moth into his mouth, and chews it with crunchy, exuberant bites.

I guess he also considers the human tongue to be optional when shapeshifting.

The marquess hands Mishal another black robe, muttering under his breath. "Amateurs."

A dry branch cracks near the edge of the clearing. The others glance up to investigate, but the sound's sizable echo is easy enough to identify.

A radiant aura of green and gold illuminates the mass of black fur as it bursts into view, smashing headfirst into an oak tree, splitting it like lightning.

Disoriented, the enormous black dog takes a few cautious steps backward, shakes its shaggy, menacing head, and turns toward the coals, unbothered.

Unlike the salamander, the barguest's blatant disregard for stealth is earned. He's a freight train of chaotic energy, intimidating lesser creatures with a complete carelessness for traveling unnoticed. The hellhound is easily seven feet long, with ears that point upward like horns atop his head and claws that dig into the ground with each step forward.

Loath as I am to admit it, his sense of smell is superior to my own. He lifts his nose momentarily, and upon catching our scent, swiftly transforms. Unlike most shapeshifters, whose senses can be easily tricked by magical spells, barguests are highly sensitive to magic, able to detect living creatures behind most wards or barriers.

The barguest brazenly walks toward us with naked, confident strides. His shift from beast to human is quick and without apparent flaws. I nearly compliment him on it until he gets within three feet of us and I'm overwhelmed by the hellhound's stench. His usual scent is a mixture of dead tissue, wet leaves, and burnt hair, but tonight I detect something else. Processed cheese, perhaps?

Marquess DeLucia interrupts my train of thought. "Finally. A few more minutes and we would have started without you."

The barguest tosses a lock of hair from his eyes and replies, "Don't care."

He grabs the last robe from the marquess and throws it on, unfazed by the feeling of fabric on his recently shifted skin. Despite only doing this for a few months, he seems immediately comfortable in his human form.

He nods to us in greeting. "Mishal. Saphir."

"Dog," I reply, causing Mishal to stifle a giggle. "You smell worse than normal tonight."

The barguest narrows his eyes. "You know that foxes are considered canids, right? That means that you're in the same family as wolves and dogs, sister."

His term of endearment is laced with venom, but I'm not too concerned. Even with his massive form, this dog is still mostly bark. Too green to be a real threat—at least, for now.

I nudge the burned owl carcass with my bare foot, flipping it to get even char. "The fact that you think we're anything alike shows just how simple you are."

He raises an eyebrow. "All right then. If you're not a dog, what are you?"

"If you must know, gray foxes behave more like cats than the average fox. And I am far, far, more agile and cunning than any of the stick-chasing members of our 'family.' If you don't believe me," I bare my teeth at him, pushing down the instinct to growl, "I'd gladly provide a demonstration."

In response, the barguest gives me a look of ambivalence, unsure if my last sentence was flirtatious or threatening. I rarely draw the line between such things, but in this case, I feel the need to clarify that no, dog, I don't find your large, pointy ears attractive in the slightest, even if you are rather adept at shifting.

But before I can say as much, I'm interrupted by Marquess DeLucia clearing his throat.

"Oh yes. By all means, waste our time with petty rivalry. It's not as if our lives are hanging in the balance or anything."

We all pause for a moment, each remembering how we were approached for this task, and what is at stake, should we fail.

I bow my head. "Apologies, Marquess."

"Thank you, Saphir."

DeLucia raises a large stick to poke the charred bird through one of its eye sockets. When the skull begins lifting away from the meat, he shows a thin smile.

"Good. Let's begin."

We sit in the grass and partake of the bird, silently. This part of the ritual isn't necessary, but it is tradition, and I'm never one to say no to a free meal, even if it is prepared in a way I don't prefer.

If human bodies weren't so prone to illness, I'd demand that we eat the owl raw, as nature intended.

I chew at some gristle while the barguest and fire salamander hungrily devour their portions, fat and muscle and all. The marquess, however, takes his time eating. He has the audacity to use a paper plate, as well as a knife and fork. When I give him a look, he pulls out a napkin and lays it flat on his lap.

"Never embrace the bestial nature completely, my dear. It'll consume you. I've had to be very intentional about how I preserve my gentility in these last few years. Living for as long as I have does that to you, I'm afraid."

We finish eating and rise. Marquess DeLucia dabs the corners of his mouth to speak first:

"Now. Mishal. The skull."

Still chewing on the skull, the salamander begrudgingly opens his mouth and removes it. He hands the skull to the marquess, disappointed to lose his chew toy.

While holding the owl's skull in both hands, Marquess DeLucia raises his eyes to the moon and speaks in a low rumble.

"For sight."

The marquess breaks off a chunk of the skull and hands it to me.

I let out a high-pitched bark. "For silence!"

That done, I break off my own piece of skull. The bones' edges splinter and spray onto the grass beneath me.

I offer the remaining skull to Mishal, who bellows, "For strength!" He breaks off his piece, smaller than the other two, and hands the remainder to the barguest.

The barguest looks at us and announces, "For science!"

We look at him for a moment, confused.

"What?" He fights the grin creeping across his face. "I thought we were just yelling out random 'S' words?"

I glare at him. "I hate you so much."

"Okay, okay." He laughs to himself, happy that his antics broke our concentration.

Well, the dog can laugh all he wants, but if this doesn't go well, he'll be the first to die.

"Tough crowd." The barguest says to himself. Then, he takes a steadying breath and says, "For sinew," before breaking off a final piece of the owl's skull. He tosses what remains of the original skull back into the coals.

The marquess continues the incantation.

"Wheels of time, turn. The fire must be lit."

Then, the four of us finish it in unison: "Tonight, it awakens."

Marquess DeLucia nods to Mishal, who arches his neck back for a moment and unhinges his jaw. Despite his humanoid form, he's able to release a fireball from his mouth, hot enough to melt the remaining bits of skull within the coals. Once Mishal is finished, the skull fragment in my hand vanishes from sight.

We glance around to verify that all four pieces have disappeared—which, thankfully, they have. That done, the salamander, barguest, and I settle into the grass and watch the fire die while the marquess opens a bottle of bloodwine and pours us each a glass. Then DeLucia speaks again. "Humans are wasteful and messy and needlessly sympathetic, but they do serve one purpose."

"They're quite tasty," Mishal offers.

"No doubt. But beyond that, they're willing to sacrifice each other's lives for the sake of safety, or progress, or whatever else they might hold dear. That natural-born selfishness is their survival instinct, and it's what we'll need to weaponize if we're to complete this task." The marquess raises his glass, inspiring the rest of us to follow suit.

"To never-ending night!"

"Never-ending night!" the three of us repeat and take a drink.

I empty my glass and look across the fire at the barguest, who takes a hesitant sip of his bloodwine. When it hits his tongue, he makes a sour face, but forces himself to finish the drink.

Smart. He knows that the smallest sign of disloyalty will put a target on his back.

It's only until after he's finished the drink that I remember the unfamiliar scent trailing him. It's a smell I'd normally recognize when not intermingled with a barguest's natural stench.

Young, fresh meat.

More specifically, young human meat—the kind that wears their hair in scrunchies and plays on their cell phones and loiters outside of movie theaters at night.

I cock my head to the side and focus on the scent. This isn't the smell of a dead human. Not yet, at least.

So, the barguest is toying with his prey and showing some restraint. Hm.

I ask the marquess for a refill of the bloodwine and shoot the barguest an approving look. Perhaps he's ready to grow up, after all.

Chapter Five

Ellie

I jolt awake, shivering. The details of my dream are already gone, but I'm left with the taste of copper in my mouth.

My shoulder is still asleep. Even after stretching, it takes a minute for blood to circulate back into my elbow, wrist, and fingertips.

I lift my phone with my other hand to check the time. 3:34 a.m.

So, I've got a few hours before I need to wake up for school. Once my dead arm is back to normal, I consider whether or not it's worth going back to sleep, when I notice a small, blackened hole in the top of my nightstand.

I'd put the salamander stone right there before falling asleep, next to my phone and the knife Grandpa gave me.

But now the stone is gone.

I run my fingers over the scorch marks. They're still warm.

Jumping from bed, I search under the nightstand—more with my hands than my eyes in the dark. Sure enough, there's another hole beneath it, burned into the hardwood floor.

No. There's no way the stone could burn straight through that many layers of wood.

Crawling on hands and knees, I feel the tell-tale sign of heat through the floor.

Is it coming from downstairs?

I peek through the hole in my floor and make out the shape of orange flames:

Fire.

Standing back up in the dark, I consider opening my door. The air grows thicker with smoke by the second. I cough, take a deep breath in, and cough some more.

It's not just dark in here because of how late it is.

Smoke is rising.

What do I do what do I do?

My chest tightens, but I fight the urge to hyperventilate. Instead, I take a final breath in and hold it as I grab my phone and knife.

I run over to the window above my bed, unlatch it, and try to push it open. One corner lifts, but the other won't budge.

The top of my door cracks, burns, and falls in on itself, allowing thick clouds of smoke to billow into my room.

With one last push, I'm able to open the window. It's barely big enough for me to fit, but I shimmy through the small opening, phone and knife in hand. I pull my comforter through the open window and sit on the roof in petrified awe.

The entire first floor is up in flames.

I have seconds, not minutes.

I walk to the roof's edge, crouch, and jump off.

A few feet of freefall—then a pine branch hits me in the face.

I lean into the tree, letting broken bark and twigs scratch into my skin. My hands are quickly coated in needles and sticky sap, but I hold on, determined not to fall.

The tree, however, has other plans. It bends and bows under my weight, and I barely take two steps down its trunk before my foot slips on a broken branch and I fall on my back, knocking the wind from my chest.

Struggling to breathe, I stare up at the empty, dark sky above, all too aware of the burning cuts and sap painted across my skin.

Is this how I die?

Not today.

I sit up and cough. I cough and cough and cough until air reenters my lungs. Each new breath is a wheeze, heavy from the smoke and the fall.

But I'm no longer suffocating.

Nearby, my knife is tangled up in the comforter, still intact—but my phone's not so lucky. Its screen is chipped and shattered, and when I push the power button, it stays black, clearly beyond resurrecting.

Well, at least the knife is still okay.

Wait.

Where's Grandpa?

I grab the comforter and sprint up to the porch, hoping to use my blanket as a shield from the fire. When I open the front door, a backdraft flings it inside.

A burning beam has collapsed in the kitchen.

The smoke is thicker downstairs, the heat more intense. I can't see more than a foot in front of my face. There's no way to know if Grandpa's still in the house.

"Grandpa!" I yell, "Where are you?"

But there's no response, and no clear path to find him.

Why didn't he wake me up?

Is he outside, looking for me?

Is there a chance he's still asleep?

The heat is too much. I grab a pair of boots, toss them outside, and reach for my jacket when I spot Grandpa's axe, propped up next to the front door. Before the flames can destroy it, I grab the axe and throw it, too, onto the lawn.

Seconds later, I'm back outside. I bundle what's left of my belongings in the blanket and carry them away from the house. Once I reach a safe distance from the fire, I drop the pile and sit, exhausted.

Waves of realization hit me at once.

The house is on fire, and Grandpa is nowhere to be found.

I get up and rush toward the far side of the house.

"Grandpa? Grandpa!"

A pillar of smoke looms above me, sprinkling the ground in ash. I watch as it consumes what's left of the upstairs.

And panic creeps in.

Grandpa's not out here because he didn't get out.

"You don't know that, Ellie. Get it together!"

I slap myself once, determined to focus. If only my heart would stop pounding in my ears.

The fire would have started in the cellar. Maybe it spread to the living room, catching on rugs and furniture before setting to the structural parts of the house. Grandpa's room is on the bottom floor, while my room is upstairs. He could have woken up with the fire already outside of his room and decided to escape through his window, rather than trying to extinguish it.

But as I approach the farthest side of the house, I see Grandpa's window.

It's still shut.

Tears fill my eyes and I start to shake, fighting to catch my breath again. Only this time, it doesn't matter how much I cough. I can't get enough air.

He's gone, and it's my fault.

I fall to the ground, sobbing. "I can't do this. I'm too weak."

As my mouth forms the words, the bones and muscles of my shoulder tense, spasm, and pop out of place. I scream as a force twists one elbow unnaturally and arches my back under an invisible, crushing weight.

And I begin to change.

The world blurs with smoke and shadow as my limbs stretch like taffy, gaining mass and height, and my bones snap and sizzle to construct something new and jagged. Eventually, the stretching slows and settles into a dull ache, and I can breathe.

I lift an arm in front of my face and extend each finger in turn.

My hand is wider now—still with four fingers and a thumb, but no longer human. This hand is calloused with long, sharp nails.

No, not nails. These are too long to be fingernails.

The word rolls around in my mind before I can name it.

Claws?

A howl erupts from my chest as I revel in the fresh power coursing through my veins.

Maybe I don't need to cower in fear.

I press into the earth on all fours and run, though it's less of a run and more of a push and pull against the ground. I pull the dense, packed patches of earth toward myself and push into the shifting, soft dirt.

Once I, a new creature, reach the house, I burst through the front door only to be greeted by a wall of heat and smoke. The devouring fire assaults my senses until my eyes and lungs adjust to their new surroundings.

Before, I had to stumble around in the dark.

Now, I can see.

I push past the surrounding flames and land in the kitchen. The walls creak and groan, and with most of the house broken or burned, there's a good chance that it will fall on top of me if I don't get out soon.

Finally, I'm in the back hallway. The door to Grandpa's room is still shut.

I ram my shoulder into his door—hard—half expecting it to burst free from its frame and fly across the room. Instead, the solid oak door absorbs the blow, barely bending at the hinges.

Annoyed, I pinch and turn the knob, and sure enough. There's Grandpa.

He's in bed, sleeping.

Most of Grandpa's room is still intact, despite the south wall catching fire at my entrance. I throw him over my shoulder like a rag doll, surprised that I can carry him as easily as a book-laden backpack, and recognize the open, nearly melted, bottle of pills on his nightstand.

His sleeping pills. No wonder he's still asleep.

I toss a quilt over his body and run for the front door, careful not to hit him against any walls or doors.

The house seizes and buckles with a groan.

We emerge on the porch, and I race for the woods, hoping to get far from the house before it collapses.

But no less than ten heavy steps away from the house, the second story falls into the first.

All our memories, gone in an instant.

I lay Grandpa down on the grass and lean in to hear his breathing. After a few tense seconds, he coughs and rolls onto his side.

"Grandpa?"

The word comes out in a gravelly, basso rumble—a voice that's not my own.

I slap a hand over my mouth.

What am I?

He blinks up at me, still groggily asleep. "Wha . . . what?"

At the sight of me, my grandfather's eyes widen in horror.

Then he blinks, closes his eyes, and returns to sleep.

I lean over him, listening. He's breathing at an even rate.

Grandpa is the first human I've seen since becoming this . . . thing, and that moment of fear in his eyes reveals a few things.

First, his reaction tells me that this new form isn't all in my head. So something's definitely happened to me.

But standing over him also shows me how easily my new senses can recognize the small, subtle changes in a human's physiology. The fear that overwhelmed him, if only for a moment, made his pupils dilate, his heart rate increase, and his sweat glands perspire.

I could already tell that my vision was better in the dark, but now, at rest, I can hear small creatures scurrying in the pile of leaves to my left. Some sort of beetle, a few worms, and a burrowing rodent expanding a tunnel.

And I can smell a million things—fallen pine needles, coyote droppings, a dead rabbit being eaten by an owl. The owl's feathers smell like bark and dirt and fresh blood.

My stomach starts to ache.

I open my mouth as drool, collecting under my tongue, spills out onto the ground.

My grandfather, wrapped in a blanket, is not unlike a burrito.

But before I snap my jaws over his neck, I turn and take off into the woods.

I run and run and run until the passing fir trees blend into the surrounding darkness. My hands, or rather, claws, give me better grip as I turn around trees and rocks in my way. Running takes my mind away from the hunger and the pain of knowing.

In this form, I can't go back.

There's no home for me to go back to, anyway. Even if I wasn't like this, by the time a neighbor calls the fire department and they arrive, I doubt there will be anything left.

I stop abruptly at a stream full of tiny, scurrying fish. Hoping to catch a few in my mouth, I dunk my head hungrily beneath the surface and open my jaws wide, like a net.

When I lift my head, however, all I've done is fill my mouth with dirty water.

I drink it down anyway and shake the excess mud from my head, thinking. If I head upstream, I might find a larger body of water, which means larger fish.

Taking off in that direction, I run faster than ever before.

The stream's path leads me uphill, but I'm not winded from the journey—I'm only slowed when climbing over a great heap of rocks. Once ascended, I find what I'm looking for.

It's a vast pond, deep and still. The moon casts a clear reflection on the water's surface, and with it being so quiet, the pond's slightest ripples of movement give away the game lurking beneath.

I watch and wait, then plunge my arm into the water, breaking the mirrorlike surface with choppy splashes as I pull a dark snake from beneath.

The large snake—a water moccasin—snaps at me, its white mouth gleaming. It jerks around to break free, but without success.

I crush its skull like a raw egg.

With the dead snake now limp in my grip, I take a bite from its midsection, easily cutting through bone with my new teeth, and consider its taste.

It's cold, tough and fibrous, like a waterlogged slice of steak.

As I lean down to eat the remaining bits of snake, the choppy water calms preternaturally. A new thread of wind whistles through the trees.

I hesitate, bloody snake in hand, and look across the pond.

Moonlight suddenly floods the woods with a brilliant, phosphorescent glow that spreads and radiates across the water. It appears to be lit from within, highlighting the silhouettes of fish and other wildlife as they swim below.

I squint at the abrupt change in lighting and notice a lone figure, sitting on a pile of rocks not too far off.

He wasn't there before.

The young man, not much older than me, has long, dark, curly hair and almost bluish skin. He's dressed in silver and white, but despite being drenched from head to toe, his clothes are still dry and vibrant as they reflect the moonlight.

He holds a violin.

Upon seeing me, the boy stares straight into my eyes without fear or judgment.

He looks sad.

I drop the remainder of my snake into the water and stride toward the figure, wondering how I might destroy such a luminous creature until I'm stuck, knee-deep, in the muddy pond floor. That's when the mysterious boy stands, lifts the violin to his chin, and begins to play.

The fiddler's first note is low and solemn, and hangs in the air. He follows that note with another, and a third, quickening his pace to add runs of three and four and five notes in the same minor key.

Despite the distance between us, the fiddler's playing makes it seem like he's right next to me, sharing his story in a sad whisper.

His song is lonely and hopeful and broken. All too aware of his past mistakes, the blue-skinned being is worried that he's incapable of change.

The fiddler returns to the chorus a second time, with each note gaining strength from the last. His music wipes away the monster's instincts and brings me back to myself.

To Ellie.

I'm five years old again—one of my earliest memories. My grandparents and I are at the mental hospital to visit my mother. Grandma tidies the room, Grandpa reads a book to me, and my mother sits in a chair, facing the window.

Grandma turns around, carrying a large, chocolate cake, topped with five lit candles. She starts singing, "Happy birthday to you!"

Grandpa joins in, "Happy birthday to you!"

Together they finish, "Happy birthday, dear Ellie! Happy birthday to you."

I close my eyes tight, make a wish, and blow out the candles.

When I'm finished, I open my eyes to see my mother, who's suddenly turned around to watch. She's staring at me, and for a moment we're locked in silent eye contact. I notice the corner of her lip twitch as if to smile, until she forgets why she looked over her shoulder in the first place and turns back to her window.

"There's a man outside," she murmurs.

Even then, I spent all of my wishes on her.

I come back to myself all at once, lying prostrate on the hard ground, crying.

Back at the pond, I can feel my body shifting again, shrinking back to the pathetic, small form of me before.

The girl whose negligence burned down her own house,

who almost killed her grandfather,

who was born wrong.

I try to slow the jagged breaths as they push into my chest. Then, despite the agonizing pain that spreads into my legs and arms and back, I crawl on all fours until I'm beneath a nearby tree.

Naked, cold, and exhausted, I curl up into a ball and fall asleep.

When the sun comes up, I'm warm.

I burrow deeper into my soft, fuzzy blanket, trying to piece together the broken strands of my dream. When I roll slightly to one side, my entire body lights up with pain. If I'm this tense, I must have thrashed around in my sleep again.

A gentle breeze blows against the bare skin on my shoulder. I blink into the sunlight, only to see that I'm still outside, and still very much naked.

"Ah!" I bolt upright.

The blanket beneath me is not a blanket. It's a large, red-orange fox tail, attached to an oversized red-orange fox, sleeping next to me.

Terrified, I jump off the fox's tail and land in the mud. "Ah!"

The gigantic fox, nearly the size of a moose, sleepily opens one eye at me, and then another. It stands up, arches its back, and then takes off into the trees.

I stare at the empty clearing around me, stunned.

"I'm sorry, what?!" I yell to no one in particular.

A hoodie and a pair of sweatpants come flying at me from the trees. When they land at my feet, I notice a familiar emblem across the front of the sweatshirt. It's the outline of a fighting gopher, Errolton High School's mascot.

"Um," I squint at the hoodie, hoping to decipher an explanation from the gopher and his boxing gloves.

Cyndi emerges from behind a tree, decked out in a similar red sweatshirt and pants, only her hoodie has the words *Go Gophers!* written across the front in funky black lettering. Her orange hair is spikier and more disheveled than usual.

"Sorry about the clothes. I stole these from the track coach's office a while back. Not because I like stealing or anything. Just for emergencies." She shrugs. "It's all I could bring on such short notice."

I blink at her, confused, "Cyndi?"

"Mornin' Ellie. We should talk."

Chapter Six

Ellie

I look up at Cyndi, bedecked in her stolen sweatshirt and wolfish grin. Though it's more accurate to say she has a foxlike grin: less menacing and aggressive, more smug and self-satisfied.

That is, if my eyes are to be trusted. Which they are not.

"That . . . huge fox," I finally say, dumbstruck. "Was that . . . did you . . . ?"

Two red-orange fox ears sprout from the top of Cyndi's head, peaking out amidst her messy orange hair. A fox tail of orange and black fur swishes out from behind her.

"Ah." She grins wider. "That's much better. No matter how much time I spend in my human form, it's always a struggle to keep those hidden away."

My jaw drops. Even if Cyndi's ability to transform is just another symptom of the new, monstrous world I live in, it's still a lot to take in.

My mind whirs with questions, each fighting to be asked first.

"What do you mean, 'my human form?'" I pull the red hoodie over my head. "As in, you're not human?"

"Yep! I'm actually a fox. I just look like a human sometimes." Cyndi takes an exaggerated bow. "Carnelian the fox, at your service."

"Carnelian?" I squint at the unfamiliar word while stepping into the oversized sweatpants she threw at me, double-knotting the drawstring. "So, hold on. Your name isn't even Cyndi?"

Cyndi the human, Carnelian the fox, pops a stick of gum in her mouth. Her fox ears twitch as she chews.

"I've had other names; Cyndi's just my most recent human name, but I think it's a good fit. I chose Cyndi after seeing Cyndi Lauper in concert. She's so flashy, funky, and cool—everything I like about humans." She pauses for a moment to reminisce. "That would have been before you were born, though. Sometime in the eighties."

"The eighties? But . . . you're . . . "

"A teenager? Yeah, I am. Well, sort of."

"Uh-huh." I purse my lips. "Cyndi—Carnelian—whoever you are. I'm very confused."

Cyndi blows a bubble and pops it. "Well, about two hundred years ago, I was born as a regular fox. At least, I think it was two hundred years ago. It could be more. I wasn't paying attention to human history for the first few decades, so it's hard to tell."

My eyes widen at her response. "Two . . . hundred . . . ?"

She tries to blow another bubble and fails, nearly spitting out the wad of gum.

Annoyed, she continues. "Yeah. I lived as a normal fox for about three years before I started to change. When that happened, I kind of . . . stopped aging? I've been stuck at that same age since then, which would be . . . hm." She pauses. "I used to know this. I think it's five human years to every fox year, so if I'd already been alive for three years . . . " Furrowing her brow, she asks, "How much is that?"

Sighing, I answer, "Fifteen."

It dawns on me that I've been attending high school with a magical, centuries-old fox who, rather than providing me ancient knowledge and wisdom, still struggles with multiplication word problems.

"That's it!" She puffs her chest out with pride, despite doing nothing to solve the math problem on her own. "So, I'm at least fifteen 'human years' old, and have been for the last two hundred years."

"But . . . " I rack my brain for a logical explanation. "What about the meteor shower? The Supernatural Tectonic Disruption? The . . . the vampires? That stuff only started a year ago."

Cyndi shrugs. "Who's to say weird things only started happening this year? Maybe this is just the first year people have been paying attention. Cell phone cameras and all that."

I stare at my hands, trying to piece it together. "Right. Okay. Maybe."

I want to dismiss her story as a dumb prank, but I can't. Not after what happened last night.

Oh, right.

That.

I fall back into the grass, fighting the alternating urges to hyperventilate and vomit.

"This is a lot to take in, Cyndi." I press a hand against my forehead. "I mean, we've been friends for years now, and you never . . . " My headache sharpens, then subsides. "Why wouldn't you just tell me?"

Cyndi joins me on the ground.

"Ellie, it's not exactly safe for me to tell people about this. Especially when someone's grandfather regularly hunts supernatural beasties."

"What? But you're not—"

"A monster? Then what would you call me?"

"You're . . . " I pick at a few brittle blades of grass on the ground. "Look, maybe I don't know everything, but I know you. You don't hurt people. You antagonize them sometimes, sure, but I can't think of a time you've ever acted evil or weird like that." I throw a piece of grass and dirt at her. "You are a turd sandwich for not telling me, though."

She brushes the dirt away, laughing. "Well, I'm glad you see it that way. Not everyone would. Maybe I should have told you sooner."

"Yeah, maybe you should have." I bite the inside of my cheek. "So, do you mind telling me how a normal fox becomes . . . whatever it is you are?"

Cyndi gives a nonchalant stretch of her tail. "I guess I can tell you, since I'm such a good friend." She extends her arm, waving it with a flourish to set the scene. "It happened randomly one day, back when I was still a normal fox. I was off doing normal fox things—tracking, snacking, the usual—when I came across a patch of woods I'd never seen before. It was getting late, and I couldn't find my way home, and I was hungry, so I foraged for berries until my belly was full. I was hoping to catch something else to eat, but the animals in this part of the woods were weird."

"How so?"

She twirls the gum around her index finger. "So, okay. Some of the birds flew upside down, as if they were meant to fly that way. And the only fish I could find was a salmon that kept playing tricks on me. He looked delicious, but was too smart for me to catch." She shrugs. "Anyway, the berries smelled fine at the time, so I ate as many as I could find.

"Of course, I got sick. I was sick for hours afterward, puking next to a bush. And then, after my stomach was empty, I dry heaved until this came out."

She pulls the wad of bubble gum from her mouth to show me.

"Your gum?"

"What?" Cyndi looks at her hand, "Oh. Not that."

It takes her a few seconds to peel away enough gum for me to see it—a glittering, red-orange stone, smooth and flat, about the size of a quarter.

"This. It's Carnelian. That's what the stone is called, anyway. I took the word to be my fox name, since it's the source of my consciousness, or power, or whatever."

"Whoa." My eyes widen. It's eerily similar in size and shape to the salamander stone. "Can I see it for a second?"

Cyndi pops it back into her cheek. "Sorry. I can't let anyone else hold onto my stone. Coming into contact with it might do something to you, like it did to me."

"It could do something to me?"

Had the salamander stone done something to me, too?

I fire a follow-up question at her. "What happened to you once you found it?"

"At first, nothing," Cyndi replies. "I carried the stone around for days—purely out of curiosity—and didn't notice any changes until the day a pair of merchants traveled by my den.

"As a fox, I'd always enjoyed listening to human conversation, even if it made no sense to me. The shape of each word, the color and tone of dialogue, the way a sentence can be cheerfully shared with a friend and also painfully spoken alone—it fascinated me, like a foreign song, or the chatter of birds. Only this time, when I listened in on their conversation, I began to understand the words they used, and I was never the same.

"Decoding different languages quickly taught me more about humans and their world beyond the woods than I ever could imagine, and I had to know more. I would run into town and spend entire days people-watching, studying their mannerisms and customs, before retreating back to the woods to practice what I'd learned.

"Once I figured out how to shapeshift into a convincing human form, though, I realized that this stone is able to do more than that. It doesn't just change me—it changes how others perceive me. At least, I think that's how it works."

I raise an eyebrow.

"It's true!" She continues. "So long as someone can sense me, I can manipulate their senses to perceive whatever I want. So far I'm only able to change myself into a human and a larger version of a fox, but I could do more if I practiced."

I think for a moment. "Has anyone ever seen through your illusions?"

"Nope!" Cyndi beams. "The Carnelian stone allows me to tell convincing lies to an observer's senses, and humans are doggedly attached to their senses, so most don't question their first assumptions unless something appears out of place. The only way someone could see through one of my illusions is if they knew about my powers and used magic or something to look around it." She smiles like a benevolent professor.

I'm tempted to check her ego with a few multiplication problems, but all that comes out is, "Huh."

She goes on. "The weird part of it is that changing my appearance impacts the observer's perception, but it also rebounds back to me and changes me, somehow. Like when I'm a big fox, I'm not just tricking you; I'm also tricking myself."

"Wait, really? How?"

"I have no idea. It's very difficult to draw a line between what humans can actually perceive, what they want to perceive, and what is 'real.' The fabric of reality is made of malleable thread, apparently."

I shoot her an incredulous look. "So, you can discuss complex details of metaphysics and human psychology, but when I ask you for help on a history test—a test that covers events you actually lived through—you have no idea what I'm talking about?"

Cyndi scoffs, "I tell you that I'm a fox whose gained conscious awareness, learned how to shapeshift, and developed a wicked sense of humor—"

"That last one's debatable."

"—and you're upset that I'm not a better study buddy?"

"Last week you asked me who JFK was!"

She throws her hands up, exasperated. "I don't care who he was! I'm a fox!"

We both laugh. It feels good to laugh, to momentarily forget about the night before.

"And anyway," Cyndi looks my way, still chuckling, "I know about the Kennedys. I only asked to make sure you knew who he was."

That's when it dawns on me all over again. Grandpa almost died last night. Or perhaps he's already dead, while I'm off in the woods discussing magical stones and shapeshifting foxes.

Cyndi notices my change in expression and says, "Your grandfather's okay, by the way. Sorry. I should have started with that."

"No, no. I mean, yes, but we needed to address . . . you being a giant fox." I sigh, still hesitant to mention the full truth of the previous night. "Do you know what happened to the house?"

Cyndi nods her head sadly. "I saw the smoke on my way home from kennel duty. By the time I got to your house, the fire department was already there." She pulls at the skin on her hand. "I'm so sorry, Ellie. They were able to put the fire out, but there's not much left."

I stare at my feet, buried in the legs of the oversized sweatpants.

"Thankfully, the barn was far enough from the house to not catch fire. Your grandfather's horse Declan is safe, though it took a while to settle him down. He's with Colonel Adams. She offered to board him at Farrowfield Farms, since the dogs are already over there."

In the insanity of the fire, I'd completely forgotten my grandfather's horse. Part of me was holding out hope that someone from the Beowulf Brigade would offer to help with the fire's aftermath, so hearing that Colonel Adams was the one to care for Declan and the dogs gave me a rare instance of comfort. She's Grandpa's second in command, after all, and one of the few people he trusts in town. Finding his trust to be well-placed is a welcome relief.

My relationship with the Beowulf Brigade has always been one of distant interest and curiosity, wondering if and when I'd have the opportunity to join. But if I change into that . . . thing, again, the only connection I can possibly have with them is that of a monster being hunted.

I don't expect the younger recruits to put up much of a fight, if it comes to it.

The image of meat on a spit intrudes my thoughts, and I consider how the age of a kill might contribute to the tenderness of meat on the bone.

Ignoring my stomach's renewed desire to feed, I bury the monster's thoughts and add AVOIDING THE BEOWULF BRIGADE to my growing list of concerns.

"And Grandpa? Where is he?"

Cyndi nods. "He's in the hospital for now. After they admitted him last night, I called, pretending to be you."

I raise an eyebrow. "Something you do often?"

She raises her hands defensively. "Sorry! You were nowhere to be found, and I can imitate your voice well enough over the phone. Just to get an update on him, so that I had some answers for you for . . . whenever I found you." She pauses. "Are you mad?"

I shake my head and look away. I'm angry, but not at her. Not really.

"Okay, well, all they could tell me at the time was that he's stable. He wasn't awake when I called, but it was late. He could be awake by now."

"What time is it?"

Cyndi checks her phone. "Nearly noon. We should probably head back." She reaches around to grab her backpack, unzips it, and pulls out a water bottle. She hands it to me. "Here."

When I take it, she returns to digging into the bag. "I think I have a few candy bars rolling around in here, if you're hungry. I know I am."

I watch her search in the pockets of her backpack while anxious, unanswerable thoughts creep back into my mind, wondering about the nature of my transformation and the new life I have to live.

My future will always be measured by this moment; my past will always be marked as the "time before."

"Ah-ha!" Cyndi pulls out three chocolate bars from her backpack. "Want one?"

I shake my head and take a sip of the water, looking around. Aside from the tree I slept beneath, this pocket of wilderness is mostly inhabited by moss and large rocks. It'd be rather picturesque if it, too, wasn't marred by the events of last night.

After putting two of the candy bars into her pocket, Cyndi unwraps the third and takes a bite. "We can walk slowly, since you don't have any shoes. Did you want to stop by the house first, to try to recover what's left? Or should we go straight to the hospital?"

I stare into the pocket of trees ahead of us. "I . . . don't know."

Cyndi zips up her backpack and throws it over her shoulder. She stands up and offers me a hand. "We can decide on the way. C'mon."

While we kick through the underbrush, I wrestle with how much I should tell Cyndi about my monster transformation. She's been hiding her shapeshifting abilities from me for a while—since we met, which was about three years ago. And while her reason for not telling me makes sense, it still doesn't explain why she befriended me in the first place.

What does a fox have to gain from being friends with a human?

Was she looking for protection from hunters, or did she just want help with her math homework?

And why is she attending high school, anyway?

She did say that her stone's power allows her to tell very convincing lies. What if that can impact a person's memory and personal history as well?

My brain lingers on her potential motives. Behind all the jokes and smiles, Cyndi's always seemed . . . restless. Bored, and a little lonely.

Maybe she did target me for protection, or maybe she was just bored, but I can't deny that she's been open and transparent with her secret when she didn't have to be. She also took action amid my personal crisis, checking in on my grandfather and coming to get me when I needed help.

Not one for elongated silence, Cyndi fiddles with the wrapper of her candy bar.

"You know," she starts, "the firefighters were surprised that your grandfather made it out of the house alone, considering his condition. One of them mentioned that with all the broken windows, he was probably thrown from the house before it collapsed. That happens sometimes, from an appliance or something exploding inside. But it doesn't explain how he was wrapped in a blanket without any bad injuries."

Cyndi shoots me a sidelong look. "Another firefighter said that, with all the new creatures around these days, he wouldn't be surprised if your grandfather was rescued by a fairy or something. Apparently, the guy's seen one before—or a friend of his has. I don't remember."

That catches me off guard. "There are fairies now?"

She shrugs. "There could be. I've never seen one, but anything's possible."

I'm suddenly reminded of the violinist in the water. Maybe that wasn't just a fever dream?

Does that mean I ate a snake, too?

"Anyway," Cyndi steps over a log, "that's not what happened, is it?"

I keep walking, unsure of what to say.

She presses, "I can tell that you saved him. It's written all over your face. I just don't understand how you did it, or what possessed you to go running miles into the woods without a flashlight, or, you know, any clothes?"

"Okay, okay. When you found me last night, what did you see?"

Cyndi cocks her head to one side. "What do you mean? I saw you beneath that tree, sleeping."

"There wasn't anything weird going on when you got there? You didn't see anything else?"

"Anything else?" She thinks for a moment. "It was pretty dark. I could see you, but that's about it. You were asleep. And freezing. Did something else happen?"

Following a deep breath, I decide to tell her everything. She's the only one who might believe me, and I doubt that my friend, the magical fox, will be upset to learn that her friend might also be a shapeshifter. She'll probably be supportive, even if what I turn into isn't cuddly and approachable as much as it is ugly, lumbering, and bent on destruction.

So, I start from the fire, explaining how I escaped, how I transformed, how I rescued Grandpa, and most importantly, how I ran into the woods to avoid eating him. Cyndi nods silently as I tell the story, and I can tell that she's listening for once, instead of pretending to listen while she gears up to tell some prepared joke in response.

She only interrupts me once, asking, "So when you changed—do you remember what you looked like? Any distinguishing features, like fur or scales? Maybe some ears or a tail?"

I shake my head. "Not really. Other than longer nails and sharper teeth, I didn't have any new accessories. I just felt like myself, but larger, and . . . hungrier."

Cyndi nods. "Okay. Did anything else happen?"

I mention the pond, the snake, and the fiddler. At that, her eyes go wide.

"You ate a water moccasin?!" She punches my arm in excitement. "That's so metal!"

I shake my head. "I don't remember many details after that. I vaguely remember the blue guy's music, but that felt more like a dream than anything else, and then I fell asleep. And changed back."

I stop walking.

Cyndi turns back to me. "What is it?"

Looking down at my hands, I realize they've been shaking.

"I don't know what's happening to me."

"I know," she says, reaching out. "But you will."

I take a step back. "You don't know that. I have no idea when it's going to happen again, why it's happening, or if it's fixable."

I tug at the shorter strands of my gnarled black hair, only for my fingers to get trapped in the knots behind my ear.

"How am I supposed to live like this now? How can I possibly live like a normal person when I'm . . . I don't know. Cursed?"

Cyndi gives me a pitying look. I want to punch her in the face for it, but I don't. She doesn't know what to say, and it's not her fault she's being confronted with such a pathetic display.

Instead, I shake my head. "Sorry. We don't have time for this right now. Let's go to the house first. I think I was able to save a pair of boots last night before running off."

She nods. We keep walking.

My stomach growls.

"Can I have one of those chocolate bars now?" I ask, embarrassed.

"Ha. Sure." She pulls a Butterfinger out of her pocket and hands it to me. "We still have a few miles to go until we get to the house. Wanna go for a run?"

"I can't run right now. I'm not wearing shoes."

She laughs. "Not you, dummy."

Then she falls to all fours and magnifies in size, as she transforms back into the oversized fox. Her grinning face towers over me.

While I watch, speechless, she begins chasing the brush of her tail in leaping, childish bounds until she slams into a tree. A few birds erupt from the tree's higher branches, clearly agitated by the impact of a giant fox hitting the tree trunk, but Cyndi is unphased. She flips over and starts rolling on the mossy ground, solely concerned with how to grab her fluffy, red-orange tail.

"Your clothes . . . " I realize, "They're not ripped up or in a pile. Does that mean your shapeshifting can account for clothes, too?"

Distracted by a new itch, Cyndi nods her monstrous fox-head while she scratches at her ear with a front paw.

"So, then why did you wear that dumb hoodie and sweatpants?" I ask. "You could have been wearing anything!"

The fox shrugs and lowers a shoulder. Does she mean for me to climb aboard?

I look around to check for anything we might need, and upon seeing Cyndi's backpack, throw it over my shoulder. Then I climb up the side of her torso until I'm perched on her back.

"Did you wear the sweat suit so that we would match? Out of solidarity?"

She gives a noncommittal bark. Then, in a voice that sounds like Cyndi's, but more distant and ethereal, she says, "I couldn't let you be the only one looking stupid."

My eyes grow large as saucers.

"And now you're a talking fox. I knew to expect it, but it's still too weird."

Cyndi, the giant fox who is also my friend, snickers. "Life is weird, Ellie. Now hang on. I'm about to go fast."

She wasn't lying about her speed. Being carried by a running, gigantic fox is like riding a horse at full tilt, but without a saddle or reigns. So really not at all like riding a horse.

My hands ball up around tufts of her red-orange fur as I hold on for dear life. At this size, I'm more like a mouse to her than a fully-grown human. How easy would it be for her to throw me off without a second thought? Was that candy bar from earlier really enough to feed this giant beast?

Before I can consider the logistics of a shapeshifter's diet and ever-changing gastrointestinal structure, we take an abrupt right turn at a familiar set of trees.

The blackened timbers of Grandpa's house are visible from this edge of the woods.

Cyndi also wasn't lying about the extent of the fire's damage. Other than a few burned beams, some peeling sections of drywall, and large piles of ash, very little remains. Even less is salvageable.

As I dismount from Cyndi's back, a gust of wind kicks some debris in our direction, which covers the front of my sweatshirt in gray ash.

I take a tentative step forward, illogically expecting that if I make the wrong move, the house might reignite.

How could I have been so careless?

I go to take another step when my foot thumps against something heavy. I stop walking and look down.

The handle of my grandfather's axe rests on top of my foot.

"This is my fault," I whisper.

Still a large fox, Cyndi asks, "What is it?"

I scan the plot of land for any recognizable sign of what used to be there. With effort, I can imagine the roof's outline against the trees.

I remember the way the sky looked from my bedroom, nestled between the two towering pines that flanked my window. I remember the loose rain gutters that Grandpa gave up on fixing because of how often they'd freeze over. I remember the crooked kitchen cupboards, the squeaks in the floor, and the one perfect spot in the living room for watching TV.

The memories are there, but trying to place them physically is painful with the evidence of the fire all around me.

This was our home. It was Grandpa's for decades before I was born, and now it's gone. All because I found a shiny rock that I wanted to keep as a fun secret at a time when strange events should not go unreported.

I take another heavy step forward.

"Last night, back at the ice cream shop. You remember the fire salamander's attack?"

Cyndi scrunches her fox nose. "What does that have to do with—"

"The salamander dropped something," I say, interrupting her. I push aside melted furniture and appliances until I find what remains of the cellar door. "I thought it was just a scale from the lizard's back, like how a snake sheds its skin. And it looked cool, so I put it in my pocket."

She follows me forward. "Okay, and . . . ?"

I open the cellar and search the scorched shadows that fill it. Most of the room is intact, since it's made from concrete and brick, rather than wood.

But the stairs are gone.

A ray of sunlight spills into the corner of the cellar, illuminating something the size and shape of a coin among the debris.

I glance over to Cyndi.

"That thing I found started the fire, I think. I need to get into the cellar to see if I'm right."

Clearly wary of my suggestion, but also too curious to disagree, she nods.

With the cellar's opening too small for an oversized fox to enter, and the cellar itself too deep for me to safely jump, we're forced to search the wreckage for a makeshift ladder or rope. I finally locate a wooden beam about twice my size, which Cyndi slides into the cellar and leans against the opening. Then she shrinks her large form into the size of a normal red fox and scurries down the beam.

I climb in after her, and right as my feet hit the concrete floor, Cyndi yips in the corner. She's standing over something glowing softly in the shadows.

Sure enough, it's the salamander stone—and it's not alone. The glowing stone is encircled by four bone shards equidistant from one another. The shards appear intentionally placed, and despite everything else in the cellar being covered in soot and burn marks, the bones are intact and stark white.

Cyndi lets out a concerned bark. "Ellie, are you sure you should . . ."

But despite her warning tone, despite the strange arrangement of bones, and despite the room's dark aura, I pick up the still-glowing ember.

I can't stop myself. It's as if the stone is calling to me, compelling me to hold it.

And just like the day before, it cools to black in my hand.

I lift the stone between my thumb and forefinger to show Cyndi its change in color. When I do, she pushes the Carnelian stone out from her cheek and holds it between her teeth to compare the two stones in size and shape.

I was right. Aside from the color, they're the same.

When the two stones get within inches of each other, they begin to glow and thrum with power. Hers is a brilliant orange-red, like a sunset, while mine is a deep red on one side and matte black on the other, like low-burning coal. The glow fills the room with light, and then, I hear a word:

Volcan.

The glow fades in an instant.

We both look down at the stones, baffled.

"Huh." I laugh. "That's new."

Cyndi's fox-face is incredulous. "Why would the salamander have one of these?"

I walk back toward the cellar door. "No idea." I place the stone in the pocket of my sweatpants. "Have you ever seen another one of these?"

She shakes her head. "Never."

I sigh. That means that this trip offered no new answers, only more questions.

I start to climb out, and Cyndi follows behind, helping to push me up the beam so that I don't fall backward.

When we return to the surface, I notice that she's looking tired. It's no surprise what with all the running and shapeshifting she's had to do in the last few hours. "Do we need to take a break?" I ask.

The small fox shakes her head. "I just need to stay in this form for a bit to conserve energy. Sorry. But what about that stone? Have you been carrying it around since yesterday?"

"Yeah. I meant to tell you and Grandpa about it, but things kept getting in the way. And then it lit the house on fire while I was sleeping last night."

Her eyes go wide. "Seriously?"

I nod. "As much as I want to throw it into the ocean and never see it again, now that I know what it can do, I worry what will happen if I leave it for someone else to find. I think if I'm wearing or holding it, it might be less likely to cause property damage? I guess I'll have to sleep outside from now on, to prevent that from happening again."

Cyndi and I discuss how realistic it would be for me to find camping gear to buy or borrow as we start to walk away from the house. I give the remaining piles of ash a cursory glance before approaching my grandfather's axe, as well as the pile of other items rescued from the house. They're still wrapped in the blanket I'd used in my escape from the fire.

After pocketing the knife—the one Grandpa gifted me just the night before—and lacing up my salvaged boots, I lift the double-edged axe over my shoulder and head back into the woods.

Cyndi runs to catch up with me. "Hey, now. Wait a minute!"

She's switched back into her human form, but this time she's wearing jeans, an iridescent purple shirt, and a rainbow of brightly-colored clips snapped into her spiky orange hair.

Her shapeshifting even accounts for cute costume changes. It's just not fair.

She pulls a neon green windbreaker from her backpack and throws it over her shoulders. "Do you know where you're going?"

"To the hospital, whichever way that is."

Cyndi points to the right. "Okay. Well, it's that way. But that's a pretty far walk from here."

I sigh. This axe is already getting heavy. "Well, what do you suggest?"

She grins like a fox.

Chapter Seven

Ellie

Cyndi's idea for quicker transportation is an annoying one—she thinks we should take the bus.

I hate taking the bus. It's rarely on time and it takes forever to get anywhere, even though it's usually empty. Errolton is a pretty small town, so I can normally walk or ride my bike to get around. On the rare occasion I need to go further than a few blocks, like getting to work or going to the library, I try to bum a ride from Grandpa or a friend, to avoid taking the bus.

I never want to ride the bus. Nobody wants to ride the bus.

And yet, Cyndi does. She's fascinated by public transportation. On mornings when we get fast food for breakfast instead of showing up for homeroom, she demands that we take the town transit line, even though McDonald's is a short walk from the school.

I'm always quick to remind her: "Walking's just as good. It's not like we're rushing to get back to class on time."

But she doesn't listen. She loves riding in cars, and the idea of riding in a large car that she can stand and walk around in makes her feel crazy. The last time we rode the bus, she ran around asking strangers, "How does physics even work?!" and tried to shove her head out the window.

I had to use all my strength to pull her back inside before the bus driver kicked us off.

I always assumed that her excitement at mundane things was the result of drinking too many energy drinks or bumming some Adderall from the neighborhood narcotics peddler. It never occurred to me that she could be genuinely excited at the idea of moving vehicles due to her being a fox in girl's clothing.

Now, as I sit on the bus next to Cyndi, a teenage girl ecstatically staring out the window, it's clear that I've been too distracted to notice her obvious tells.

I look across the aisle to the other passenger joining us for this trip. He's an older gentleman with wispy gray hair, a cheek full of dip, and an empty soda can. Occasionally he lifts the can to his lips to collect the spit gathering in his mouth. When I make eye contact with him, he lowers the can too soon. Saliva dribbles out from his mouth and onto his shirt, but he doesn't notice the growing wet spot on the fabric of his flannel.

He's too busy giving us a look of calm, unblinking derision.

We must be quite the pair to him. Aside from Cyndi's bright clothing and poorly contained excitement, my choice to bring a double-edged axe on a bus was bound to get some stares. Most of our town is quick to admit that we have a beast problem, just like the rest of the country, but there are some older folks that still fervently deny it.

I've heard some older restaurant patrons complaining about the curfew to my grandfather before, saying things like, "When I was younger, we didn't have monsters in the woods. I've never seen one, anyway. This is just a problem created by the media, to keep people scared and locked in their homes."

At least my axe is encouraging any strangers to keep a safe distance from us. These days, two teenagers traveling alone are asking for trouble, especially with all the recent disappearances. Errolton is pretty safe to walk around during the day, but who knows what North Bern, the next town over, is dealing with.

We don't have much choice in the matter, though. Our town doesn't have a hospital big enough to deal with issues more complicated than the flu or small household injuries. Smoke inhalation from the fire is bad enough, but with my grandfather's lungs already damaged from decades of smoking, he'll need a lot of care to get better.

I'm all too aware of Grandpa's health these days. Since the creation of the Beowulf Brigade, I've been driving with him to check-ups and physical therapy appointments, to ensure that he's in fighting shape. He stopped smoking years ago, but the damage to his lungs was pretty bad, and the doctors are regularly checking for signs it's getting worse.

Frustrated and guilty and scared, I bite at the raw spot inside my lip.

I hope he's okay.

The bus stops in front of the familiar doors of North Bern General Hospital, and I stand, nudging Cyndi to get off with me. She does, begrudgingly, and we step onto the sidewalk alone. The wind blows hard now, and I can feel the sun lowering, settling into the afternoon chill of New Hampshire's autumn.

When I approach the hospital's front desk, the woman sitting behind it gestures to my axe without even looking up. "No weapons allowed in the hospital. You'll need to check your items in with our security officer and leave them here if you want to enter."

I give her a frustrated look. "Are you serious?"

"Can't have you chopping up patients, dearie. Those with dementia might think you're the grim reaper or something." She returns her gaze to the computer behind the desk and begins typing. "Them's the rules, sorry. Name?"

Growing annoyed, I reach into my pocket to check the salamander stone. It's still there, but as I graze it with my hand, it sizzles against my fingers.

I quickly pull my hand from the pocket and say, "Ellie Adair. I'm here to see Peter Karlsen, my grandfather. He checked in last night?"

The front desk attendant pauses her frenetic typing to point to a clipboard. "Sign in here. Who's the one behind you?"

Cyndi looks over my shoulder. "My name's Cyndi. Hello!"

"She's my friend," I say, elbowing Cyndi. "She's also here to visit."

The woman behind the desk looks us up and down. "Are either of you over eighteen?"

We both shake our heads.

"I can't let you in here without an adult. Is there one with you?"

"Um, no, I . . . " I let out a long breath. "I don't have anyone else. Just my grandfather, who we're here to see."

"Well, I'm not sure—"

"Ma'am." The words fly from my mouth before I can pull them back. "My grandfather almost died last night. I almost died last night when our house was burning down. That's why I'm here to see him, and your hospital . . . protocols or whatever, are not working for me."

The stone in my pocket grows warm with each newly aired grievance.

"What do you suggest I do? Find a pair of new parents outside? Wait two years before reentering? Break down the doors myself? Because it seems like the easier answer is just to let me in to see my grandfather, rather than following a dumb rule that says a sixteen-year-old can't be in the hospital unsupervised."

The shadow of my axe falls across the woman's face, and she looks up at me, uncomfortable.

"I mean, if I'm allowed to get my driver's permit, then you'd think I'd be allowed to walk down a hallway by myself. I swear, if I wasn't—"

A hand clamps down on my shoulder.

I turn my head to find Colonel Simone Adams standing behind me. In her everyday clothes, I almost don't recognize her as the same woman in camouflage and chainmail from the night before.

Today, she's dressed in jeans, a cozy pink sweater, and an unzipped tan jacket lined in navy blue flannel. Her hair is no longer tied back; it frames her face in voluminous, textured curls, proudly displaying a gray streak, as well as a scar on the left side of her face. Up close, the scar looks like a deep scratch that barely missed her eye. It cuts across her left temple and ends mid-way down her brown cheek in a thick, dark line.

If it wasn't for that scar, I'd think she was a regular civilian off to run errands, not a retired military officer trained to fight monsters.

Her grip on my shoulder reminds me that looks can be deceiving.

"She's with me," Colonel Adams says. She lessens the pressure on my shoulder while she hands her license to the woman behind the desk, who sighs with relief at the colonel's intervention.

I can't say I'm not thankful for it myself. I didn't mean to get so upset. Normally, I wouldn't be.

Once she's signed in, the colonel nods to me. "I think the two of us should go in to see Pete first. Why don't you hand Cyndi the axe for a bit? She can wait here with it," She looks over to Cyndi, "if that's okay with you?"

"Sure." Cyndi reaches out to take the axe. She points to a chair by the front door. "I'll be right here."

Nodding, I turn back to the woman behind the desk.

"Sorry. I just . . . " I let out a gruff sigh. "Sorry."

She nods back to me. "You'll find your grandfather through those doors over there, in room 418."

I take a deep breath.

They would have already told me if Grandpa was dead.

He's going to be okay. He always is.

I follow Colonel Adams through the swinging doors, trying not to notice the number of eyes on me. It could just be from my earlier outburst, but moments like these make me wonder if people know who I am for some other reason: namely, my mother. Those that know about the court case have this look in their eye when they meet me, wondering if they can catch crazy, or when I'll break, like she did.

Though, it's not like my recent actions have given them a reason to think otherwise.

After walking down a few hallways, the colonel and I enter a second set of doors and another waiting room. We sign in and sit for a few silent minutes before Colonel Adams turns to me.

"You know, your grandfather talks to me about you all the time. He says you're pretty easy to take care of, as far as kids go. But what I've seen in the last few hours—partying in the woods, being out all night away from home, skipping school the following day when multiple people are looking for you?" She frowns at me. "I don't think I agree with him. I'd say you've been pretty difficult so far."

I sigh. I did not come here to get lectured.

"I wasn't skipping school. I was," I pause, choosing my words carefully, "lost. In the woods. The fire started when I was still in bed, and after I got out of the house, I ran off into the woods to, um, find help?"

The colonel raises an eyebrow. "Why weren't you there when the emergency vehicles arrived? Why didn't you wait with your grandfather and go with him in the ambulance last night?"

"I . . . " I look away. What am I supposed to say?

"They sent men back into that burning house multiple times looking for you, only to find you were already gone. Did you know that?"

My eyes start to well up with tears. I hadn't thought about that, but her words make sense. With the fire and me nowhere to be found, it's obvious to expect the worst.

I sniff, trying to fight back tears. "Did anyone . . . get hurt?" I ask.

"No. Thankfully." She sighs and eases up. "But they could have. Meanwhile, I've been all over town, driving between here and your school and your last-known hangouts. I expected you'd be with Cyndi, but she's had her phone off since yesterday."

While wiping my nose, I look over at the colonel. "Why were you looking for me?"

"Before this last hunt, your grandfather asked me to take care of you in case anything happened. So you're staying with me until we can confirm a more permanent living situation for you. He never mentioned this?"

I shake my head, surprised.

"Well, you obviously need a place to stay. I stopped by the house this morning. You can't stay there."

I nod. "Do you know how long Grandpa will be in here?"

Colonel Adams hesitates. Before she can answer, a doctor enters from a side door. "Family for Peter Karlsen?"

We both stand.

The doctor gives us a look of forced cheerfulness. "You can follow me. Come on in."

We follow him past a few rooms. This hallway is much quieter than the previous areas we've passed, with signs posted that say, "Quiet Zone" and "Shh" on the doors of various rooms. As we round a corner, I notice a handwritten note posted on someone's window. Something like a prayer.

When we arrive at Grandpa's room, the doctor opens the door and stands aside, to let the colonel and I walk in. But I can't. I just stare into the room as the weight of my grandfather's condition crushes me in place.

He's lying in the hospital bed with his eyes closed, hooked up to a breathing tube and a machine that lets out rhythmic wheezing noises every few seconds. A heart monitor next to him beeps occasionally, marking jagged lines up and down to declare that life, however quiet, still rattles in his bones.

The doctor takes my look of horror as a sign to ignore me and speak directly to Colonel Simone about Grandpa's condition. Because naturally, I don't matter.

I'm just a kid.

"Mr. Karlsen's been in a coma since we operated on his leg," the doctor says. "He was breathing on his own when the ambulance first brought him in, but after the surgery, he lost consciousness and had to be put on a ventilator. We're working to wake him up and remove the ventilator, but it's been slow-going."

The colonel holds her no-nonsense expression in place. She asks, "What happened to his leg? I thought you were concerned with his lungs?"

"Initially, the paramedics were focusing on his smoke inhalation and any burns he received from the fire, but once he was stabilized, they found a few wounds on his leg growing infected. We ran some tests and recognized the pattern of cuts to be from a large bite."

I lock eyes with the doctor. "A bite?"

He nods. "The cuts went deep into the muscle and connective tissue of his leg—nearly down to the bone—and the wound started showing signs of infection at an accelerated rate. Honestly, this bite is unlike any I've ever treated. It must have been a rather large creature, but we haven't been able to determine what kind. The bite pattern doesn't match any we have on file or any in the Beowulf Brigade's database."

My ears begin to ring.

I didn't bite him.

Did I?

I fight to remember the details of that pivotal ten minutes between last night's transformation and my sprint into the woods, but I can barely think, much less focus with the heart monitor beeping this loud.

And that ringing. I've got to turn off the ringing, somehow.

I pull the salamander stone out of my pocket and slam it into the palm of my fist. It sears my skin immediately, but the burning pain is enough to distract me from the ringing in my ears.

For now, anyway.

Nearly doubling over from the sudden pain in my hand, I turn and run down the hallway, pushing a supply cart out of my way. It clatters and falls behind me, spilling metal instruments and bandages across the floor.

The bite must have come from me. Who else could it have been?

I have to get out. If I transform again, in here . . . well, I don't want to think about the kind of damage I could do.

My boots squeal around the corner as I turn down a narrow hallway. If I follow the arrows that point to nearby restrooms and vending machines, then I maybe can go hide in an empty bathroom stall while I wait this out.

Or maybe I'll smash a few toilets to calm down.

Or maybe I'll find someone else and take a bite out of them, too.

My stomach growls again, reminding me just how little I've had to eat in the last twenty-four hours.

I take a sharp left turn toward the restrooms and smack into someone's shoulder. As I turn, pausing awkwardly to apologize, I recognize their startled expression.

"Wade?" I ask, surprised.

Wade lets out a surprised smile. "Ellie. Hey."

He looks casually cool in a black band tee and blue hoodie, unzipped. The t-shirt's lettering is cracked, its white ink fading to gray.

Glancing down at my salvaged hiking boots and oversized red tracksuit, I instantly feel self-conscious. "Right, this, I . . . "

From behind Wade, I see Bear, peeking out from the side of the vending machine. "Ellie?" He's holding an unopened bag of chips. "What are you doing here?"

"Oh, hey Bear. You're here too." Their sudden appearance, my outfit, and the absurdity of the last day crash down on me all at once.

"I'm sorry." I take a few steps backward. "I don't . . . You don't need . . . " I turn to go, only to be stopped by Wade's hand on my forearm.

"Hey," Wade says gently, "are you okay?"

I tear my arm away from his grip, angrily. "Why do you care?"

He looks away.

I need to scream or punch the wall to scare him off, but I don't, because I notice something important.

Unclenching my palm reveals the salamander stone in my hand. It's once again matte black and cool to the touch, no longer burning my skin.

More importantly, the ringing in my head has stopped.

Exhausted, overwhelmed, and relieved, I collapse right there. Tears fall without stopping, but I don't care.

I can't believe how close I came to transforming again.

Grandpa, I am so, so sorry.

Wade crouches beside me and places an arm across my shoulders while Bear hovers, unsure of how to help. After a few seconds, he opens a bag of chips with an audible pop and starts snacking.

"Bear!" Wade yells at him, "Now is not the time for chips!"

I laugh despite myself. "No, it's fine. Bear, Cyndi's in the waiting room near the main entrance if you want to go see her. I'm headed there too, in a minute."

Thankful for an excuse to leave, Bear nods and rummages into his bag of chips for a minute. He takes an unbroken chip out of the bag and offers it to me.

"Sorry you're sad. Here: salt helps with fluid retention."

I take the chip and laugh again. "Thanks. Are these sour cream and onion? They're the best."

"Well, actually," Bear raises a hand to debate my claim until he makes eye contact with Wade, who's glaring at him, and remembers why I'm sitting on the ground.

"Right. You need a minute. We can argue the merits of competing chip flavors when you're better." Then Bear turns and walks away, munching with each step.

"He's hilarious," I say, wiping away a new tear as it rolls down my cheek.

"Oh, I'm aware. I get to live with him," Wade replies before turning to me. "More importantly, are you okay?"

I nod and take a minute to catch my breath. "I just wasn't expecting my grandfather to be so hurt. Last night, the house caught fire, and . . . "

"I heard. I'm so sorry about your grandfather."

My chest tightens at the rush of memories that suddenly flood my mind. Happy moments and arguments with Grandpa unravel in order, each now tinged with the fear that it might be too late to say goodbye.

It's all my fault. It's all my fault.

I lean forward and hug my legs as I start to cry again, too tired and overwhelmed to suppress the tears. Eventually, I gather myself and glance back over at Wade, who looks concerned.

"I'm sorry." I cough. "You don't have to stay either. You barely know me."

He smiles; his eyes stir with competing emotions.

"I know that you're someone going through a rough time." He moves to sit across from me. "That's all I need to know. Do you want to talk about it?"

I shrug, noncommittal. "Not really. Why are you and Bear here, anyway?"

"Oh. That." Wade rubs the back of his neck and glances away from me. "I mean, we come here once a week to volunteer with our mom. She works in one of the labs in this hospital, and she set it up for us to stop by and help out. Volunteering here is meant to help with our college applications."

"Huh." The phrase "college applications" is so far from my list of concerns these days. But then, it usually is, even on days when I'm not fighting the urge to hulk out.

Hearing someone mention college so casually, ignoring the pivotal, life-changing step that it is, baffles me.

"But," Wade continues, "I may have stopped by today specifically hoping that I'd run into someone."

I look up at him, "Someone?"

He nods. "Someone who never replied to my over-enthusiastic text. Someone who I was so excited to talk to, I had to beg my brother for her number, because I was too impatient to wait to see her at school the next day."

My stomach churns with indecision. I remember seeing his text and avoiding a reply because he'd come on so strong. And now, in person, he's coming on just as strong.

I should walk away, but I can't. Instead, I force a laugh. "Someone wearing a dumb sweat suit because all her other clothes are burned up?"

"Yeah. But hey, it looks cute on her."

I blush again. This isn't my first time flirting, but I'm not sure if awkward flirting in middle school counts. The last time I even talked to a boy like this was when one asked me to a dance in seventh grade. He did it on a dare, so after I said yes, he immediately ran back to his friends to laugh about it.

"Guys, she said yes! What a dork!"

People aren't generally nice to me for no reason.

I avoid Wade's eyes. "Well, I guess I should get out of your hair, so you can go find her."

I push up to stand, only to have Wade reach out to me again. This time, his hand grabs mine.

Our eyes meet, and it's then that I notice his dimples.

I'm stuck.

"Um," he laces his fingers through mine and hesitates before asking, "Can I . . . see you later tonight?"

"Tonight?" I ask, unable to say much else. My stomach is flip-flopping all over the place.

"It doesn't have to be tonight. I know you have a lot going on, and I'm not even sure if you've figured out where you're staying yet, but . . . "

I look down at our hands, confused by his warmth. It feels unearned, but I'm thankful for it, nonetheless.

"I'll ask Colonel Adams," I answer. "She's watching me until we . . . until I find a new home, I guess." The words feel so foreign and horrible to say. "So I probably can't do anything tonight or tomorrow. But I'm planning to meet Bear on Saturday to study, so maybe . . . you could come with us?"

Wade nods. "Okay. Saturday, then. I'll text you."

"Oh. You can't. My phone is destroyed."

He tilts his head. "Wait, really?"

"Yeah. I broke it when I jumped out of my window. When the house was on fire."

His eyes go wide. "You what?"

"I'll tell you more about it tomorrow. I should be able to get a new phone this weekend, but until then, I'll use Cyndi's to text. Or maybe I can find a computer to chat online or something. I don't know." I let out a tired sigh. "You'll hear from me?"

"I'm holding you to it. Can I walk you up front?"

I'm still holding Wade's hand when we stand up, and as we take the long way back to the hospital's entrance, I listen while he explains what I missed at school that day. It doesn't matter what he says; his willingness to share the mundane details of his day—including a poorly executed food fight and a trip to detention—is a refreshing distraction.

But once we approach the main lobby, I let go of his hand. I'm not looking forward to facing the colonel after my dramatic exit from Grandpa's hospital room, and I doubt she's going to be happy to see me, either. She might be relieved that I've willingly reentered her custody, but I can't imagine my presence causing her happiness. Not when all I've done since last night is run away from her.

Soon enough, I spot Colonel Adams with Bear, who's now holding Grandpa's axe, and Cyndi, standing near the exit. A middle-aged man is with them, wearing orange scrubs and holding a clipboard. I sheepishly approach, fully expecting to be yelled at.

The first to see me is Cyndi, who runs up without a word and hugs me.

I'm surprised at her overt act of affection. She's rarely one for hugs.

Cyndi takes a step back and asks, "You all right?"

I shake my head. "Were you able to see him?"

"I can't," she replies. "Visiting hours just ended for the day. But they said that I can come back tomorrow after school?"

"Okay, I'll come with you." Looking to the colonel, I ask, "Is that allowed?"

The colonel glares at me. "We'll talk about it at the house. I'm assuming Cyndi is sleeping over?"

Cyndi nods enthusiastically, and I try not to smile. "Only if that's okay. I don't want to make more problems for you."

Colonel Adams uncrosses her arms and sighs. "Well, your actions so far say otherwise. Speaking of which," she gestures to the nurse to her right. "I believe you owe this man an apology. He's one of a few nurses who had to clean up the mess you made in the hallway."

I look over to the man in scrubs. "I'm sorry, sir. I wasn't looking where I was going. I . . . "

The nurse shakes his head. "Don't worry about it. The doctor told us about the news you'd just received, and you're not the first person to need a breather. Though you are the first to topple a supply cart." He laughs at his own joke while opening the folder in his hand. "Just be more aware of your surroundings the next time. Now, before you leave, I need to go over a few things with you."

The nurse and I walk away from the group to go over the paperwork at a nearby table. As I take my seat, I notice Bear, Wade, and Cyndi talking quietly in a huddle while the colonel answers a phone call.

What are they up to?

"So, on this sheet . . . " the nurse explains, "we just need you to verify some of the information we've already collected. Most of your grandfather's information is already in the system, and you're set up as his emergency contact, but the phone number we have listed for you isn't working." He hands me a silver pen. "Is there another number we can use to reach you?"

"This one is good for now." I write down Cyndi's number, hoping she doesn't leave my side in the next few days. "I should have a new one soon."

He nods. "Good to hear. We'll fill out this form again when that happens."

As the nurse tucks a few papers back into the folder, I take a closer look at his pen. A repeating pattern of engraved violins spiral around its barrel.

"Um," I say, gesturing to the nurse's nametag, "Hal. Do you play the violin?"

"Hm?" he asks. When he notices me inspecting the pen, he chuckles. "On occasion. Not much these days though, on account of all the monster attacks. I'm kept pretty busy here. What about you?"

I press my thumb against the pen's cool surface for a moment—when I lift it, a blue thumbprint remains for a few seconds before fading back to silver.

"No," I finally answer. "I just . . . never mind."

Hal hands me the next pack of papers, unbothered by my lackluster small talk. "This is literature on what to expect in the coming days with your grandfather's condition. We spoke to your guardian about most of this, so she should be able to answer any concerns you have, but be sure to write down any questions you think of. That way, you'll remember to ask them when you come back."

I look over at Colonel Adams, who is now off the phone and shooing the boys away from Cyndi. Bear and Wade wave goodbye as they walk back toward the main swinging doors. Before stepping through the doorway, Wade catches my eye and mouths something that looks like, "See you later!"

I wave back and try to fight the butterflies in my stomach.

Nurse Hal, who's been talking this entire time, notices me waving and stops midsentence. He looks over his shoulder to see the guys, looks back at me, and snickers.

"Teenagers."

He pulls out a new sheet of paper. "As I was saying, there are a few other pages in this folder I'll need you to fill out and bring back tomorrow. Does your grandfather have any living relatives you're aware of?"

"Other than my mother, no."

"Okay. Right." He says, turning the page over, "Speaking of that . . . "

I freeze. There's a name at the top of this last page that doesn't belong to me or my grandfather.

It says Roen Adair.

My mother.

"So, ah, your grandfather never gave us permission to release his medical information to your mother."

I look up from the paper in front of me. "What?"

"The last time he was in for a checkup, we discussed it with him, since you and Colonel Adams were the only people on his medical release forms. He said he intentionally didn't want to add her to that form, because he preferred that she hear about any serious medical situations from a close, trusted family member. Which, ah, means you, as far as I understand."

I grit my teeth in anger and fight the urge to flip the table. "Did my beloved grandfather say anything else?"

The nurse avoids my eyes while replying, "No. Just that he hoped you would be the one to tell her directly. If you . . . "

"Yeah, I'm done with this." I push myself up from the chair and storm out, away from the front desk and the swinging doors and Cyndi and the colonel, into the swirling darkness of the early evening.

Chapter Eight

Ellie

I turn Cyndi's cell phone over in my hand, examining it. The phone's soft plastic case is covered in Lisa Frank rainbows. There are lightning bolts, purple hearts, chocolate-covered strawberries, and a pair of green aliens riding in a convertible, offering me a peace sign.

Like so many things Cyndi surrounds herself with, it's an explosion of color and life and vibrancy.

I want to chuck it across the room.

I don't, of course. Cyndi was kind enough to lend me her phone, and she has every right to wear accessories with excessive pattern and saturation. Today's just been an exhausting trudge, and her ever-present optimism—while helpful—has been a lot.

Perhaps that's the benefit of being a centuries-old fox. When someone lives for that long, they have more time available to use, and they're less worried about wasting a little bit of it on silly or childish pursuits.

Has she ever, truly, been stressed in front of me?

Have I ever seen her upset?

I was never bothered by how little I knew about her until this week. Granted, she's been hiding things from me for years, but I could have pushed harder to learn more.

Cyndi is just too good at putting on a brave face.

I am incapable of doing that.

I roll onto my back and stare at the ceiling. It's one of the spare rooms in Colonel Adams' house, which used to be her daughter's bedroom before she went off to college. Now, with only the bed and an empty dresser, the room feels like a sparse shadow of what it once was. The closet contains echoes of a past childhood: stuffed animals packed away in cardboard boxes, crates stacked full of trophies and ribbons from athletic and academic achievements, small handwritten scribbles near the baseboards announcing, "Ayanna was here!" and "Aya loves J" in pink and purple marker.

My eyes trace the pattern of small, glow-in-the-dark stars stuck to the ceiling. I attempt to draw different constellations in the air with my finger until I remember why I'm sitting in this room in the first place.

Annoyed, I sit up and return to the phone in my hand.

To say that I'm having a bad week is an understatement. It's more like I've had a weird, messed up life for a while now—like a manure cart filled to the brim with cow patties. Only this week, the cart's decided to collapse in the middle of main street during a parade.

After my grandmother passed away, I've been silently worrying about Grandpa's health with each passing birthday. Now, on top of the very real possibility that he is going to die, I have to wrestle with how many of his injuries are my fault, while fighting the urge to scream at his comatose body for essentially forcing me to reach out to my mother, when neither of us is all that keen to talk.

Oh, and meanwhile, I still have the whole "occasionally turning into a monster" problem to worry about.

My thumb hovers over the dial pad. I nearly lost it back at the hospital, and that was before the nurse mentioned my mother. Who knows what kind of a trigger a conversation with her might be?

So far, the monster transformations have happened (or almost happened) in moments of extreme emotional upheaval. When I'm angry,

I can usually express it and move on quickly, but I've never been good at moving past fear. Fear often visits, lingers, and suffocates until I'm trapped in my head for days.

I take a deep breath. If I'm able to keep my emotions in check and focus on what I need to tell her, it should be okay.

I quickly dial the number and hold the phone to my ear.

An older woman answers.

"North Bern Community Mental Health. How can I help you?"

"Hi. Yes. Sorry," I begin, plucking the words from the air. "I'm calling to speak to Roen Adair. It's about a, um, family medical situation."

"One moment." There's a pause on the line, followed by, "I'm sorry. Roen isn't available to take calls right now. If you'd like to leave a message with me . . . "

"I can't leave a message with you. I have to speak to her directly."

"And what's your name?"

"Ellie Adair. I'm her daughter."

Another pause, then the woman says, "Ah, Miss Ellie. Sorry about that—you're name's right here on the list. Can I place you on hold for a minute?"

I nod, realize that the woman can't hear a nod through the phone, and reply, "Sure. Go ahead."

The hold music is a garbled mess of static and loud, bouncy jazz piano. I put the phone down on the bed and start picking at the cuticle on my middle finger.

My left hand is shaking.

I don't know why I'm always so nervous to speak with my mother. I guess it's because she knows exactly what to say to bother me the most, even if she doesn't mean any of it.

I glance back at the closet, full of carefully preserved childhood treasures, and wonder what it might have been like to have parents so directly involved with my life.

The music cuts off suddenly and the woman from before returns.

"Miss Ellie?"

"Yes?"

"I'm going to transfer your call now. Your mother should pick up after a ring or two."

"Okay."

The line beeps for a second, then it rings once, twice, three times.

Maybe she won't pick up. If I call and she won't pick up, isn't that on her?

I won't have to visit her, will I?

"Hello? Who is it? No one . . . no one . . . "

My mother's voice is loud on the other end, though she sounds more hoarse than usual.

"Hello. It's Ellie," I reply, used to her strange phrasing by now. My mother doesn't speak directly like a normal person would—at least, she hasn't since I was born. She likes to talk circles around what she's trying to say, as if she's speaking in code.

I can hear her inhale sharply on the other line. "Elijah. So good of you to call."

She refuses to call me by any name that isn't the one she gave me, and I hate her for it. But there's no use in correcting her or getting upset. It's been this way my entire life.

She follows up her greeting to say, "There's a man outside."

"There's a man outside" usually means that she's not alone, or that the conversation will be overheard. It's a phrase she uses constantly. There are nurses everywhere, so she's rarely left alone.

"That's fine. I'm calling you about Grandpa."

My mother doesn't speak for nearly a minute. Then, in a whisper, she asks, "Is he dead?"

I'm stunned. A direct question. The first in a very long time.

"No, he's not dead. But he's in the hospital, and he's not doing well."

I wait for her reply. At first, she says nothing. Then, softly, I hear her sniffling through the phone. She's crying.

I can't listen to her cry. If I do, then I might cry, and I know the sound of me crying will send her into a fit. So, I try to fill the silence with something, anything, so that she won't linger on the tears while we talk.

"Grandpa has really good doctors," I blurt out. "They're doing what they can. The house . . . caught on fire the other day. The smoke hurt his lungs, but the doctors are trying their best."

"Doctors!" she shrieks. "Doctors and nurses standing around on pills and needles. Prick me again, pricks!"

I expel a slow breath, thankful that the topic of doctors and nurses distracted her. She especially loves yelling about nurses, since she sees them every day and hasn't found one that she likes. She's convinced that they're trying to make her crazy, and that if she were to walk out of the hospital, she'd be sane as anyone.

She asks, "The fire. Did you do it?"

Did I do it?

It's not something I know how to answer.

She takes my silence as assent. "Elijah with two faces. Something happened . . . didn't it?"

I should say no, but her words are starting to fit together in my head in a way I don't like.

"What are you trying to say?" I ask, nervous to hear her response.

She sings back a refrain I know by heart, one she's sung since I was a little girl. Only now, the words take on new meaning:

Elijah, Elijah, fire and flame,
take a seat here at the table.
Two hearts, two souls, and two rows of teeth,
hungry, ready, and able.

My hands shake wildly. Questions escape before I can stop them.

"Do you know what's happening to me? Do you know what I am?"

My mother cackles into the phone.

"You're maggot food. We all are."

Then she coughs into the phone three times and says, "There's a man outside. There's a man outside."

This is her signal to end the call. It means there's someone nearby and she doesn't feel safe talking anymore. Or she's just bored from messing with me and wants to go eat some Jell-O.

"Mom, wait, you can't—"

She hangs up.

I place Cyndi's phone on the bed, shaking with anger and terror and frustration.

I hate her clanging, broken brain.

Cyndi's cell phone buzzes beside me, indicating a text message. Out of habit, I turn it over to see a text from Wade . . . on Cyndi's phone. I'm tempted to leave it and ask her about it later, when I see the beginning of the text:

Ellie.

How does he know I have her phone right now?

I open the message to read the rest. It says:

Look out the window.

No way.

I drop the phone and nearly run to the window behind me. It faces the street, the mailbox, and the yard in front of Colonel Adam's house. Most of the street is dark, but pockets of the cul-de-sac are lit by the occasional lamppost or front porch light.

And there, standing in the shadow of the house, is Wade.

The anger from talking with my mother instantly melts away. I don't need to worry about what she knows: it's all locked away in her mind anyway.

I don't want to keep begging my mother to treat me as anything other than the catalyst for her breakdown—not when I can take the time I spend worrying about her and invest it into relationships that give me something in return, with people that take the time to see and know me.

And after today, I can talk to her as much or as little as I choose.

I race down the stairs, slamming into the wall at the bottom with an "oof." After a brief pause in front of the mirror to collect myself, I notice Colonel Simone, Cyndi, and Bear in the living room, chatting pleasantly over a game of checkers.

They all look at me with knowing smiles.

I guess this is just a surprise for me, then.

I look back at the mirror, tug at the bottom of my t-shirt, and say to my reflection, "I'll, um, be right back." Then I run through the front door, poorly hiding the grin on my face.

The cold air hits my bare arms and feet, reminding me that I've forgotten socks, shoes, and a coat, but as my eyes settle on Wade's dark outline, silhouetted against the dusty purple sky, I decide not to care.

A puff of vapor escapes my mouth as I speak.

"You're . . . why are you here?"

His white teeth shine brightly despite his face still being cast in shadow, and as my eyes adjust, I can make out the shape of his honey-colored eyes in the dark.

They almost glow.

"Bear and I talked to Cyndi at the hospital, and the colonel approved for us to come by tonight for a bit," he says, taking a step toward me. "We can't stay for dinner or anything, but we wanted to stop by. To check on you."

I look down at my hands, clasped in front of me. "We?"

"I mean, Bear's the one who wanted to stop by, mostly."

With another step, Wade is mere inches in front of me.

"Right. Bear."

I don't dare to look at him. Being this close to Wade makes me feel incredibly small and scared and also ready to fly off into the clouds.

"Ellie, I . . . " Wade trails off, clearly distracted by my shivering. "Are you cold?"

"Cold?" I can't possibly be cold right now. My blood is pumping too fast to be cold.

He unzips his hoodie and opens it. "Hey, come here. It's windy."

"Windy. Right. I could . . . " I gesture toward the house with no intention of walking inside.

Instead of answering, he reaches out and closes the distance between us, wrapping me up into his hoodie. "You're not even wearing shoes. You'll freeze."

I fight the tightness in my chest and stomach as we stand there, letting the wind swirl leaves to the ground around us. Strands of hair blow into my eyes and mouth, but before I can brush them away, Wade's hand is at my temple, pushing the hair from my eyes. His thumb lingers on the side of my face, cupping my cheek.

Without thinking, I ask, "Why me?"

My question prompts him to smile again, shining brilliantly. "Why not you?"

"I mean it. We just met, but you seem so invested in getting to know me. Why?"

"You're making it hard for me to appear mysterious with all these pointed questions."

"Humor me."

He traces the line of my cheek with his forefinger. From our spot in the driveway, the streetlight creates a halo atop his dirty blond hair, a tousled mess that's far too tempting to run a hand through.

While I study the angles of his face in the dark, Wade finally speaks again.

"Okay, so, last year, I went on a ski trip with a group of friends."

"Ah. So you like spending time with me because you enjoy boring things."

"No." He rolls his eyes. "We took the trip only a week into the new semester, and at the time, I was really worried about missing class. The idea of borrowing notes and having to catch up on work was driving me crazy. How could I possibly know everything I'd missed just from looking over someone else's notes?"

Wade lets out a rueful laugh. "I was still like Bear then, obsessed with my grades and planning my time outside of class according to what activities would look best on college applications. That's why the ski trip was so important—as much as I didn't want to go, part of me knew that taking a break would be good for me. My parents knew too, which is probably why they let me go.

"Anyway, a friend suggested we try a steeper slope, and even though it was my first time snowboarding, I was doing fine on the easier courses, so I didn't think I needed to be cautious." He takes a difficult breath. "I should have been. I flipped going around a turn and flew off the course, over a wooden barrier. My head smashed against some rocks and I fell into a ravine, I guess. I don't remember much after that."

I look up at him, horrified. "Are you serious?"

Wade nods. "It took hours for someone to finally get to me. According to the search party, I came close to freezing to death. Almost lost a hand." He pauses, recollecting. "Thankfully, I woke up in the hospital with only a broken arm and a concussion. But with how close I came to dying, it scared me."

He breathes in, steadying his rapid heartbeat.

"The night I first met you, I saw how guarded and scared you were. You reminded me of those days back in the hospital, when I was coming to grips with how little I can control, how short life is, typical near-death-experience stuff. Now that I've come out on the other side of all that, I'm thankful to be alive and walking around, and I don't want to waste the second chance I've been given."

His free hand reaches for mine, almost in pledge.

"I don't know everything you're going through, but I'd like to help you get to the other side of it, if I can. Maybe I'm overstepping, but I think we're more similar than you realize, and I . . . "

Wade pauses, locking eyes with me. Then he lowers his voice. "I want to get to know you better, if you'll let me."

His words, vulnerability, and proximity convince me.

I lean in and kiss him.

Wade's breath catches at the sudden, wordless kiss, but that doesn't stop him from kissing me back. He holds me tight, like he's afraid that I'll change my mind and run off like a spooked deer.

But I don't want to run.

You should.

We stay there for a moment, two lost souls entangled in one another's arms, thankful for a place to rest. But then my arm starts to cramp, and I slowly pull away from him.

"Sorry. Hold on." I stretch my arm out to loosen the cramp, but pulling the muscle only makes the pain radiate up the side of my arm. "Ow. Why is that . . . "

Wrong. It's all wrong.

Then my back begins to bow, and the muscles in my legs start to pull and stretch away from the bone.

No. This cannot be happening right now.

Howling, my legs grow and twist, pushing me upward. My torso expands as it gains mass and sharp teeth push through the gums of my newly formed jaws.

He's maggot food. We all are.

I scream in momentary pain until the transformation is complete, and I'm once again large and hungry. My claws seem somehow sharper and longer than before.

It's then that I look beyond my hands to see Wade, shivering a few feet below. He's pointing at me, mouthing wordlessly in fear.

"Wha . . . what . . . Ellie?"

I take a deep breath to get a better sense of my prey.

No, not prey—he's just a teenage boy. All scrawny bones and messy hair and lean, gamy muscles seasoned with microwavable pizza rolls and Mountain Dew.

And something else.

Still, if he turns and runs, I might be up for the chase. I doubt it'll take me more than four steps to catch him.

Wade takes a hesitant step back, and with his outstretched arm still shaking, falls backward. He gets up again with panicked speed, but the sign of weakness encourages me to amend my earlier prediction:

It'll only take me three.

I crack my neck to loosen my newly formed spine. Why are my instincts shouting to attack the boy who just promised to care for me?

Wade. His name is Wade.

Smells. Wrong.

I grind my teeth in anticipation of the coming hunt, but right before I lunge, a patch of branches rustles to my left.

Turning reveals the animal dumb enough to step between me and my meal. It's a wayward moose, lazily chomping on the branches of a fir tree planted in Colonel Adams' yard. The colonel's backyard connects to a larger stretch of woods, so she must get regular visits from deer and moose, especially if she leaves out feed for them.

I'm tempted to try to catch both the boy and the cloven-hoofed beast, but I know better. I'll lose the moose if I waste time on the human, and after all: one moose in hand is worth two meals in a bush, or whatever.

Instead, I cut to my left and charge at the beast, knocking it over in an instant. The moose bucks, pushing its antlers into my eyes and mouth as a last attempt to avoid my teeth, but it's too late. The animal is on its side like a tipped cow, and I'm using my body weight to pin it down. I hold down its chest and neck with one arm before tearing off an antler with the other.

The moose bellows in agony at the broken antler, but I'm unfazed. With the bludgeoning tool removed, I can sink my teeth into its neck and drink greedily of its blood, which I do before chomping into the muscle and sinew of its shoulder.

I find myself crouching over the moose's body for a time, grateful to have caught a large enough meal for my monstrous appetite. I'm still curious about human meat, of course, but it's not like there's a shortage of them. I'll find one to snack on soon enough.

Maybe even tonight. If I'm not too full after this.

As I rip off the animal's hind leg and bite into the meat of its thigh, a small light is cast onto the grass at my feet.

I turn, hoping to find the source of light and turn it off, when I see another boy. This one is holding a lantern, aimed right at me.

It's . . . a bear?

No. It's a boy named Bear.

I blink into the small light, irritated. I can't see well with that thing aimed between my eyes.

The light-bearer stands next to a few others—Wade, Cyndi, and Colonel Adams—humans whose names I only remember after a few seconds of determined focus.

Not safe.

They're joined by someone I can only assume is the colonel's husband, whose car is now parked in the driveway. Mr. Adams is a lawyer, so working late is probably normal for him.

Coming home to a large monster on his lawn, covered in the blood of a dead moose, is probably not so normal for him.

The CAH-CHUNK of Colonel Adams' rifle cocks loudly between me and the group, and for a moment I'm tempted to test her aim against the strength of this new body.

But then I hear the scurrying of deer in the woods, and I remember the taste of fresh prey.

Wade. I'm . . . so sorry. I can't be the girl you want me to be.

I turn and lope into the dark.

Chapter Nine

Dani

The school bus bounces in and out of a pothole. It sends me and two other girls flying into the aisle.

Coach Lewis turns in her seat, glaring at the three of us who fell. "Excuse me! Everyone better be wearing a seatbelt! The streets are still wet from the rain, and we're at least twenty minutes from school. The next person who falls out of their seat will not be running at our next race."

As I climb back into a seat, Errolton High School's draconian cross-country coach returns to her clipboard to check attendance for the hundredth time. "Also, if you haven't contacted your parents yet, be sure to let them know that we'll be back soon. It's been a long day, and I'm not trying to wait in the cold. Understood?"

"Yes Ma'am!" The bus erupts in a scattered choral response.

Satisfied, Coach Lewis turns back to the front and sits down.

I grab my backpack and slide into the seat next to Nadia.

"Man. She's in a sour mood," I whisper.

Nadia laughs and whispers back, "Isn't she always?" She pulls her track hoodie over her head—a red sweatshirt with our mascot, the fighting gopher, outlined in black above the letters XC, for Cross Country.

"That's true." I pull out my phone to check for any new messages. "I think she's smiled once this year."

There's a new text from Sara.

I glance across the aisle at Sara, who's sitting diagonally from us. She's wearing headphones and resting her forehead against the bus window.

She looks upset.

Confused, I open the message.

Hey. Vlad keeps texting me. I'm starting to freak out.

My eyes widen in surprise. I lean across the bus aisle, avoiding Coach Lewis' scanning eyes as she checks off the roster, and whisper loudly, "Sara! Psst!"

When she doesn't respond, I tap Ynez, Sarah's seatmate, on the shoulder.

"Hey, Ynez, switch places with Sara."

Ynez looks over at me, annoyed. "Why should I?"

"Because you're in the way. I need to talk to her."

"I just want to do my English homework!" Ynez gripes. "Why can't I be left to work in peace?"

Nadia looks over my shoulder. "Maybe we'd care more if you were doing your own work, instead of copying someone else's."

Ynez purses her lip at Nadia, glancing at the papers in her lap. Sara's completed study guide is layered behind Ynez's paper, which is still two-thirds empty.

Realizing that she can't deny the obvious plagiarism, Ynez grumbles, "Fine. Hold on." She nudges Sara on the shoulder. "Hey. Switch seats with me."

Sara takes off her headphones. "What? Why?"

Ynez rolls her eyes. "You're being summoned."

With lots of grumbling, they switch seats. Once Sara's in the aisle seat, she doesn't look at me. "Yes?"

"What do you mean he's texting you? I thought things were over with Vlad. Your parents said you're not allowed talk to him anymore, right?"

"Hey! Keep your voice down." Sara whispers. "They only said that I'm not allowed to date him. They didn't say we couldn't text. And anyway, it's not like that." She shows me a set of messages on her phone while Coach barks at another student to sit down. "I'm just worried about him. He said he's tracking something in the woods. Do you think he'll be okay?"

I laugh at her question. "He's a bloodsucker! Of course he'll be okay!"

Eavesdropping—and chewing ferociously on a protein bar—Nadia asks, "Who's a bloodsucker?"

"Sara's boyfriend."

"He's not my boyfriend!" Sara hisses.

Nadia bounces in her seat. "No freaking way!"

Coach Lewis shushes us, and I can tell she's writing something down on her clipboard. I drag Nadia back into her seat, only to have her shove past me to get closer to Sara.

"So, um," Nadia sheepishly laughs to herself, "what's it like?"

Sara narrows her eyes. "What's what like?"

"You know . . . being bitten by a vampire?" Nadia waggles her eyebrows suggestively.

Sara picks up her biology textbook and throws it at Nadia.

"I told you, it's not like that!"

"Yeah, Nadia, it's not like that!" I can't help laughing at Sara's overreaction. "He doesn't even sparkle."

Sara shoots me a death glare before turning back to Nadia. "Listen. Dani and I met him when we were getting ice cream. He rescued us from a monster, and he and I text sometimes. But we're not dating. Now go away."

Nadia stops laughing. "Wait, what monster?"

"What difference does it make, what monster?"

"Well, if there was a monster attack nearby, I'd like to know what it was. What if that thing—"

The bus driver slams on the breaks and cuts hard to the left.

I fall out of my seat and back into the aisle as the bus continues swerving. I have to grab the leg of a passing seat to stop myself from sliding to the front.

Coach Lewis stands to look at me.

"Dani, what did I say about buckling your—"

The bus swerves to the right and bounces off the road, knocking Coach into another set of seats. She leans to steady herself just as our bus smashes into a massive oak tree.

On impact, Coach Lewis flies forward and crashes into the already shattered windshield. Her body crumples and falls over, unconscious.

For a moment, there's nothing but empty, shocked silence.

The bus driver shakes his head groggily and pushes away from the airbag as he slowly collects himself. "What the . . . "

Still on the floor of the bus, I check my arms and wrist, which are red and banged up from the crash. Other than a few scrapes and a bump on the head, I feel fine. Bracing myself against the chair legs on the floor may have just saved my life.

I stand up slowly and take note of the floor of the bus, now covered in notebooks, backpacks, and rolling glitter gel pens. Many girls are rubbing their foreheads, groaning from hitting the seats in front of them.

Did they see what happened to Coach Lewis?

Did they see that thing outside?

"Hey," I start to say, "I think we should—"

I'm interrupted by the sound of scraping metal.

Frozen, we pause to hear something scratch along the bus's exterior for seconds that feel like minutes.

"I think it's coming from over there," Nadia whispers, pointing out the window.

I follow Nadia's hand and look out the window, but see nothing. It's probably just a tree branch making that noise. Whatever I thought I saw, there's no way . . .

The bus door suddenly wheezes, twists, and collapses as it's torn off of its hinges.

Sucking in my breath, I duck down into a nearby seat. I can hear the sudden, muffled scream of the bus driver, which, once quieted, is replaced by the relentless munching of bone and muscle.

I fight off the rising panic in my chest and try to catch the gaze of someone sitting in the back of the bus—so that they might open the emergency exit—but it's not happening. All eyes are fixed on the gory display at the front of the bus, which they watch in stupefied horror.

I will not look. I will get out of here, and I will live, and Mom will pick me up from school, and everything will be okay.

If I run fast enough, maybe I can get to the exit in time.

If I open that door, maybe some of us will live.

Ready to lunge toward the back of the bus, I turn to grab my backpack, only to find a dark figure looming above me.

The beast opens its bloody mouth to reveal a set of sharp, uncomfortably large teeth, itching to attack its cornered prey, and the last thing I see are two glowing, unblinking eyes.

Chapter Ten

Ellie

At 6 a.m., I'm shaken from sleep by the sound of eighties synth-pop. I squint in the music's direction to find Cyndi's phone propped up on the nightstand just out of my reach, blaring "Girls Just Wanna Have Fun" as a morning wake-up alarm. The song's relentless cheer and bubble-gum beat make returning to sleep impossible. I sigh, roll over on the mattress, and glance around the room.

Cyndi is sitting in a rocking chair in the corner of the room, eating a Pop-Tart and drinking coffee from a white mug. Its green logo is scratched and faded from overuse, but after squinting, I can make out the words, "Minton College School of Law" printed along one side.

"Morning, sunshine." She chuckles into her collegiate mug, ignoring the obnoxiously loud alarm still playing next to my head.

I glare at her, snatch up the phone, and turn off the song, growling in her direction.

"Oh, now," Cyndi waves her Pop-Tart at me. "I don't think the Great Cyndi Lauper deserves that kind of treatment. Not when she's paved the way for girls everywhere to have fun. Honestly, the fact that this song has been demoted to nothing more than a generic soundtrack choice for shopping montages is insulting. It should be the anthem for rebellious teens everywhere!"

As her argument crescendos, the Pop-Tart breaks in half. She narrowly catches the broken piece before it lands on the ground.

I ignore Cyndi's presence and rub my eyes, trying to focus my vision until I can recognize where we are—back in Colonel Adams' spare room.

"Why are you in here?" I ask, stretching.

Cyndi fluffs her spiky orange hair.

"What, you can't even give me a 'Thanks for saving my butt, Cyndi. Couldn't have done it without you, Cyndi. I owe you my firstborn child, Cyndi.'"

I look her in the eyes, annoyed, "Thanks for waking me up, Cyndi. Now get out."

"I'm not talking about the alarm, idiot. You really don't remember? Look at your sheets!"

I toss aside the comforter to find my legs caked with dried mud. My feet are cut up, too, and it looks like they've painted streaks of blood across the colonel's white bedsheets.

"Wait. Do you mean . . . "

"That you turned into a beastie, again, and I had to cover for you, again, and go rescue you, again? Yes, to all of the above. You owe me a cheeseburger."

I pinch the bridge of my nose, "Oh no. I thought it was a dream. I . . . " I stop, suddenly remembering. "Wait, Wade saw me!"

"Wade's not the only one." Cyndi barely hides a smirk behind the mug as she sips her coffee.

"What do you mean, he's not the only one?"

"Well, he's probably the only one who saw you transform, but the colonel, her husband, Bear, and I all saw you as the big bad thing. I think one or two neighbors saw you too, since animal control was called." She bites into the Pop-Tart. "Gotta say, Ellie, you are a gnarly thing. I'm pretty impressed. You took down that moose way too easily."

I shake my head. "Oh no. Do they know it was me?"

"The colonel provided you with a plausible alibi before I could come up with one. She just assumed that you ran off into the woods after seeing the monster, er, yourself, and that Wade was too shocked to follow. He didn't correct her. Honestly, he didn't say much of anything after you ran off. He just nodded and got into Bear's truck without a word."

"Well, that's . . . good? In the sense that him not telling anyone about my monster transformation is . . . a good thing?" I bury my face in my hands. "I have no idea what's good anymore!"

"Okay, pause the existential drama for a second," Cyndi says walking over to me, "and check this out." She lifts her phone from the nightstand and unlocks it. "I snapped a picture of you before you ran into the woods. By the way, you're lucky I was able to run off after you when the colonel wasn't looking. It took me hours to track you down. Next time you go on a bloodthirsty rampage, could you do it at a more leisurely pace, instead of running at full tilt for six miles?"

I stop listening to Cyndi the instant she brings up the photo. It's dark and blurry, but I'm able to get a sense of shape and size from it.

In the image, my bones are larger and more pronounced, with shoulder and elbow joints pulling my skin taut against newly formed muscle. My hair looks the same—it's still black and straight—but it hangs limp from the back of my bloated, grotesque head, which has an elongated jaw and visible razor teeth. The scariest part of the change isn't my teeth or claws or increased size, however.

It's my eyes.

Compared to my newer, more pronounced features, the eyes look small and beady, but no less fierce. They're sunken into my face, giving me an almost alien expression, and entirely black, with nothing human remaining.

"Thankfully, after running and eating enough things, you finally collapsed out of exhaustion and transformed back. That's when I brought you home." Cyndi crosses her arms triumphantly. "Do you remember anything that happened?"

I shake my head again. My eyes are locked onto the image and I can't break free of it.

I'm a broken, cursed thing.

Should I be put down like a rabid dog?

Cyndi turns off her phone screen. "Well, enough of that. You need to shower now if we're going to make it to school on time."

I blink for a minute, coming back to our conversation. "When have you ever cared about getting to school on time?"

"When Bear scolded me last night." She rolls her eyes. "He says it's my fault that you're not doing well in Bio, because I'm a 'bad influence' for skipping homeroom with you."

"Right. Biology." I'd nearly forgotten about last week's failed biology test. The idea that grades should be a priority right now feels almost laughable, but I did promise Grandpa I'd do better.

"All right. I'll shower now." I stand up and notice the red sweatshirt I'm wearing. It's the same one Cyndi handed me yesterday, after my night in the woods. "Did I sleep in this? Does that mean . . . "

Cyndi takes a sip of coffee. "Yep. You were naked. Again."

"Well, thanks for taking care of that." I look away. "And for everything lately. I never . . . "

I can't seem to find the end of that sentence. I never could have gotten through this without you? I never want to do that again? I never thought anyone would care enough to chase after me like that?

"Anyway," I rub my eyes, exhausted. "Thanks."

She smiles. "No worries, champ. You can make it up to me by buying lunch."

"I can do that. Any chance you have more clothes I can borrow? I seem to be destroying them at a ridiculous rate."

"Oh, I have clothes for you." She laughs like a fox.

Thirty minutes later, Cyndi and I are running down the stairs, trying to catch the bus before it leaves without us. The colonel mentioned that the bus stops at the corner at 7 a.m., but with only five minutes to spare, we're cutting it close.

We stop at the bottom stair to put on shoes. Per Cyndi's request, we're wearing matching outfits—both with layered fishnet and matching black beanies. Thankfully, she picked the plaid skirt and neon pink sweater, leaving me with a long-sleeved tee and a pair of black, distressed overalls. I don't love the fact that we're dressed in coordinating emo/grunge/alt-girl uniforms, but at least I'm not wearing a skirt in forty-degree weather.

And hey, the beanie is warm.

I begin zipping up my coat when Colonel Simone Adams appears around the corner, holding two paper bags with our names on them.

"Headed out now?" she asks, offering the paper lunches. Cyndi greedily reaches for both bags and puts them into her backpack.

I nod to the colonel. "Yes."

"Well, let me give you this before you leave." Colonel Adams picks up a box from a table by the door and hands it to me. It's a new cell phone.

I look up at her. "You didn't need to . . . "

She waves a hand dismissively. "My husband was able to pick this up last night on his way home from work. He used your grandfather's card information to purchase it, so you don't have to worry about paying us back. I just didn't want you to be without a phone in case anything else happens." The colonel gives me a grim look. "Trouble seems to follow you, Ellie."

"No doubt about that," I reply, opening the box and looking over the phone. I'm tempted to take it out and activate it when Cyndi tugs at my arm.

"Hey. The bus is coming around the corner now."

"Right. Sorry. Thanks for this, Colonel!"

Cyndi and I dash out the front door and run to the bus. After a few steps, I can hear Colonel Adams yelling from the stoop.

"Come right back after school lets out! You have a meeting with your caseworker this afternoon!"

I shoot the colonel a thumbs up and jump onto the bus.

Walking into homeroom before the morning bell is a strange experience. It's not that I've never been on time for Biology, but I can't remember the last time I was early. Riding the bus to school means that I have an entire twenty minutes before class to do . . . whatever I want to, I guess.

Before the fire, Cyndi and I would walk to school together from Grandpa's house, which was just a few blocks away. We'd usually take the long way, unconcerned about what time class started or which ones we missed. Even on the days we showed up for homeroom, Cyndi and I always loitered behind the gym until the bell rang, and usually walked into class five to ten minutes later than everyone else.

And yet, as I walk into Miss Raposa's room ten minutes before the bell, I can't help noticing the students already seated. Some hunch over their notebooks to finish last-minute assignments, others poorly hide their smartphones while they browse social media, and one senior rests his head on top of his desk, snoring loudly.

It never occurred to me that other students might prefer getting to class early. I guess it's a less chaotic way to start the day, when compared to my typical rushing in after the bell to find a seat.

With no idea of the work I've missed, I sit down and drum my fingers restlessly on the desktop, waiting for Cyndi to come in. She'd mentioned needing to stop at her locker before class, which usually means stopping at Bear's locker to harass him on the way.

I would have followed her, but after last night's transformation, I'm not ready to goof off as if everything's okay. Seeing Bear—or worse, running into Wade in the halls—might trigger another episode, and I can't afford for that to happen at school.

"I just need to keep my head down and focus on classwork until the final bell," I mutter to myself. "Collect the work I've missed from different teachers. Then Cyndi and I can focus on getting this monster problem under control."

But before I can even pull out my notebook, Miss Raposa strides up to my desk. Her brown hair falls over her shoulders in soft, natural waves, complementing the feminine swoosh of her long floral skirt. "Ellie Adair, is that really you?"

I sigh and look up. "Yes, Miss Raposa. It's me."

She places a hand on her heart. "You poor girl. After your absence yesterday, I didn't expect to see you at all this week. I heard about your grandfather." Miss Raposa whispers her last sentence in an attempt to discuss my business privately, but even her whisper is loud, drawing the attention of a few students nearby.

My biology teacher lets out a whine of remorse. "Oh, and the last time I spoke with him was about your grades, isn't that right? If I'd known that the very same day . . . " She winces, awkwardly. "Well, we can't fix that, I suppose. I'm glad you're honoring his memory by showing up today."

She reaches out to pat me on my head, but I raise a hand to stop her.

"Miss Raposa," I squint up at her in confusion. "He's not dead. He's just . . . in a coma right now. But they're working to improve his condition."

Her sympathetic expression fades at my words, with a new emotion lurking behind her façade of forced sweetness.

Was that anger I saw?

"Yes, of course. I'm sure he'll pull through any day now." Miss Raposa breaks eye contact then, looking over my head at the clock. "Well, I need to check on some things before class starts, but it's good to see you, Ellie."

She says my name with an air of heavy, smothering softness before returning to her desk. The faint scent of honeysuckle lingers as she walks away.

I blink a few times, caught off guard by the interaction. It was nice of her to talk to me about my grandfather, I guess, but something about it felt off.

Cyndi and a few other students mill into the room just as the bell rings, finding their seats. She plops down next to me, pulls out a pack of gum, and offers me a piece.

"Want some? I stole it from Bear." Cyndi tosses a piece into her mouth, crunching the gum's hard shell between her teeth.

"No, that's okay. How is he?"

She shrugs. "He's fine. Worried about some upcoming test, but otherwise fine."

With my finger, I trace a wobbly shape onto my desk. "Good. And . . . was Wade there, too?"

"Nope. I don't think he came to school today." Smirking, she wags a finger at me. "Aw. You miss your new friend?"

I shoot her a glare. "It's not that. I just . . . "

"Settle down, everyone," Miss Raposa announces from the front of the class. "Let's get started with this warm-up. Without talking to your neighbor, answer the questions on the board."

Grateful for the distraction, I open my notebook and start to read the questions on the whiteboard. It's not that I miss Wade. I'm just concerned that I scarred him for life after he saw me transform into a monster. And, you know, tried to kill him. Just normal teen stuff.

And yeah, maybe I miss him a little. It was nice, having a cute boy go out of his way to see me.

But that's all over now. I have no delusions of him accepting my monster form and wanting to go for milkshakes this weekend. If he's smart, he'll run in the opposite direction.

Resigned to a romance-less existence, I reach into the pocket of my overalls for a pen and find the salamander stone.

Oh right. This thing.

Right before catching the bus, Cyndi and I debated over whether I should leave it at the house or bring it with me. The stone seems to have a mind of its own regarding heat transference, but it's less prone to burn down buildings if I'm carrying it than if it's sitting somewhere unsupervised. Cyndi thinks I should put it on a necklace or something, so that I can't lose it even when I'm sleeping, but I'm not so sure.

I look around the room to see students diligently writing down answers in their notebooks and not talking to each other. Even the sleeping senior from before, who's normally disruptive in this class, is quietly working on the assignment.

Could the dynamic of my biology class really change this much in the month since school started? I know I've skipped a lot of homeroom, but I could have sworn things were rowdier just last week.

Puzzled, I confirm that Miss Raposa is still sitting at her desk and everyone else is preoccupied before I take the salamander stone out of my pocket. I absentmindedly hold it between my thumb and forefinger and allow my thoughts to wander.

Why did I transform after kissing Wade? It's not like I was angry or sad, like I was during the fire. Standing there with him, especially after that phone call with my mother . . . I felt safe.

Not safe.

No, I was safe. Until I transformed and almost killed everyone.

I guess both moments had a surge of sudden emotion that could have triggered the change. But what about the hospital? How was I able to stop transforming after seeing Grandpa, when I couldn't stop later that same day?

My thumb slips, letting the salamander stone fall softly into my lap.

"Ellie? Are you finished?"

On instinct, I cover the stone with a fist and shove it into my pocket before looking up at Miss Raposa, hovering over my left shoulder. She must have gotten up from her desk when I wasn't paying attention.

I drop the stone in my pocket and grab a pen, lifting it proudly. "Found it!" I announce louder than expected. A nearby student shushes me before I add, "I'm still working on question number three."

Miss Raposa's eyes settle on my pocket, but before she can ask me about the salamander stone, the school PA system turns on for announcements.

Everyone glances up at the speaker as it reverberates with static. Normally, the principal waits to announce upcoming sports games and school-wide events until the end of first block. It's strange for them to make an announcement this early into the class period.

"Good morning Errolton High School teachers and students. After receiving numerous reports from local law enforcement this morning, I can confirm that the town of Errolton is officially on lockdown until further notice. We'll be dismissing early today. Please travel home immediately following homeroom and stay with your families until you hear from a town official. Teachers, please check your emails for further details and instructions to share with your classes."

The PA system then screeches with interference before cutting out.

Each student slowly looks around and begins talking on top of one another in urgent sentences.

"Students! Everyone!" Miss Raposa returns to the front of the class and attempts to yell over the growing din, but is unsuccessful. Shaking her head, she strides back to her desk to check her email.

Glancing at Cyndi for the first time since class started, I find her comfortably napping in the seat next to me. I shake her.

"Wake up, you hooligan!"

"Huh?" Cyndi snorts, still half asleep. "Come here you chicken! I'll . . ."

She swats at the air for a minute, locks eyes with me, and, realizing she's in class, lets out a boisterous laugh.

"Dang. I almost had him." She wipes some drool away from her mouth and looks around at our visibly upset classmates. "Did I miss something?"

"Only that the entire town is now on lockdown. Do you know anything about this?"

She shakes her head. "I'm just as clueless as you."

"Okay, students, settle down! I found the principal's email!" Miss Raposa finally pulls the class back in with the promise of more information. Pockets of students shush each other until we're all able to hear.

Miss Raposa reads from the screen of her laptop. "It says that the girls' track team never returned from their track meet last night in North Bern." She looks up, nervousness dancing in her eyes. "Am I okay to read this?"

Everyone nods.

She continues:

The Department of Public Safety found the bus transporting Errolton High School's girls' track team a few miles north of town, damaged from hitting a tree on the side of the road. They speculate that inclement weather caused the bus driver to lose control and hit the tree. However, irregular damage to the bus indicates an alternate cause of the accident. Three bodies were found dead inside of the bus with evidence of an attack from either a wild animal or supernatural being.

Thirteen students remain missing. As a result of this unexplained event, as well as several reported monster sightings from the same night, town officials are instituting a state of lockdown for the town of Errolton. Town residents are to remain inside and follow supernatural protection protocols until law enforcement can confirm it is safe to return to public spaces.

My eyes go wide. I lean over to Cyndi and whisper, "Hey, you don't think I . . . "

She sucks in a slow breath. "Honestly? I don't know."

Biting the inside of my cheek, I fight to remember the night before. No images of school buses or teenagers come to mind, but then—aside from the occasional flash of a moose antler or the rustling of leaves—there's not much I do remember.

Wouldn't I have some memories of kidnapping or killing a dozen teenagers?

How far gone am I?

"One thing I do know," Cyndi whispers back, "is that you need to get your monster stuff under control, like, now. Two unintentional full-body transformations in two days do not bode well for how things are going to go in the future."

"What do you mean?"

"So, for me, shapeshifting takes a lot of concentration. It took me a while to learn how to do it without weird inconsistencies, but your situation seems different. You're not having any trouble changing from one form to the other, you've only been doing this for a few days, and—most importantly—you're not making the willful choice to change. Right?"

I nod. "Pretty much."

"Okay, so then something else is causing you to change against your will. And if you don't figure out what that is soon . . . then you might not be able to change back."

My eyes widen, terrified.

"You mean, I could get stuck like that?"

Well hidden amongst the chatter around us, Cyndi shrugs before whispering back.

"Maybe? But, it's probably the salamander stone, right? I can't think of anything else with enough power to trigger that kind of transformation."

"I thought that too, but now I'm not sure. The two times I've transformed, I haven't had the stone on me."

Cyndi furrows her brow. "Are you sure?"

I tug at my hair, growing anxious. "Yeah."

The bell rings and everyone rises from their seats, rushing for the door. Cyndi and I follow.

"You know, about the track team," I say to her. "Grandpa mentioned something about people going missing the other day. I wonder . . . "

But just as we're about to enter the hallway, something tugs at my sleeve.

"Just a minute, you two."

I peek over my shoulder to see Miss Raposa standing to my right with an open binder.

"Ellie, Cyndi, can you wait a minute?"

"What is it?" I ask, stepping out of the line of students funneling into the hallway. Cyndi follows behind.

"Oh, I just wanted to go over a few things," Miss Raposa chirps melodically as she returns to her binder. "You two have missed a lot of class, so I hoped we'd have time after school today to review some material for the upcoming test. Are you able to stay? I can drive you home afterward."

Cyndi and I exchange looks.

"Shouldn't we be heading home immediately, just like everyone else?" Cyndi asks.

"Oh, I'm sure everything's fine. Someone bored or half-blind reports a coyote nearby and the Beowulf Brigade is ready to spring into action, locking everyone in their homes," Miss Raposa says in a sing-song tone. "Staying here for an extra hour shouldn't make a difference, but it's up to you. Is following the Beowulf Brigade's suggestion more important than your grade?"

Her question dangles in the air, as if to test my reaction.

I raise an eyebrow. "Um, yes? I think we should follow law enforcement's advice and head home now. I'll try to stay after next week to catch up."

My biology teacher purses her lips, nodding. "I'll be waiting."

I turn and walk out of the classroom without replying.

Cyndi follows, laughing and skipping behind me.

"Ha. The look on her face was priceless!" After catching up to my strides, she continues, "But, are you sure you don't want to stay after?"

I shrug. "I don't know. Staying here feels like the wrong choice, no matter what it might do for my grade."

I have too many questions and not enough answers, and that needs to change.

"Do you mind taking a detour on the way back to the colonel's house?" I ask, turning to Cyndi.

"You have somewhere in mind?"

Chapter Eleven

Ellie

Mary Shelley's novel *Frankenstein* was originally published under a more telling name: *The Modern Prometheus*. For those unfamiliar with Greek mythology, the god Prometheus is best known for gifting humans fire from Mount Olympus—a task for which is he brutally punished."

Cyndi and I sneak in behind the audience seated in rows of plastic, foldable chairs. There are nearly fifty people in attendance, which is more than I'd expect for a midday event being held at the Errolton Public Library. Though, if any event was to have increased attendance today—the first day in months that our town prepares for lockdown—then Lord Vance's Vampire Book Club, sponsored by the Beowulf Brigade, would be it.

We find a few empty chairs next to the refreshments table and take our seats. My eyes return to the speaker, a man with short, neatly styled brown hair and a flamboyant mustache that curls at the ends. His position at the podium, as well as his neat black suit and nametag that reads, "Hello! My name is Lord Vance," gives me the sneaking suspicion that he's Lord Vance—the organizer of this event, and the one I'm looking for.

"Like Prometheus, Victor Frankenstein seeks to test the limits of existence without considering the long-term results of his pursuit. Dr. Frankenstein claims that only 'cowardice or carelessness' creates the boundaries of scientific inquiry, essentially removing the burden of ethical responsibility from his shoulders. So, his descent into mad science begins."

I glance at the snack table to my left and notice a platter of sugar cookies, each topped with a thumbprint of what appears to be strawberry jam. The cookies' sweet scent lingers in the air, tempting me to reach over and grab one for myself.

"And who wouldn't be excited to test the limits of life and death? Dr. Frankenstein claims that, following his experiments, death is a solvable problem rather than an existential requirement. He states: 'Darkness had no effect upon my fancy; and a church-yard was to me merely the receptacle of bodies deprived of life, . . . food for the worm.'"

A hunched, elderly lady walks up to the table of refreshments and pours herself a glass of fruit punch. She turns around, leans casually against the table, and takes a sip, slurping it through her teeth like a wine connoisseur.

"Losing his fear of death turns Victor Frankenstein into the true monster of the novel. Once he discovers 'the cause of generation and life' and decides to move ahead with his experiment, 'bestowing animation upon lifeless matter,' he no longer sees life as a precious resource.

"In doing so, Dr. Frankenstein forgets to consider what giving life to dead matter will do to the being he's creating. His analytical approach ignores the element of the soul, or at the very least, the personality of living things."

The cookies smell too good to stay seated. I stand up awkwardly, trying not to block the view of anyone behind me, and step over to the table as quietly as I can. Then, before I lose my nerve, I turn my back to the speaker, grab a dessert plate, and begin piling cookies onto it.

Still leaning on the table, the older woman chuckles to my right.

"Eat up," she whispers. "When Vance starts talking about romantic literature, he can go on for a while. It's best not to listen on an empty stomach."

I nod, balancing the paper plate of cookies on my arm, and extend my empty hand to her. "Thanks. I'm Ellie."

She looks at the hand for a moment before shaking it. "Well, aren't you a polite one? Ellie, I'm Miss Virginia. If you need anything, let me know."

Miss Virginia smiles in an attempt to set me at ease, but her mouth is stained from the fruit punch. It leaves her teeth a glistening, vibrant red, which is unsettling to look at.

"Thanks." I shoot her a tentative smile back before returning to my seat.

"Fellow vampires," Lord Vance addresses the crowd, "remember that our absence of a pumping, bleeding heart does not negate our responsibility toward those with them. Yes, we are dependent upon humans for food, but they are willing to cooperate with us despite our existence threatening their way of life. The creation of hema is just the beginning—local and state governments everywhere are promoting cooperative efforts between vampires and humans, despite those governments being run by mostly humans."

Once seated, I pop a cookie into my mouth. The soft, buttery shortbread melts on my tongue, quickly followed by a swirl of sweet, berry jam.

They taste like heaven.

There's a third flavor in the cookie that I can't place, but I'm too preoccupied with the mechanics of eating the pile to care. I grab two more cookies and continue munching happily.

Cyndi, who's been playing a game on her phone since we arrived, absentmindedly reaches over and grabs a cookie from my plate. After taking a bite, she spits the cookie into her hand.

She looks at me, wide-eyed, and whispers, "Ellie!"

"Yes?" I keep my eyes on the speaker.

"These have blood in them!"

"What?" I ask out of the corner of my mouth.

"Well, not blood. But something like it. Didn't you read the sign?"

I squint at her for a minute before looking over my shoulder at the snack table. There, Miss Virginia is straightening a banner above the punch that reads, "Don't eat your friends! Have an Impossiblood™ treat!"

There's some smaller text at the bottom of the banner, stating, "Please be advised that our food may have come in contact with or contain peanuts, milk, eggs, wheat or hema."

Hema. The vampire dietary substitute for human blood.

I look down at my plate of cookies. "So, the red jam on these cookies . . . "

"Is most likely hema. Yep."

My brain tells me to go to the bathroom and vomit them up, but my tongue and stomach protest. If Cyndi hadn't said anything, I wouldn't have noticed.

What's more, I'm starting to feel full in a way I haven't felt in days.

The speaker places a hand on his chest, pulling my attention back to the front.

"In the same way, friends, do not forget your past humanity. Use those memories to inform how you treat new people you come across. If you struggle to fight your bloodlust, remember that there are crisis counselors available around the clock, both online and over the phone. And remember to meet regularly with your sponsors to discuss your journey. No vampire is an island, and no real growth can occur without the support of others. Many have tried solitude and isolation as a way to protect humans, only to eventually break and appear on the evening news after devouring shoppers in their local supermarket. Don't end up on the evening news. Instead," he gestures to the crowd, waiting for a response.

As if on cue, three vampires in the front row respond in unison, "Find a bloody-buddy!"

"That's right." Lord Vance chuckles over various pockets of laughter throughout the library. "Thank you all for coming. Before we dismiss, there's one specific item to mention regarding the western region—is Marquess Bayard here?"

A man with coppery-red hair and a long, braided beard stands suddenly. He responds, "Yes, Lord Vance?"

The vampire leading the group waves a hand at him. "Be seated. I know this is your first meeting, but there's no need to be so formal here." Lord Vance references his papers for a minute before speaking again. "Marquess Bayard, as well as Marquess DeLucia. This involves you as well, since your province flanks his to the south."

Another man rises slightly, waving a hand to the crowd in silent greeting. His long black hair is tied back in a black and red ribbon, which touches the collar of his dark green coat. The man makes eye contact with various members before turning back to Lord Vance and sitting down with a bow.

Vance continues, "Ah yes. There you are, DeLucia. In the western region, the numbers of thralls and new vampire converts are increasing at higher rates than any other region in the state. I realize you cannot control the acts of individual vampires, but our coalition made a treaty with the state of New Hampshire not to prey on state residents unless they willingly registered with their local ordinances. Humans are supposed to submit to testing before joining a family, to guarantee that those individuals are submitting themselves without manipulation on our part. Not only am I not seeing an influx of thrall registration in those areas, but I'm hearing rumors of vampire pop-up bars appearing throughout the state, encouraging 'membership' and offering 'eternal life.' Are either of you aware of this?"

Marquess Bayard responds first. "Lord Vance, sir, I have groups of vampires in my province searching for members of what we suspect to be an underground cult. These illegal gatherings have been tough to track; those involved are incredibly organized and tight-lipped. They may be actively recruiting, but they're incredibly selective of who they let in." Bayard sighs in defeat. "I'm afraid we haven't found anyone willing to talk to us about these meetings as of yet, but we will. My trackers just need more time."

Lord Vance shakes his head wearily. "I'm afraid time is something we don't have enough of these days. Many of you are aware that Errolton will soon be in lockdown due to a recent attack on a group of young people, but things like this are happening across the state. These targeted attacks are not just the work of rabid beasts looking for dinner: they're precise, coordinated, and often too quick to track. I appeal to the other marquesses in attendance today: please, lend Bayard your aid. We must root them out."

Marquess DeLucia responds with a haughty eyeroll. He stands slowly and turns away from the podium to address the crowd directly. "Do we honestly still believe that underground cults are happening here, in New Hampshire? This state has been nothing but accepting of vampires. What need do we have of recruiting thralls and enlisting baby vampires in secret?"

DeLucia begins to fiddle with one of his many gold rings, continuing, "I mean no disrespect, Lord Vance, but you have accused multiple marquesses of intentional mismanagement for months without presenting any hard evidence. You link together isolated events with conspiracy theories and offer statistics that, to be honest, appear fabricated or just incorrect.

"As I've mentioned before, this feels like an issue of paperwork, not one of organized crime," he scoffs. "The registration process for thralls and new vampires can take up to nine months, and that isn't taking into account the delays caused by monster attacks." DeLucia removes a smartphone from his coat pocket and waves it to the audience. "Nearly everyone here has a computer in their pocket, and yet individuals waiting for their state identification are unable to purchase hema until their physical ID arrives in the mail. Even if you are including the number of pending applications in your data, Lord Vance, I'm sure that the discrepancies you're seeing are of those vampires who prefer to opt out of the registration process altogether. Many are skeptical of the local government's intentions with registration, and to be frank, I can't say their worries are unfounded."

The room is quiet for a moment, allowing a palpable tension to stretch between the vampires and humans in attendance. Then, before Lord Vance can respond, the silence breaks with an ear-ringing smash.

Everyone turns in the direction of the crash to find Miss Virginia, the older lady from before, holding her wooden cane above the now-shattered punch bowl. With its serving vessel in pieces, the fruit punch pools atop the plastic tablecloth and runs down the table legs in rivers of, well, what looks like blood.

Miss Virginia lowers her cane sheepishly. "So sorry to interrupt. There was a fly in the punchbowl."

She walks up to the podium, leaning on her cane in a way that's intended to attract attention rather than for actual support. When she reaches Lord Vance, she bows her head in deference and turns to the crowd.

"As a more recent convert," Miss Virginia begins, "I don't have centuries of experience or a fancy title, but I do remember my humanity. As such, I ask you to remember what it felt like in life to fear death. Lord Vance mentioned earlier that losing that fear can turn us into monsters, and while I think we should enjoy our lives without that fear, we should never, ever forget what fear and loss look like. The availability of Impossiblood™ products and blood donors makes it easy to be a vampire today, but these dietary options don't remove from us the responsibility of ethical improvement and communal support. Vampires are still every bit the predators they've always been, with or without hema, and backsliding into a life of reactionary bloodlust is far too easy if we don't hold one another accountable."

Miss Virginia gestures to Marquess DeLucia. "I do understand the marquess' criticisms; he's right to question the registration process' timeframes and intentions. However," she leans forward, comfortably pressing on her cane, "I find it convenient that you overlook months of collected data on this subject so flippantly, DeLucia. You know as well as anyone the dangers of unregistered vampires hunting privately and creating new members without the proper paperwork. When new converts go unregistered, human families are torn apart. They often go years without knowing what's happened to their loved ones."

I look down at my hands. I know that feeling all too well.

"I believe Lord Vance is only asking for us to redouble our accountability efforts. I certainly hope DeLucia is right, and that we're wrong about the underground cult. However, if there is a cult and we do nothing to stop it, not only will lives be lost, but it will cast doubt on our community as a whole. If that happens, it's likely the state will get involved."

She pauses to let her words sink in before raising her cane into the air. "I call for a vote. Those who support Lord Vance's suggestion of lending available resources to Marquess Bayard's operation, please stand."

Seven vampires stand up out of their seats. Seeing the number, DeLucia begrudgingly stands up as well, muttering to himself.

Miss Virginia smiles widely and lowers her cane. "That's eight votes, one from each region. Let the record show that the vote is unanimous." She bows to Lord Vance. "Apologies for my big mouth, sir. Sometimes I don't know when to keep quiet."

Lord Vance returns her smile brightly. "No problem at all, Virginia."

"On that note," he says to the crowd, "marquesses, be sure to stay in town tonight. We'll need to meet privately after this to outline our plan of attack. Aside from that, I think we can end our meeting here. I'd say let's adjourn for snacks and punch, but as most of the punch is soaking into the carpet, how about we all work together to clean up the mess?"

"Aye!" the crowd yells out boisterously. Within seconds of the closing statements, vampires swarm the soaked refreshments table, either to eat the remaining snacks or to drink "fruit punch" out of the carpet.

Not wanting to attract the attention of unknown vampires, Cyndi and I walk briskly away from the snack table, leaving my plate of cookies behind.

Goodbye cookies. You were weird, but also tasty.

"Are you sure you want to talk to Lord Vance now?" Cyndi asks as we weave through the crowd. "That last part of the meeting seemed intense."

"He's got to talk to me," I answer her, determined. "He's the one being who might actually know if the track team was taken down by vampires or . . . something else."

"What about Colonel Adams? She seems pretty knowledgeable, and the Beowulf Brigade has a lot of resources, right? Wouldn't they have access to the same information that Vance does?"

"Maybe, but it's not just about the missing track team. I can't just ask Colonel Adams about my monster transformations, can I? 'Hi Colonel. Thanks for inviting me into your house out of the kindness of your heart and all. By the way, I've been a monster this whole time. Any idea what type? Also don't hunt me, okay?'"

"Yeah, I don't see that going over very well." Cyndi lets out a slight laugh as we stop behind the small group gathered around Lord Vance, taking turns asking questions.

"You know," she says, "I've been assimilating into society for so long that I've forgotten what this feels like."

"What what feels like?"

"Just all the hectic running around that happens during a major life change. I've already gone through my initial experiences with shape-shifting, so other than working random jobs, making new friends, and creating new personas, I haven't faced any real hurdles in decades. None worth dwelling on, anyway."

For a moment, Cyndi's fox ears perk up alongside her messy bun. Then, before I can blink, they're gone.

"Anyway," she grins, "thanks for bringing me along for the ride. This week has been a fun change of pace. Much better than pretending to take notes in class."

I narrow my eyes at her. "Uh-huh. Well, I'm glad you're enjoying yourself. Next time I go through a life-shattering experience like this, I'll be sure to include you."

She shoots a pair of finger guns in my direction. "That's all I ask!"

Before I can give her a snarky response, a man in a green velvet coat bumps into my shoulder.

I look up to find the dark stare of Marquess DeLucia, one of the vampires that spoke during Lord Vance's meeting. His earlier arguments were persuasive and self-assured, which gave off an air of manicured confidence; the creature before me, however, is barely able to hold its mask together. His eyes, rimmed red with growing irritation, contain dark blue irises that look nearly black, and the decadence of his many rings does little to disguise his long, sharpened nails, itching to dig into the nearest artery he can find.

His unhinged appearance reminds me of Vlad, the starving vampire from Howard's Frozen Treats, as he requested Impossiblood™ just days before.

But why would a vampire, a marquess, be struggling to find food in a time with so many alternatives nearby?

The looming vampire draws up the corners of his mouth, baring the tiniest points of his fangs, until a flicker of recognition enters his eyes.

Then he blinks, looks away, and stalks out of the room without a word.

I glance at Cyndi, who shrugs. Thankfully, after the marquess' departure, the group blocking our path begins to break up. We step toward Lord Vance, who's in the middle of telling Miss Virginia a joke.

Despite the apparent age difference between them—Miss Virginia's body appearing twenty years older than his, Lord Vance's life lasting centuries older than hers—the two are obviously flirting when we approach.

Miss Virginia notices us first. "Ellie! Our newest member. How are you, sweetheart?"

"Oh, um," I scratch the back of my neck, "that's not . . . "

Cyndi interrupts me, "That's what we're here for! Yep! To talk to Lord Vance about new vampire things and, um . . . " she looks back at me, unsure of how to finish the lie.

"And to report possible information about the missing track team?" I add. "Yeah. That's it. We saw something strange last night, and Cyndi thinks that it might have to do with the track team. Right, Cyndi?" I nudge her.

She nods enthusiastically. "That's why we're here! No other possible explanation!"

The two vampires exchange puzzled glances before Miss Virginia replies, "Well, okay then. I'm curious to hear what you two have to say, but I'll leave you in the capable hands of our fearless leader here. I need to help with the snack table, anyway." She bows her head to Lord Vance. "Vance."

He lifts her hand to his lips and leaves a light kiss on her freckled knuckles. "M'lady."

"Oh, you!" She withdraws her hand playfully and turns away, giggling to herself.

Lord Vance watches Miss Virginia as she wedges herself back through the crowd. He laughs to himself.

"Even after centuries on this planet, people never cease to surprise me."

He glances back at us. "Anyway. Ellie, Cyndi, you mentioned being new vampires?" Lord Vance squints at us before adding, "I'm sorry, your names sound familiar. Have we met before?"

"You might have heard of me from my grandfather," I reply. "His name is Peter Karlsen."

Lord Vance's eyes grow wide. "Wait, you're Pete's granddaughter?" He looks between the two of us before piecing it together.

"So, you're not vampires then."

"Most likely not," Cyndi replies.

His brow wrinkles deeper into the creases of his forehead.

"And you already know more about Pete's condition than I would. Which means . . . " Lord Vance snaps his fingers. "Ellie, you're here about the curse!"

His words knock the wind out of me. What else could "the curse" be but an explanation of the monster I'm becoming?

The idea that Lord Vance, someone I've never met before, could know more about what's happening to me than I do, fills me with rage. Why is it that the adults in my life are determined to withhold this kind of information? Don't they know that hiding the truth doesn't preserve my childhood?

It just makes growing up that much scarier.

I'm hit with the sudden urge to lunge at the vampire and rip off his curly mustache, but I decide against it. It's not Lord Vance's fault I'm out of the loop.

Instead of acting out, I place a hand into the pocket of my overalls, hold the salamander stone in my clenched fist, and ask him, "What do you know?"

Cyndi coughs loudly before he can answer. Then she whispers, "Are you sure we can talk about this here?"

The vampire shrugs, unconcerned. "This might be the best place to talk." He gestures to the loud pockets of conversation surrounding us.

"It would take someone with powerful magic to pinpoint our conversation out from those around us, so long as we speak quietly."

Lord Vance sits in a nearby folding chair and Cyndi and I do the same. The vampire lord hesitates, clearing his throat.

"It's not that I know much, you see. I've always sensed a sort of curse or dark burden being shared between you and your grandfather. Being as old as I am, I've learned how to spot supernatural details in everyday life. There's always more going on beneath the surface than people show. You see . . . " He looks up at the clock. "Oh, but we're running out of time."

"What?" I blink. "What happens when time is up?"

Lord Vance chuckles. "Nothing too serious. It's just that the librarians asked for us to be out of here within the hour."

I let out a steadying breath, thankful for one less surprise. "Oh. That makes sense."

He continues: "I'll try to be brief. I always assumed the darkness following your grandfather was due to your mother's condition, and the mysterious details surrounding her disappearance and apparent loss of sanity. But now, I'm starting to think it has to do with you."

I blink at him. "What do you mean?"

"Well, the last time I met with your grandfather, I realized why he's been so resilient to that darkness. He gives off an incredible amount of protective and defensive energy, which is probably why the Beowulf Brigade does so well against monsters—not just because they're a group trained to fight against beasts, but because they have a wall of defensive magic going into battle before them."

Lord Vance leans in to whisper. "This layer of protection is a natural repellant to creatures of the night—vampires included—so I've always been able to sense this shield of protection around you and your grandfather. That is, until today."

The salamander stone burns against my skin, but I don't yell or cry; instead, I tighten my fist around it. If I focus on the pain in my hand, then I don't have to think about the tidal wave of emotions churning in my stomach.

I turn to Cyndi.

"Show him the photo you took."

"Are you sure?" she asks, concerned.

"I'm sure."

Cyndi sighs and opens her smartphone. "Here. What can you tell us about this?"

Lord Vance tilts the phone up to better see the photo. After a minute of examining it, he asks, "What is this?"

"That thing," I work to suppress feelings of self-loathing and disgust as they bubble up. "That thing is me."

"How . . . what do you mean?" He looks up at me, baffled.

Excluding the details about Cyndi being a fox and the salamander stone, I tell him what we know so far about my transformations: what happens to my brain and body before, during, and after each shift.

Then, after describing the scenes in as much detail as I can, I mention my mother's words from the other night:

Two hearts, two souls, and two rows of teeth,
hungry, ready, and able.

It takes a full minute for Lord Vance to respond. I can tell he's searching for the best way to share what he knows without overwhelming me with the truth.

Finally, he says one word: "*Strigoi.*"

"Gesundheit," Cyndi replies. I hit her on the shoulder.

Lord Vance smiles faintly. "It's an umbrella term from Romanian mythology that describes the undead, or those that are not alive, that often feed on living things for their life force. Vampires are included in this classification, but there are other types too, like the *strigoaica*—one who sells their soul in exchange for dark powers. But the term *strigoi* is sometimes used in connection with the *strzyga*, which originates from Slavic folklore."

"*Strzyga*," I repeat, listening.

"In English, I believe it's just pronounced, 'striga.' Your mother's song mentions 'two hearts, two souls, and two rows of teeth.' This is a common phrase specifically used to refer to *strzyga*. It means that a person is born with two souls, and after one dies, the other one brings the body back to life and begins hunting animals or people for nourishment."

"So then, I'd be a . . . striga?" I say, testing it out. I'm willing to go along with the idea until I realize a very important detail.

"But, Lord Vance, sir." I look up at him. "I'm not dead."

The vampire lord reaches up to tug on his mustache, thoughtful.

"Are you sure?" he asks.

"Um," I glance at Cyndi, who shrugs in response, and say, "I'm pretty sure."

"Harumph." He twirls his mustache. "Well, sometimes with curses, death can be more symbolic, such as a metaphorical death of a former self, or a major life transition, IE: 'The old me is dead,' or something of the like."

Lord Vance tilts his head to one side, as if to blow dust from the stacks of information that clutter the rooms of his mind.

He returns my gaze after a minute. "You could be something else, like a werewolf. Their transformation is usually temporary, and they dance on the line between human and nonhuman. Was it a full moon when you transformed?"

Cyndi shakes her head before I can answer. "Nope. I always spend the full moon hunting with . . . " she pauses, remembering that Lord Vance is unaware of her true identity as a fox, and says, "some locals. Anyway, the last full moon was nearly two weeks ago."

"Ah." He nods, understanding. "Occasionally the full moon in mythology refers to a period of magical amplification, so being near a magical hot spot or some powerful totem could be enough to trigger your shapeshifting. In the case of a werewolf, however, the full moon is a standard part of the deal, so that's probably not it."

The vampire lord sighs in defeat. "I'd like to answer this question for you, but unfortunately, I've never come across something like . . . " he points to Cyndi's phone, "what you are. I do apologize."

I look down at my shoes, frustrated. This was a waste of time.

"What about the missing track team?" Cyndi asks.

Lord Vance looks at her quizzically. "What about them?"

"Do you know anything about them?"

"Cyndi," I shake my head, "we don't need to ask about that. I doubt he can tell us anything anyway."

"And why couldn't I?" Lord Vance asks me. "I offered my guidance to your grandfather only days ago. At the very least, I can give you the same information I gave him." He smiles again. "Think of it as a way to make up for my lacking help before."

Cyndi nods at his response. "Sounds good to me! We're trying to find out if what happened was Ellie's fault."

"Cyndi!" I yell at her, annoyed.

The vampire glances at me then, his earlier familiarity retreating.

"Did you attack anyone last night? Did you knock over a bus?"

"No! At least, not that I can remember." Sighing, I add, "But unlike my first transformation, I don't remember much from last night."

"I see. Blackouts like that aren't uncommon, though they usually occur following a feed . . . " He narrows his eyes warily. "It's hard to prove that you did anything either way, since the students are still missing. Though the damage to the bus makes me think it was something other than a vampire that attacked them."

Lord Vance goes on, "Still, I struggle to believe you wouldn't remember the taste of human blood. That sort of event would shape you . . . significantly."

Cyndi presses the issue. "So then, if she didn't eat them—sorry Ellie—then she, or something else, must have taken them, right? But what's the point of kidnapping a bunch of teenagers? Wouldn't the typical monster response be to attack them all on the bus?"

"It's a good question," the vampire purses his lips. "I can't speak for other predators, but it's common for vampires to keep their prey alive for some time, as a source of food. We usually refer to this type of prey as a thrall—at least, we did until the term gained popularity amongst humans who desired companionship with vampires. Now, usage of a thrall as a food source is outlawed, but some continue this practice in secret."

I think back to my last conversation with Grandpa, in which he mentioned the missing girls throughout Errolton, and ask, "Why do you think young girls are being targeted?"

"I doubt it's only girls, but the majority of those who have gone missing in the state are under thirty," Lord Vance replies. "And if this is related to the other kidnappings, then the Reformed Vampire Council should also look into it. Among the more savage vampires who still try to hunt humans for sport, there's a preference for younger prey. They say the younger the human, the sweeter the blood."

The vampire's eyes take on a glazed, faraway look as he speaks, until he shakes his head. "I realize how that sounds. It's unfortunate that a vampire's natural tendency is to destroy those that are so full of life. It's just that younger blood has a higher amount of potential energy, and with such, it can be drained for more magical properties that way. Not just by vampires, but by anyone with enough skill to distill someone's lifeforce into its pure magical essence."

"Um," Cyndi replies.

"What?" I ask.

"Apologies. I'm getting off into theoretical magic again. It's been an interest of mine over the last century to observe and track how magic and natural forces push and pull against one another. I have notebooks full of theories, but so far, no concrete proof of any of them. Perhaps, another time . . . " He stands and begins walking toward the podium to collect his papers.

"Perhaps," I repeat, glancing at the clock. "Um, sir, if my friend and I wanted to, say, go looking for the missing track team, do you have any suggestions for where we should start looking?"

Lord Vance taps his papers together to straighten the edges of his pile.

"Well, the Beowulf Brigade is having a raid tonight to search for them. Isn't that right, Colonel Adams?"

I spin around to see the furious outline of Colonel Simone Adams, hard as iron, wearing a bright yellow coat and hand-knit purple scarf.

She inclines her head in greeting. "That's right, Lord Vance. The Beowulf Brigade is gathering supplies as we speak."

Then, with a scowl etched across her face, the colonel leans down to look at me, her nose mere inches from mine.

"And you're not coming with us."

Chapter Twelve

Ellie

"But I can help!" I yell in protest.

Colonel Adams slows at the oncoming stoplight. Her fingers tense around the steering wheel of her tactical SUV.

"Even if I wanted you to come on tonight's raid," she begins, "which I don't, by the way. But even if I did, I wouldn't be able to guarantee your safety. And your grandfather would never allow it."

I cross my arms and glare out the window. "Yeah. Well. He's not exactly here to complain, now is he?"

Despite being in the wrong for running off with Cyndi again, as well as not following lockdown protocol, I hold on to my indignance. I'm not about to let this opportunity slip by.

Sighing, the colonel accelerates the car forward. "Be that as it may. You don't know how to hunt, Ellie."

"I know enough!"

"Subduing one fire salamander with your friends is not the same as fighting an unknown threat in the woods. At night, visibility is horrible, and if you're not careful, you'll likely hurt yourself with your weapon before you get a chance to attack anything."

"But—"

Colonel Adams hits the turn signal before turning left.

"We can talk about this later. Thankfully, because Miss Virginia called me, I was able to find you just in time for your meeting with the social worker. They should be arriving at the house right around now, and I suggest you change your attitude before talking to them. This is a very important meeting."

Sunlight sprinkles through the trees as we drive, heating the skin of my arm in small patches.

I know what I'm asking for is ridiculous. I'm only so good on horseback, and I'm not a trained monster hunter.

But I'm sick of sitting around, waiting for something else to happen to me. I want the next action I take to be one of my choosing, without interference from dark forces or monstrous urges or low self-esteem.

My talk with Lord Vance gave me something I haven't had in a long time: answers. Even if most of them were no, the more I learn about supernatural things happening in Errolton, the more likely it is that I'll find out what's happening to me.

And out in the woods, I might find new information that I can't hope to understand from a secondhand source. I have to see the monsters with my own eyes, and, if necessary, bludgeon them into talking.

Because, like it or not, I'm changing.

It would be nice to know why.

"Hey." Cyndi leans forward, clearly not buckled into the back row of seats. "Why do you think it's called a 'Vampire Book Club?'"

I shrug. "Probably because their meetings are at the library."

"Fair point," Cyndi says. "What do you think, Colonel?"

Colonel Adams replies, "Sit back. You could go flying through the windshield."

Cyndi scoots back. "Sorry. I just wanted to be included in the conversation."

"Well, now I've scolded both of you. Feel included?"

"A little." Cyndi grins. "So why do you think it's called that?"

"Called what?"

"A book club! Do the vampires ever sit around and talk about books?"

"Oh." The colonel pulls into her neighborhood. "Back when the Reformed Vampire Council was formed, locals were worried about a group of powerful vampires meeting nearby, even if it was just to discuss basic vampire business. That's why Lord Vance made the meetings public—so that no one could accuse them of 'dark, nefarious plotting,' as he put it. Letting humans and other non-vampires attend the meeting allowed local officials to learn about the council's plans, which were to ensure safety and promote positive relationships between humans and supernatural beings."

"Huh," I say, looking over at the colonel. "But how do public meetings turn into a book club?"

"That was probably Miss Virginia's doing. I heard her say once that using a story to illustrate an argument might cast a wider net of understanding across a room of beings, despite their differences in age and background. But it's probably just her way of livening up the meetings. Most that I've attended are just debates between marquesses about their regional dividing lines."

Cyndi yawns. "Huh. Well, I think Miss Virginia has the hots for old Vance-y. Right, Ellie?"

I roll my eyes.

"Really?" Colonel Adams arches an eyebrow. "I mean, stranger things have happened." She stops the car in her driveway and looks into the backseat. "Sorry, Cyndi. You can't stay over tonight, and we're already running late for this meeting, so I can't drive you home. Is it a far walk?"

I start to say, "Uh, I don't—"

But Cyndi cuts me off. "No worries. It's only a few minutes from here. Bye Ellie!"

She hops out of the car and skips down the sidewalk without a care.

I wonder what she'll do during her break from me and my personal chaos. Maybe she'll shift back into her fox form and sleep under someone's porch or go through their garbage for snacks. Maybe she'll stay in human form and ride the bus around town. Maybe she'll become the large fox and just go running.

I smile, envious of her freedom. It'd be nice to have an inconspicuous form to transform into, instead of the beast I'm stuck with.

"Look." The colonel points to another car parked near her mailbox. "That's probably the social worker's car. Let's head in before we're any later."

Begrudgingly, I exit the SUV. I'm all too familiar with the red pick-up truck parked along the road.

We walk into Colonel Adams' house to find Mr. Adams, her husband, seated with a smiling, middle-aged man wearing round-framed glasses. As we enter the living room, the bespectacled man looks over the top of his lenses at us. He then leans back, drops his papers, and reaches out to shake the colonel's hand. "Ma'am. I was just getting on with your husband here. The name's Mickey Reyes."

The cheery face of Mickey Reyes is one that only appears at the worst times in my life. He's been my caseworker since I was an infant, when the issues with my mother first started. As such, Mr. Reyes attends every one of my custody hearings and mental health evaluations.

And each time I see him, he does his best to couch bad news with a smile.

He doesn't understand that hedging around the truth, pretending that things aren't as bad as they seem, just makes it worse. His unwavering smiles create a barrier of pity between us, arming him against the pain of my misfortune.

As if my bad luck is something he can catch.

Once the colonel sits on a nearby couch, Mr. Reyes offers me a million-watt smile.

"Ellie! It's been years! Well, and it looks like you're all grown up."

He laughs at his own sentence, as if it was a witty observation and not just a statement of fact.

I sit across from him, avoiding his eyes.

"Yeah," I say, "well, almost anyway. I just turned sixteen."

"That's great!" Mr. Reyes responds enthusiastically. When I don't reply, he picks up a sheet of paper from his stack and looks it over.

"I guess that's part of what we're here to talk about. I heard about your grandfather's condition. Have you visited him in the hospital?"

I nod. "Yeah. Grandpa's not doing well. He still hasn't woken up."

"That's what the doctors told me. Your grandfather told the hospital to contact me in case things ever got . . . " he pauses, ever tactful, and says, "serious."

Mr. Reyes takes his glasses off and places them on the coffee table. "I'm sure it's been rough for you, having him in the hospital. But there are certain things we have to discuss in case your grandfather doesn't get better."

His eyes remain full of light and love as he speaks.

I wonder how his expression might change if he could see my monstrous form.

"So, the last time we changed your custody arrangement was when you were an infant, back when your mother, ahem, disappeared."

As I nod, I fantasize about shapeshifting into the monster right in front of Mr. Reyes, the colonel, and Mr. Adams. It's not an elegant way out of this uncomfortable meeting, but some problems require a cartoonishly large hole in the wall as a way of escape, rather than a well-timed excuse.

The salamander stone glows hot in my pocket.

"Your mother never lost custody of you, because your grandfather was sure that she would be rehabilitated and eventually return home to care for you. If he passes away, however, then we'll need to have another custody hearing to determine whether or not your mother should have sole custody over you."

I openly glare at my caseworker. "I'm sorry. What?"

The possibility that my crazy, absent mother could potentially make decisions about my life if she ever convinces those in the looney bin that she's ready to leave, is insane.

It makes my eye twitch.

"I don't want her to have custody over me," I say, gritting my teeth.

Mr. Reyes reaches out to place a comforting hand on my shoulder, pauses, and returns his hand to his stack of papers.

Coward.

He lifts another piece of paper. "Okay, well, if we don't want her to have custody, then we'll need to build a case to prove that she's still mentally unfit to care for you."

His use of the word "we" grates against my patience. As if "we" are a team. No, Mr. Reyes—you are someone who has never cared what happened to me, and up until this point, you've always had my grandfather to mediate between us.

How does it feel, Mickey, speaking directly to me for once? How inconvenient that my grandfather isn't here to be chummy with you. I'm so sorry for your loss.

"But," lowering the paper in front of his face, he finally looks me in the eyes and says, "I don't know if it's a good idea to change your custody arrangement."

"And why not?" I challenge.

"Because if you take away your mother's custody, and you have no other living relatives, then you will become a ward of the state. It means you might have to go into the foster system."

I jump out of my chair. "What?"

Mr. Reyes raises his hands defensively. "I'm sorry, Ellie. You're not eighteen yet. You can't just take care of yourself."

"As if I haven't been taking care of myself for the last sixteen years."

"Be that as it may . . . "

I don't wait for him to finish.

Instead, I let out a guttural scream, grab Mr. Reyes' stack of papers, and throw them across the room before running upstairs and slamming the door to the colonel's spare bedroom.

I press my fists to my temples and do my best to calm down. This room is a safe place, a small pocket of space I can call my own.

For the time being, anyway.

Where will I go if Grandpa doesn't get better?

Even if he does come home, where will we live?

I drop my backpack on the floor and let my arms hang limp while exhaustion and fear bite at me in shaky, feral pulses.

If I can just focus on something else, then maybe I won't tear out Mr. Reyes' throat. Maybe I won't chase his car and crumple him up like a metallic burrito.

I grab a pillow, press my face into it, and scream as loud as I possibly can. After a minute, I pull my face away and try to count my breaths.

Breathe in for five.

Hold for four.

Breathe out for six.

I've got to stop this madness pressing against my humanity.

Eventually, the fire in my veins cools and my vision settles on my backpack, half unzipped. The unopened box for my new cell phone peeks out.

I unwrap the phone and go through the steps to set it up, confirming that my contacts have imported over. Once done, I shoot Cyndi a text:

Hey. It's Ellie. Sorry you had to leave earlier. I finally got the new phone working. Also, I'm about to bust out of here.

Cyndi replies minutes later with an image of a cat in sunglasses waving hello. She follows it up with this:

No problem. I've just been loitering outside of Badger Burger. Wanna meet up now?

Before I can answer, there's a knock at the door.

"Ellie? Can I come in?"

It's Colonel Adams.

After a minute of silence, she says behind the door, "I just want to talk."

I open the door to see the colonel, who's alone, thankfully. From the looks of it, she's not trying to broker peace between me and Mr. Reyes—something that Grandpa has had to do in the past.

Things are so hard without Grandpa here. I just want him to wake up and take care of all this.

Colonel Adams takes a seat in the rocking chair, casually placed in a corner of the room.

"I can see that you're upset, and I don't entirely blame you for the outburst. Life has not been kind to you this week. But that doesn't excuse your behavior."

I scoff at her words, but I don't interrupt.

"And I'm not just talking about your display downstairs, though that was concerning. I'm talking about deliberately disobeying me, your current guardian, as well as the town's lockdown orders. You know that my job is to protect you from harm right now, don't you?"

Her logic is annoying.

"What is the point of going through the effort to get you a new phone if you won't even use it?" She sighs. "I called both you and Cyndi the minute I heard about school letting out early. But neither of you was willing to even let me know what you were doing, let alone ask for permission. Your phone hadn't even been set up, and either Cyndi's phone was dead, or she just decided to mute my calls."

I avoid the colonel's gaze to hide the smirk on my face. Cyndi and I were well aware of her attempts to call. At the time, it seemed like a better idea to ignore them and ask for forgiveness later.

Colonel Adams snaps her fingers to grab my attention. "Hey. Look at me. This is important. You're young, but you're not invincible. You're not even trained in combat against humans, let alone monsters. And just because your grandfather was an experienced hunter and tracker does not mean that you inherited those traits. It takes years to develop those kinds of skills. If you want to work on them, fine, but running around with Cyndi like you've been is not the way to do it."

Biting the inside of my cheek, I push away all the things I want to tell her. There's too much to explain, but none of my reasons change what I've done.

"Sorry," I finally say, "I won't ignore your calls anymore. And I won't run off again."

Not without good reason, anyway.

Satisfied, the colonel nods her head. "Glad to hear it."

"By the way," I add, "you said my grandfather was an experienced hunter and tracker. He still is: present tense. He's just . . . taking a break right now."

She pauses, then nods again. "All right, then. He is."

Glancing at the open bedroom door, I ask, "So, um. How bad was it after I . . . walked out?"

"After you stormed out in a rage?" The colonel corrects me.

I throw my hands up in frustration. "Okay, but c'mon. Foster care? What am I supposed to do with that?"

"Well, if you'd stayed downstairs for a bit longer, you would have learned that Bernard, my husband, is a lawyer familiar with cases like yours." She crosses her arms. "Bernard is downstairs right now talking with Mr. Reyes about what it would look like if you filed for emancipation, or, at the very least, if they adjusted your mother's custody details. Both of them want to find a solution that lets you avoid the foster system and protects you until you turn eighteen."

I stare at her, surprised. "Really?"

Colonel Adams smiles at me. "You don't think I'd let you get sent away to some unknown family, do you?"

Her words open a door in my chest, allowing the anger and fear to float right out and escape.

Do real families make room for each other like this all the time, not just when things are going sideways?

I look down and begin to pick at the skin between my thumb and forefinger.

"Honestly," I say, "I wouldn't blame you. I've done nothing but cause you problems."

"That's true." She laughs. "But it's like you said. Your grandfather is a good tracker. He'd roast me alive if he learned that I didn't do everything in my power to protect his granddaughter."

I smile at that. "Thanks, Colonel. I'm really thankful for all of your help."

"Well, you can show that appreciation by apologizing to Mr. Reyes."

Ah. There's the catch.

"Do I have to?"

"I don't think he means you any ill will. And, if you apologize," the colonel hides a smile of her own, adding, "I might let you come with me on the raid tonight."

I stand up, surprised. "You mean it? What changed your mind?"

Colonel Adams stands as well. "Let's be honest. You'd be running off tonight to go looking for the missing students whether I bring you along or not, right?"

I sheepishly laugh. "I might have been thinking about it."

"I thought so." She extends a hand to me. "So, if you ride with the brigade tonight, I can at least keep an eye on you. What do you say?"

My hand shakes the colonel's before I can stop myself. "I'll do it."

Now all I have to do is hide the fact that I'm a giant monster from our local monster-hunting militia.

I'm sure it'll be fine.

Chapter Thirteen

Ellie

"Kill the beast!"

Two senior members of the Beowulf Brigade circle one another, readying themselves for a sparring match. The older of the two men, the "beast," is shirtless and blindfolded with a bandana over his eyes. Unable to see, he spins a gleaming machete in slow arcs in front of his bare chest.

His opponent is a man in his twenties, holding a wooden practice sword and wearing only a thin t-shirt for protection. The younger man's face is painted with jagged black stripes that amplify his fierce smile—a grin that only grows wider as he howls and taunts the blinded man.

They're surrounded by nearly thirty hollering armed militia members of varying ages, clapping and chanting back and forth.

"Kill the beast!"

"Kill the beast!"

As a beast of sorts, I make a mental note not to draw attention to myself and return to organizing my grandfather's saddlebag. I might have enjoyed watching this display of masculine aggression the week before, but the crowd's jovial mood, hungry to injure "the blindfolded beast" or his opponent, "the poorly armed warrior," feels different now.

Thankfully, using this time to organize my supplies is an inconspicuous way for me to avoid getting too close to the action. Colonel Adams recovered Grandpa's saddlebag the night of the fire, when she searched the barn for our horse, Declan, so the contents inside have been untouched since their last raid.

"Kill the beast!"

After moving around the bag's existing supplies—a flashlight, a first aid kit, extra gauze—I find a pocket within the saddlebag large enough for my hunting knife. Still resting in its leather sheath, the knife's polished, wooden handle clearly announces how new it is.

The blade has yet to be tested against any threats, perceived or pursued.

I nestle the knife into the bag's interior pocket. I won't need it tonight. I'm just here as a tag-along.

"Kill the beast!"

"Kill the beast!"

The crowd's chanting grows in volume and fervor, pulling my attention back to the sparring circle.

Still blindfolded, the older man is now unarmed and crouching on the ground. His opponent, "the poorly armed warrior," holds the wooden practice sword high and leans to attack. But just as he moves to slash down on the older man's shoulder, the blindfolded man catapults himself to the right.

His risk pays off. The man with the wooden sword chases after "the beast," but it's too late. The older man has found his machete within the fighting circle, and, with only the noise of his opponent to guide him, swings his blade to attack.

With a WHUMP, the machete meets the practice sword at the hilt.

The two men push against each other in locked, aggressive stances, while the crowd cheers on.

"Kill the beast!"

The blindfolded man breaks away from the wooden sword to thrust his machete forward, unknowingly aimed at his opponent's belly.

His strike misses, but only because Colonel Simone Adams, bedecked in chainmail, has stepped between the two men. She catches the weight of the man's blow on her forearm, grabs the machete from the older man's hand, and throws it out of the circle. She then pushes him to the ground and turns back to the younger man.

"Jones! Bingo! What is this?" The colonel grabs the practice sword and tosses it in the same direction as the machete. "Is the thought of being torn apart by monsters not titillating enough for the two of you?"

The man on the ground removes his blindfold and spits into the dirt. "Aw, Colonel. You can't fault the young men for wantin' a little blood-sport before a hunt. We were just putting on a good show for the new recruits. Ol' Pete lets us do it from time to time."

Colonel Adams turns back to the older man. "Interesting. I don't think I see Ol' Pete here giving orders. Do you, Bingo?"

The older man, Bingo, clicks his tongue as he stands up. He places an unwanted hand on the colonel's shoulder. "It ain't that serious, Simone."

In response, the colonel grabs Bingo's wrist and twists it behind his back.

"Ow! Simone, c'mon!" Bingo winces at the wrist lock. "Colonel! Let me go."

Instead of responding, Colonel Adams pushes his weight forward and keeps him subdued as she regards the crowd.

"Since Bingo so kindly volunteered, he'll be the one cleaning out the dogs' kennels tonight. And Jones," she releases Bingo to bark at the younger man, "you'll be caring for the horses when we return. Got it?"

Jones toes the ground, grumbling. "Yes."

"What was that?" The colonel takes a step toward him.

"I said yes, Colonel," Jones repeats, meeting her gaze.

Her eyes rove over the crowd of young men, covered in face paint and camouflage.

"I may not be Peter Karlsen," she growls, "but I've served in the military longer than some of you have been alive. If you have a problem with my position as your commanding officer, you're free to leave now."

She pauses, daring anyone to walk out.

No one moves.

"While I'm your commanding officer, I will not tolerate the unnecessary endangerment of any members of the Beowulf Brigade. We are not 'playing war.' We are protecting the lives of those that cannot defend themselves."

She points at the barn. "Farrowfield Farms has been kind enough to let us care for the dogs and horses here for practically nothing, because Mr. Clark, the owner of this farm, understands our purpose. All he wants is for the members of our town to rest easy while we, their appointed guardians, keep away those things that want to eat, kill, and destroy their children and their livelihoods.

"Now, we owe Mr. Clark a great debt for his support, and his daughters are among those that have gone missing in the last few weeks. Nearly thirty teenagers have been kidnapped this month, and we haven't found a single one. That's unacceptable."

The colonel waits for a minute, letting the weight of her words hang heavy on the shoulders of her recruits. Then, she continues:

"Good news is, we have our first lead in months. The same night that Errolton High School's track team disappears, I witnessed a monster with power I've never seen before."

Uh-oh.

Colonel Adams' voice lowers terribly. "Nearly eight feet tall, the jaws of this beast are powerful enough to snap a man in half in one bite. Its claws can run you through without a second thought. And its eyes?" She shudders dramatically. "Well, there's nothing more terrifying than an animal devoid of fear. This thing looked down the barrel of my shotgun as if it were an appetizer."

A bead of sweat runs down the back of my neck, despite the temperature outside being below forty.

"We must all be on high alert tonight. Any carelessness in the face of this creature will result in loss of life, is that understood?"

"Yes, Colonel!" the crowd yells in response.

She nods. "We can't let this thing get away; not if we're to find those girls. The plan is to follow its tracks into the woods, kill it, and, hopefully, bring everyone home. Are there any questions?"

After a beat, a fit man in his thirties raises a hand. "Colonel, are we sure that those teens are still alive? If the monster you mentioned is what took them, then there's a good chance it's already eaten them for lunch."

"You're right," the colonel agrees, her voice solemn. "There's no guarantee of success today. But we cannot leave this thing alive to terrorize our town any longer. I'm hoping to find the missing students alive—but there's a good chance that tonight will be nothing more than collecting evidence of their deaths. If nothing else, we'll prevent future bloodshed and provide answers to parents who, at the moment, have none."

I desperately want to correct Colonel Adams, to tell her that I'm the monster she's looking for and that I haven't eaten any teenagers lately. At least to the best of my knowledge.

But I can't tell her any of that. Her position is clear: if she sees that monster again, she will kill it, because it is a threat to everyone's safety.

She's not wrong.

Colonel Simone Adams clears her throat. "On another note, I'd like to introduce you all to Ellie Adair, Pete's granddaughter. She'll be shadowing me this evening, riding her grandfather's horse. If anyone has an issue with that, they can take it up with me. Got it?"

The crowd nods, and a few younger recruits wave my way. I recognize their faces from school, but despite living in this town my entire life, I've never spoken to any of them.

The colonel nods. "Good. Go ready your gear and get something to eat. We'll be rolling out in thirty minutes, and unlike the last few raids, once we get on those horses, we won't be stopping for a while. Dismissed."

Everyone breaks off into pockets of murmurs and nervous laughter as they walk into or around the side of the barn. Just as I'm about to follow the group back toward the horse stalls, I'm stopped by Colonel Adams.

"How's it going?" She places a hand on my shoulder. "I know this is a lot to take in."

I avoid her gaze. "Yep! Just getting ready to ride around in the woods to hunt a huge monster. Wouldn't miss it for the world."

Why did I think this was a good idea? There's a very high likelihood that I'll transform while riding along with everyone.

What if I try to eat another moose?

Or the colonel?

Or Bingo?

She laughs quietly. "You'll be okay. I'm glad to see that you're nervous though. You should be." The colonel gestures to a pile of nearby haybales. "Let's sit."

I follow her and take a seat. "Were you nervous during your first raid?"

"I'm always a little nervous," Colonel Adams replies. "It's only natural, if you're really aware of what you're about to do." She looks past me for a minute, recollecting. "Ellie, I dedicated over twenty years to the Army. I missed out on raising my daughter while I served and rose in the ranks. And you know what it got me?"

I shake my head.

"Less than nine months into my new role as colonel, I was in South Korea with my unit when one of those meteorites fell into the sea near our base. We were off-duty that night, cutting loose at a restaurant with some locals, when the building was attacked by a pack of . . . well, I guess you'd call them ghouls."

My eyebrows shoot up. "Ghouls?"

The colonel raises a hand. "I know. It sounds like the plot of a bad TV show, but that's what happened. A group of undead monsters burst into the dining room and started biting restaurant patrons."

There's that word again—undead. So vampires, ghouls, and strigas are all part of this dysfunctional family of undead monsters.

"What do ghouls look like?" I ask before I can stop myself.

It's a perfectly normal question to ask if I've never seen a ghoul before, so the colonel shouldn't be suspicious of my curiosity. I just hope she can't hear the anticipation racing through my veins as I wait on her response.

"Honestly," Colonel Adams replies, "they're what you'd expect a zombie to look like, with grayish skin and a general human shape. But a bit bigger than your average human, and slimier. Not sure why they're so slimy."

I let out a breath. Based on Cyndi's photo, my skin never changed color. And I didn't look particularly slimy, either. So I'm not a ghoul.

My relief fades to annoyance. I'm sick of searching for answers just for them all to be "No."

Too preoccupied with her story to notice my emotional turbulence, the colonel points to the scar running down the left side of her face. "That's how I got this scar. Nearly lost my eye that night fighting them off. And," she points to her chest, "a stray bullet hit me here. I was too distracted by the ghoul on top of me that I didn't see my second-in-command pull out his firearm and aim at the thing."

She exhales, irritated by the memory. "That idiot nearly killed me. It took forever for me to recover, and by the time I'd physically healed, the PTSD made it impossible to return to duty. I swear, I had nightmares for months that alternated between being shot and fighting off those monsters.

"All of that to say, we're promised very little in this life. One second you're fine, living how you'd like, and then WHAM," she punches the meat of her palm. "Something rocks your world and you're left reeling for years after. Though, I guess you'd know that more than most these days."

I tug on a hemp braid around my neck, resting behind the neckline of my shirt. The salamander stone is woven within it, tied together with some cords I found at the colonel's house before we left. The makeshift necklace isn't too tight around my neck, but it's certainly itchy, and Colonel Adams' story isn't helping me to forget about it.

But itchy or not, the necklace should help me to keep track of the salamander stone during the night's ride. As a child stuck inside on rainy days, Grandpa was always quick to give me something to occupy my idle hours. Most of the time, he'd hand me a book of knots and some spare rope, saying, "If you can learn a new one before dinner, I'll give you an extra cookie for dessert."

Naturally, I learned all of the knots in that book within months.

The image of Grandpa, now comatose in a hospital bed, hits me again, and I'm lost without words to respond.

"Ellie . . . " The colonel puts a reassuring hand on my shoulder. "I'm not trying to scare you right before we head out, but a bit of caution and nerves is a good thing, so long as you can still defend yourself. Speaking of which—have you had time to sharpen that axe?"

I nod, thankful for the change of subject. "I got that finished right before you spoke to the troops, but there are a few things I still need to pack up before we leave."

"Then I'll leave you to it. Remember, when we move out, you'll be riding right behind me. Don't let anyone tell you otherwise."

Then, without another word, she walks into the barn.

Placed near the barn's entrance, the colonel's horse is streaked with splotches of red and brown hair across its legs and torso, but its face and mane are entirely white—as if it's a white horse covered in dirt and fresh blood.

The colonel tosses a carrot to the horse from a bucket and begins brushing its mane, unfazed by its menacing appearance.

Just when I start to think that Colonel Adams is secretly a softie, she shows me how life has refused her the opportunity to be soft. And yet, while her experiences have formed callouses on her heart, they haven't made her unkind. She's decided to learn from her past, rather than allowing it to control her, so that the pain can mean something.

Perhaps my curse is just another callous forming, something new I have to work around until it becomes a normal part of life.

Could my life as a striga, or whatever I am, ever feel normal?

I vaguely remember the taste of fresh moose.

Probably not.

I follow the colonel's path into the main barn to find the rest of Errolton's monster-hunting militia readying themselves for the night's hunt. When they're not on a raid, the Beowulf Brigade boards their horses and hunting dogs here, so many members treat Farrowfield Farms as a "home base" of sorts.

The brigade also has a central office in town—near city hall—but it's mostly for processing permits and sending forms to local officials for approval. The average member isn't aware of the paperwork required to keep the militia running, but according to Grandpa, that's how it should be. It's not a volunteer's job to worry about claiming horse feed as a tax-exempt expense or submitting annual hunting certifications; they should be focused on their weapons training and equipment, to properly face any threats they find in the woods.

I approach Declan's horse stall slowly, unsure of how the dark courser will react to seeing me since the house set fire. The colonel mentioned that Declan hasn't been ridden since that night, and he's still getting used to his new living situation. Apparently, being housed with the other horses, rather than at home in the barn, has been an adjustment for him.

He's also not used to Grandpa's absence.

Well, that makes two of us.

Thankfully, Declan greets me with a chittering whinny, though whether he's happy to see me or the sugar cubes in my hand remains to be seen.

As I turn to hang Grandpa's saddlebag on a hook near Declan's horse stall, I find Bingo, the previously blindfolded man from the sparring circle. He's found Grandpa's axe amongst my supplies and decided to pick it up, to better admire its blade.

His eyes gleam with the look of a possessive lover.

The salamander stone around my neck heats up, but I push down the feeling of personal invasion. If I'm to hunt with this group, it's probably best for me to avoid a fight with him.

Bingo wipes a bead of sweat from his forehead with one hand and struggles to balance the axe in the other.

"Wow," he remarks. "They're not lying when they call this a two-handed battle-axe." When I don't respond, he looks back at the double-edged weapon. "A bit heavy for a girl, though, eh?"

He holds the axe out to me as a challenge.

Without thinking, I reach for it and lift it easily over my head with one hand.

Huh. It felt heavier the other day.

"I don't know, sir," I say, trying to hide a grin. "Doesn't feel that heavy to me."

Bingo assesses me, then bursts out laughing.

"Well, I'll be. You're Pete's granddaughter all right. Glad to have you with us, ma'am."

He offers me a fake curtsy and walks off, still laughing.

I lower the axe and shake my head, laughing despite my annoyance.

Go away, Bingo. You smell, and your name is stupid.

Hoping to avoid any further interactions, I strap the axe to Declan's saddle. My phone buzzes just as I'm tightening the final buckle.

I open it to see a new message from Cyndi.

Hey. I got bored waiting for you and went running.

Oh, right. I was so excited to be hunting with the Beowulf Brigade that I forgot to let Cyndi know I wouldn't be meeting her.

I begin to write back a snarky joke about Cyndi joining Track & Field when another message comes through. It's Cyndi again:

I found Bear in the middle of the woods. He's unconscious, and it looks like he's been hit in the head.

My eyes go wide. I text back:

Send me your GPS pin. I'll be there as soon as I can.

With a tense, slow breath, I open Declan's stall and lead the horse toward the barn doors, saddlebag still in hand.

No one moves to stop me. With it being only ten minutes 'til we're meant to head out, every militia member is too preoccupied with their gear to look my way.

As far as they know, I'm just getting into position ahead of schedule.

Once we're outside, I mount Declan and give Colonel Simone Adams one final glance. She's distracted by Jones, the younger man from before, showing her his new hunting bow. The colonel holds the bow gently and pantomimes shooting with it, explaining something about form and tension.

Jones listens carefully, hoping to do something right for the first time that evening.

My phone lights up with Cyndi's GPS coordinates.

Time to go.

I know what I'm giving up by running off like this. The colonel is probably my best bet to finding out what is actually going on with this town, and what's going on with me.

But I can't leave Cyndi and Bear out there alone, and dragging the colonel away from tonight's search could be incredibly dangerous for the brigade and the missing track team.

No, this is something I should do myself. All I have to do is go get my friends and ride back. And sure, Cyndi's more than capable of bringing Bear back herself, but she might not be ready to tell him her secret—a reality I can relate to now more than ever.

I turn out to face the field in front of me. The chill in the air clings to the overgrown grass, creating occasional patches of frost across the ground.

Fighting the urge to look back, I dig my heels into Declan's hide.

He takes off at a gallop.

Chapter Fourteen

Ellie

Horseback riding does not offer the luxury of a cell phone holster. This makes following a map on my cell phone, while riding a horse in the dark as it swerves to avoid overgrown roots and scurrying woodland creatures, impossible. Fortunately, the map can give me voiceover directions.

"Recalculating . . . recalculating . . . "

Unfortunately, riding around in the woods means that there are no marked streets or highways for the GPS to use for navigation. So instead of telling me to turn right at the next tree, the only suggestion my phone can offer is: "Please turn around. Recalculating . . . "

I pull on Declan's reigns to slow him to a trot and lift my phone. Looking at the pin Cyndi sent me, I still need to head southwest on the map.

At least this thing has a compass.

I shut off the voiceover directions, however well-meaning, and turn Declan's reigns to the right. The horse lets out a harumph.

"I know," I say, patting his neck. "We're pretty much lost. But also, I have no idea where Cyndi is, so we can't be lost. I mean, if we don't know where we're supposed to be, then we can't know where we're not supposed to be, right?"

Declan snorts in response.

"Uh-huh." I check the map a second time and put my phone back into my coat before pointing to the right. "Well anyway, let's try this direction."

We take off again, at a slower pace while I adjust to the darkness ahead. The woods are denser here, with less space between trees and no marked footpath, but Declan confidently runs through each obstacle with only the light of the moon to guide him.

The waning moonlight reminds me of the previous night's transformation and my walkabout as the beast, which prompts hidden memories to flash across my mind. I can recall crashing through thick hedges and spiny tree branches in search of a gray fox, too fast to catch. And there was a family of badgers, which my monstrous form was happy to devour as a midnight snack.

I wince at the thought. Those badgers were sleeping peacefully until I came along. They didn't deserve to die—not like that, anyway. Sure, they have other natural enemies in the woods, but there's nothing natural about being eaten by a rogue striga.

Not that I am a striga. I'm not dead, so I can't be one. But with no other way to refer to the monster, it helps to have some sort of name. Even if it's the wrong one.

The memory of eating fresh kill hits me again, and as Declan pushes deeper into the pine forest, I notice a growing rigidity in my muscles.

I'm itching to run.

It's just because of these woods. They're dark and winding, and while I'm high up on this horse for now, I know that the minute I get down, I'm just as vulnerable as anyone else.

In this form, anyway.

Be quiet, Striga. If something comes after me while I'm out here, alone, then I'll just use the axe. Normal people defend themselves from monsters with weapons, instead of becoming one themselves.

And that's all I want to be. Normal.

Nothing about you is normal, Ellie.

And that settles it. No more letting the monster out, even in a life or death scenario. It's just not going to end well.

A reddish light gleams ahead.

Hesitant to approach, Declan and I pause behind a tree while I check my phone again. According to the GPS marker, Cyndi should be right in front of us.

I call her cell phone. The line connects, and after a few quiet seconds, a faint ringtone echoes through the trees. It's coming from the same direction as the reddish light, and I recognize the ringtone playing to be Cyndi Lauper's "Time After Time."

At my signal, Declan resumes trotting toward the light. I make out the shape of Cyndi, pulling her phone out of her backpack and humming the ringtone's song to herself.

She recognizes my name on the caller ID and stops humming to answer.

"Hey! Where are you?"

The horse stops right behind her as I reply, "Right behind you."

Cyndi spins around and squeaks in surprise.

"Ellie! You scared me!"

"And hi to you too." I jump down from Declan's saddle and begin tying him to a tree. "Where's Bear?"

"He's over here." She walks over to the red-orange lantern sitting on the ground and points to Bear, who is resting against the trunk of a tree with his eyes closed. "I've been trying to get him to eat something, but he's refusing food."

“That’s because I don’t need food, Cyndi,” Bear says, keeping his eyes closed. “I need painkillers and a way home, and the snacks in your pockets won’t help with either of those things.”

“Is he hurt anywhere? Is he bleeding?”

Bear opens his eyes, clearly annoyed. “Hi, I’m right here, and I’m not bleeding. I just hit my head on a branch or something.”

Cyndi crosses her arms. “You see the thanks I get? I should have just left him where I found him, face down in the mud.”

Bear glares at her. “Correct! You should have left me where you found me! I’d finally caught up to Wade before I got hurt. How am I going to find him now?”

“Wait a minute.” I look between Bear and Cyndi. “Wade was here, too? Cyndi, you didn’t tell me that.”

“I didn’t know.” She studies Bear. “When I found you, you were alone. Why did your brother leave you out here if you were hurt?”

At the mention of his brother, Bear wrings his hands. “He said he was going to go get help after I hit my head.”

He begins thinking out loud. “Wade’s been going off by himself a lot lately, so when he snuck out tonight I figured he was heading off to another party. But with all the new monster attacks, I knew Mom and Dad would have been furious at me for not stopping him. ‘You’re the older brother, Bear. You have to look out for each other.’ So I followed him and tried to bring him back. And after some convincing, it seemed like he was willing to come back with me, until I hit my head. And now,” he looks back at Cyndi, “thanks to you, he has no idea where to find me. Why did you move me to this spot, anyway?”

“That part of the woods wasn’t safe, Bear. There were . . . things circling, and I wasn’t trying to fight them on my own.”

“Did you actually see something?” He presses her. “Or did you just get spooked?”

Cyndi scoffs. “Okay, first of all, I’m afraid of nothing.” She emphasizes the word “nothing” with a pointed finger. “And second, I may not have seen anything, but I could smell something.”

“What did you smell?” I ask, concerned. It’s still too soon to know how much we should tell Bear, but Cyndi didn’t mention this in her texts. It must have been pretty scary for her to run off.

She shoots me an uncertain look. “I’m not totally sure. Blood, mostly. A lot of blood, and most of it was human.”

Bear furrows his brow. “How could you possibly tell it was human blood?”

“Look, just trust me on this one, Bear.” Cyndi starts, “I—”

“And if it was more dangerous over there,” Bear interrupts her, pushing up to stand, “then we need to go find Wade now, before . . . ” He leans on his left leg, wobbles, and sits back down.

“Oof. I guess I twisted something in this leg, too.”

“Okay, wait,” I say. “Let’s deal with one problem at a time.”

I walk back to my saddlebag and retrieve the flashlight and first aid kit. Once I return to Bear, I crouch down and give him a stern look.

“Ted, you’re hurt, and we’re in the middle of nowhere. We need to get somewhere safe, and preferably well-lit, to avoid getting eaten in the woods. But first, we have to make sure you’re not bleeding or ignoring any wounds that could get infected. Okay?”

His narrowed gaze moves from Cyndi to me before relaxing a bit. “Don’t call me Ted. It’s a stupid name.”

Cyndi tightens her spiky ponytail. “Yes, because the name Bear is much more normal.”

“Hey. You.” I turn around to glare at her. “Not helping.”

“Psh.” She waves a dismissive hand. “Anyway, now that you’re here, it’s not like we need to be worried about anything we come across. Why don’t we just . . . ”

I raise a hand to stop her. "Nope. Not yet. That sort of thing should only be shared on a need-to-know basis. As of right now, he doesn't need to know."

"I don't need to know what?" Bear demands, looking between us. "What's going on?"

I sigh in his direction. "Let's make a deal. First, you show me where you hit your head and tell us a little more about what happened with Wade. After that, we'll tell you what you don't know. Deal?"

Bear nods, annoyed but willing to play along. He points to the back of his head. "I hit something on the top of my head. Or something hit me. I don't remember."

I push away his dirty blond hair until I find the lump on the top of his head. When my thumb hits it, Bear grimaces. "Ow. Yes. That."

The bump is covered in dried blood. It's not a large cut, but I should clean it before we move on.

"Okay. Let me work on this for a minute," I say before grabbing an alcohol wipe from the kit. I try to remember the list of things Grandpa used to ask me after every fall as a child. "How's your vision?"

"Fine," he replies.

"Do you feel like throwing up? Are you sleepy?"

"No, and not really, though I guess I did just take a nap."

"How bad does your head hurt? On a scale of one to five?"

He raises a hand to his forehead. "About an eight?"

"What a wimp," Cyndi mutters to herself.

Bear snaps at her, "I didn't ask for your help, you know!"

She yells back, "Well then, next time I see that you need help, I'll be sure to leave you for the werewolves!"

"Fine by me!"

Cyndi storms off. Since she can't move more than a few steps away from our circle of light, she plops down next to Declan and plays a noisy game on her phone, angrily grumbling to herself.

I place a few small bandages on the cut within his hair and return to the first aid kit. "How are you two even friends?"

"We're not friends," Bear corrects me. "Just coworkers."

I arch an eyebrow at him. "Oh?"

Bear lets out an exasperated breath. "Cyndi just likes pestering me. She's constantly stealing my lunch and tricking me into doing her homework. The other day, she convinced me to close the ice cream shop early so that we could go to Badger Burger. Can you believe that?"

Cyndi places a hand on her chest. "Oh, what villainy!"

I laugh to myself. "She does that stuff to me, too, but that doesn't mean she and I aren't friends." I shine my flashlight into his eyes, and then away. His pupils seem fine. "Anyway, what about the other night at the colonel's house? Weren't you two playing checkers or something?"

"Aw, that was just to kill time while you and Wade . . . " Bear awkwardly trails off. "Sorry. I didn't mean to mention the other night. I know things are weird between you now, for whatever reason."

"Is that what he told you?"

"No," Bear replies, "but it's pretty obvious."

My mind replays the moment when Wade and I kissed, an incandescent memory marred only by my transformation into the gigantic, clawed thing. Holding in the stress and embarrassment from that night has been exhausting, but Bear's casual reference to things being "weird" helps me to breathe a bit easier.

At least Wade hasn't told anyone what happened. That would be so, so much worse.

"Where does your leg hurt?" I ask, hoping to change the subject.

Bear points to his left knee. "Here. But only when I put pressure on it."

I reach out a hand to pat the leg of his khakis. There's no blood, thankfully.

As I wrap a large cotton bandage around his knee a few times, I say, "I don't know how much this will help. I only sort of know what I'm doing here."

Bear smiles at me. "Thanks."

His sudden friendliness is surprising. I'm used to seeing Bear's face settled in an expression of absorbed concentration or grim annoyance, so seeing a smile up close is . . . unusual.

He has the same dimple on his left cheek as Wade.

I shake my head and try to remember that Wade is ignoring my existence right now, and for good reason. He's allowed to live his life away from me. In fact, it's better this way.

I know if the situation was reversed, I'd run from him.

You should run.

I back away from Bear and avert my eyes. This is awkward.

"We done?" Cyndi asks without looking up from her game. "Not that anyone cares about what I have to say, but I think we should get out of here."

Her words remind me that every beep, plink, and boing from her phone, as well as any audible sound we make, can be heard by passing animals and monsters alike.

I close the latch to the first aid kit. "Are we taking him back home?"

Before Cyndi can answer, Bear replies with, "No."

Cyndi turns off her phone and stomps back over to us. "Bear, you're in no shape to wander around the woods."

Bear crosses his arms. "I came out here to follow Wade and bring him home. I can't just leave him. I'll never hear the end of it from my parents. And . . . " He looks down. "I'm worried." He wrings his hands again. "What if Cyndi's right about that earlier spot? What if something attacked him?"

I tug at my hair and glance at Cyndi, who's wearing a broad smile. She knows what's bound to come next.

Bear pushes himself up again, and after a moment of straining, balances to stand with his newly bandaged leg. "I need to get back to the place where Cyndi found me. Maybe there's a clue to where Wade's gone, like footprints, or a trail or something. Only," Bear looks between the two of us, "I'm not sure how to get back to where we were separated."

Cyndi's smile widens. "If only we could track Wade's scent or something!"

"Yes!" Bear gestures toward her. "Exactly like that. Is there any way for us to do that?"

She laughs at his question and shrugs. "I don't know, Bear. If I did know something like that, it sure would be helpful at a time like this. Almost like it's . . . " she drums a finger on her chin in mock contemplation before turning to me with a cheeky expression, "need-to-know?"

I roll my eyes. "Go ahead."

In response, Cyndi the human, Carnelian the fox, transforms. Her body rapidly grows until she's larger than Declan, while her face elongates into a fox's muzzle and pointed ears. Red-orange fur spreads across her entire body and sprouts into a long, swishing tail.

Once she's fully transformed, Bear stares up at the large fox without blinking. He opens his mouth to comment, but all that comes out is a very confused squeak.

Laughing, I ask Cyndi, "Is that what I looked like when I first found out?"

She nods her shaggy head, grinning.

"Buh . . . but . . . " Bear points a shaking finger at her, then looks over to me. "You . . . Cyndi . . . you knew?"

Cyndi answers him, "Surprise! I'm a fox. Well, sort of. Ellie found out yesterday."

Bear's eyebrows shoot up. "You're . . . you can talk?"

The oversized fox barks happily in response. Then she plods to the glowing lantern on the ground and lifts it between her teeth.

"Ellie," she says, "make sure you're on the horse before I take off. I'll try not to go too fast for Declan, but if I pull ahead, follow the lantern."

I start collecting our belongings, strapping Cyndi's backpack to the saddle. Bear continues to look between us, dumbfounded.

"Are we just going to act like this is normal right now?" he demands.

Cyndi nudges Bear with her fuzzy forehead until he's standing right next to her shoulder. Once he's at her side, she angles her large nose to push him onto her back.

I climb into Declan's saddle at the same time. Once we're atop our steeds, Bear and I exchange glances.

"What is happening?" he asks me, clearly terrified.

Still balancing the lantern's handle between her teeth, Cyndi chitters. "Bear, I'll explain everything on the way, but we should leave now before your brother's trail goes cold."

"Wait, but how—"

The red fox races into the dark, with Bear holding on for dear life and Declan and I close behind.

We ride for nearly an hour before Cyndi signals for us to stop.

When I catch up to them, Cyndi's already back in her human form, devouring a bag of salted peanuts. She offers a sweaty handful to Bear, only for him to wave it away, preoccupied with his thoughts.

"So, Cyndi," I say, hopping down from Declan's saddle. "What's the verdict? Did you break Bear's brain?"

Laughing, she tosses another handful of peanuts into her mouth. "Hopefully not? I tried telling him about the Carnelian stone and how I gained my powers and whatever, but he's pretty resistant to the whole idea. Keeps saying that this is a dumb practical joke and that he's not a fan of whatever drugs we slipped into his food today."

"Oh boy. Well, if he's not able to handle this, then we definitely can't tell him about the other thing."

Bear gives me a look. "What other thing? Don't tell me you're also a shapeshifting fox."

I tug at the sleeve of my jacket for a moment before responding.

"You really want to know?"

He gestures to the surrounding darkness. "I'm a captive audience right now. And if it'll help us find Wade, then I want to know."

"Well, I don't know if it'll help us find him, but it might help us to scare off any threats we come across." I remove the water bottle from my saddlebag and open it to stall time. After taking a drink, I sit down next to Bear.

"What you have to understand is that this is brand new for me. Cyndi's known what she is for a long time, so she's used to all this. I'm still learning about . . . whatever I am. So, I need you to not be a jerk about this."

"Hey, you two just kidnapped me. I can be a jerk if I want to."

Cyndi spits a peanut in Bear's direction. "Is it technically kidnapping if the perpetrators are also kids?"

Bear squints at her.

"Well, since you're more than two hundred years old, I think you can be tried as an adult."

I reach over and grab a handful of Cyndi's peanuts.

"Bicker later, please. This is important." I pop a peanut into my mouth. "Bear. Do you remember that thing that you saw outside of Colonel Adams' house last night?"

"Oh yeah. What a monster. I had trouble getting to sleep after seeing it up close, and Wade . . . I don't think he slept at all."

Hearing Bear's response, Cyndi gives me a sympathetic look. "That's rough, buddy."

"Shut up, you." I throw some peanuts at her.

"Wait, what am I missing?" Bear asks.

"Okay." I take a deep breath and look into his eyes. "That monster was me. Is me. I transformed into it last night and the night before, during the fire at my house. It's . . . I'm . . . a striga. Or something like it."

"What?" Bear sits back. Fear and confusion cloud his eyes. "How?!"

"Honestly, we're still trying to figure it out. I have a few ideas, but nothing concrete."

He twists his face in disbelief. "There's no way that's true."

"It is!" I insist.

"Why would she lie about that?" Cyndi asks him.

"Because you're messing with me. You both are. This whole thing is a simulation, and it's been a convincing one, but I'd like whoever is responsible to remove my VR headset now, if they don't mind."

"If by that you mean we're all living in a simulation, then sure." Cyndi laughs. "Otherwise, sorry to disappoint you, my dude, but this is all very real. In the same world where huge, fire-breathing salamanders and vampires exist, your friends—I mean, coworkers—just happen to also be shapeshifters in their spare time."

"There's no way." He frowns. "I've never heard about anything like this happening, before or after the meteorites. I just don't buy it."

Cyndi shrugs. "Okay. I mean you've watched me shapeshift with your own eyes and you still don't believe me, so I won't waste my time. C'mon Ellie."

She lifts the lantern high into the air. Then, with a wave of her hand, the lantern's outer shell vanishes, and all that remains is a small, glowing stone.

Despite the red-orange glow of her Carnelian stone being our only source of light in the dark woods, Cyndi plucks it from the air and pushes it into her cheek, leaving us in darkness.

"Hey!" Bear yells.

I flip on my flashlight instantly. Its small beam of white light doesn't illuminate the area between us and the surrounding trees as well as Cyndi's lamp, but at least it can light the muddy path ahead.

"I was wondering where the lantern came from," I remark to Cyndi.

She bows with a flourish. "Behold! My abilities to manipulate perception at work! Light is especially fun to play with."

"Nice." I link arms with Cyndi and the pair of us start walking away from Bear. "So, how far do we need to walk?"

"Ahem!" Bear clears his throat behind us.

Cyndi looks back at him. "Yes?"

"Are you going to leave me back here with the horse?"

"Why not?"

Bear grabs Declan's reigns and tries to come toward us, but the horse stays put, refusing to go with him.

Defeated, Bear looks up at Declan. "Not you, too?"

"He can sense your skepticism," Cyndi gloats.

"I'm allowed to be skeptical of things I've never had to consider before!" Bear squeaks. He drops the reigns and crosses his arms. "For the sake of finding my brother, I'll believe you. I don't know what to do right now. I just want to find him and go home."

"Let's cut him a break," I whisper to my friend, the fox. "We're expecting him to accept a lot of new information within the span of an hour, when I'm still unsure about some things—and I've had a few days with it."

Cyndi nods and looks at Bear. "Fine. Come on, Teddy. You can hold the flashlight."

I follow them with Declan's reigns in hand, unbothered to take a backseat to their conversation. It's obvious that Bear needs some time to process everything he's heard, and as long as they're nearby, I'm fine with being on the edges.

After a few minutes, we approach an old, dilapidated shack flanked by trees. I can barely make out the house's outline against the night sky. The only light for miles—other than our flashlight—is a solitary lamp inside the house.

Bear turns off the flashlight and signals that I should tie Declan to a tree before entering the front yard. I'm hesitant to leave Grandpa's horse behind, but it's a good idea. If we're going to search this old house for clues about Wade's disappearance, then I can't risk bringing the horse any closer.

I pat Declan on his rump and feed him a carrot from the saddlebag before digging into the deeper pockets for my hunting knife. When my hand finally locates the blade, I take extra care to unsheathe and strap it into an interior pocket of my coat. That done, I untie Grandpa's axe from the saddle and turn back to the shack.

It's never a bad idea to prepare for a fight.

I step toward Cyndi and Bear with the axe resting on my shoulder, only to notice the salamander stone, still safe in my braided necklace.

It's glowing faintly in the dark.

Cyndi and Bear are busy peeking into the window of the old house's solely lit room when I approach. Once I'm able to adjust my vision to the room inside, I see three figures.

The first is a woman with dusty blue, almost gray hair in a short pixie cut. She's standing next to a man with large, reptilian eyes who's snacking on . . . is that a raw toad?

I stick out my tongue in revulsion. I mean, sure, I've eaten my fair share of raw food this week, but toads are covered in warts and slime. And I can't imagine the splintery bones making for an enjoyable bite.

Pulling my attention away from the disgusting, bloody stranger, eating a raw amphibian, I notice that he and the other woman are facing a third figure who's hidden from sight behind the foggy glass. The three of them are dressed in long-sleeved robes, with the two facing the window in black. The one facing away from us is in dark green, with black and red marks on the sleeves.

Cyndi's ear is pressed to the window when she sees me.

"Oh, good. Ellie, can you read lips at all? Bear is useless."

"Hey!" he whispers back at her, "I resent that."

I let out a light laugh, despite the nearby threats. "I doubt I'm much better. It's not exactly a skill I've had to develop."

"See?" Bear gestures to me. "It's not a standard skill for humans to learn!"

Cyndi rolls her eyes at the two of us. "Well, the pair of you are useless, then." She presses her ear to the window and listens again.

"Okay, the person closest to the window is talking, but it's muffled so I can't make out much. They're complaining about getting involved in human affairs."

"Do you think they're vampires?" Bear asks her.

"No idea," Cyndi replies. "The woman in the corner isn't saying much. Just the occasional comment about how humans make for better eating than befriending."

I watch through the window. "It looks like she's picking her teeth. What if she's the monster that attacked the bus?"

"Could be." Cyndi nods. "Everyone in that room smells weird, so it's hard to tell. But even though Wade's trail ends at this house, I don't sense him anywhere inside."

Bear looks over at her. "How can you tell?"

Cyndi laughs to herself. "Believe it or not, but your brother has an incredibly strong scent. It's quite easy to track him."

"Ted?"

The three of us whirl around to see Wade standing behind us, with his cell phone in one hand and an energy drink in the other. When he recognizes me, he drops the canned drink in surprise.

"Ellie?" He steps toward me quickly, whispering, "You're . . . how are you here?"

Avoiding Wade's eyes, I point to Bear.

"Your brother refused to go home without finding you first. It's, um, good to see that you're still in one piece." I look up, panicked, "I mean, not hurt, I guess."

I grip the axe's handle with sweaty palms. Seeing him this close, so soon after my recent transformation, sends my stomach into knots of shame and anger.

I didn't want him to see me like that. No one should see me like that. But there's nothing I can do about it, now.

"Oh. Okay." Wade makes a few furtive glances to the left and right before bending down to pick up his energy drink. "Well, I don't know how you found me, but here I am, so why don't you three go back home. I'll . . . see you tomorrow."

He's nervous too, though it's hard to tell if that's due to my presence or something else.

Bear joins us, while Cyndi stays at the window, alternating between watching us and peering inside.

"We're not leaving without you," Bear says, determined.

Sighing, Wade shoots his older brother an annoyed look. "Ted, I'm not going home yet, but I will soon, so stop worrying. Just take your friends and head back now, before something happens."

Bear responds with a frown. "By that argument, you should be coming home with us too. Why are you out here in the first place?"

"That doesn't matter. We can talk about this later, at home, but that's only if you start walking . . . " Wade stops midsentence, his ears perking up at a silent, distant noise.

After a beat, Wade locks eyes with me.

"You're out of time."

I blink at him. "What?"

He takes a few quick steps toward me, grabbing my coat slightly. "Ellie, listen. I'm sorry about the other night. No, about everything. I . . . You have to know that I had no idea what they were trying to do to you."

"They? They who?" I ask, looking around. "The freaks inside?"

"I thought I knew about you, but I was so wrong, and now . . . " Wade's neck twitches. "Just know that I'm sorry you got caught up in all this."

I shoot a panicked look at Cyndi, who's still keeping watch at the window, and Bear, who's without any weapons or abilities to help.

Wade's proximity and the darkening of his expression make me keenly aware of the weight of my grandfather's axe in my grip.

"All of what?" I finally meet Wade's darting, scared eyes. "You're purposefully keeping us in the dark, acting like it's normal for you to be out here with those weirdos. If you won't tell us what's going on, then why should we . . . "

My sentence never finishes. In the dark, my eyes can make out the outline of something standing beside Declan.

No, not something. Someone.

But before I can identify the shrouded figure, the porchlight behind us clicks on.

I turn just in time to see the three robed figures from inside the house running through the front door and down the porch steps. The two in black grab Cyndi and Bear, while the third one in green approaches me and Wade directly.

Wade bares his teeth at the robed figure, who quickly tosses their hood aside to reveal their true identity: Miss Catherine Raposa, my biology teacher, wreathed in a dramatic halo of porchlight.

"Well, Ellie," my teacher chirps malevolently, "you've made this almost too easy."

With strength I don't expect from my floral-print-wearing, mitosis-defining high school teacher, Miss Raposa grabs Grandpa's axe from my grasp with one hand and tosses it aside.

"And look." She gestures behind me. "You're just in time, DeLucia."

Robed in the same shade of green as Miss Raposa, Marquess DeLucia—the vampire who'd argued with Lord Vance just hours ago at the Vampire Book Club, and the figure I'd seen in the dark—steps out from the woods and into the light.

"Apologies for the delay, my lady. Vampire business ran longer than expected."

In response, Miss Raposa savagely pushes me into the waiting grip of the vampire DeLucia, who pins my arms behind my back.

"Better late than never, I suppose." She rolls her eyes.

DeLucia looks down at me with a relaxed, toothy smile. His irritated expression from before has vanished, and the slightest stain of red on his lips tells me that he's had something to eat since Lord Vance's meeting.

"Hello, Dinner," he purrs.

Somehow, I don't think it was a Snickers bar.

The salamander stone burns hot against my neck, but despite this being the opportune time for me to become the big, bad thing, nothing happens.

Great. The one time I need the monster, it's nowhere to be seen.

My biology teacher wipes her hands on the edge of her robe and chuckles.

"Honestly. Walking up to our front door? You three are very dumb, even by human standards."

I look back at her, stunned. "What . . . what do you mean?"

Instead of answering, Miss Raposa begins to change. Her long brown hair lightens to a sandy gray color, her eyes grow fierce and pointed, and her smile stretches cartoonishly wide. Then, her body shrinks and reorients anatomically from a human form to what appears to be a small fox. Within seconds, her body is covered in sections of white, gray, and tan fur, while her ears and fluffy tail appear to be dipped in black.

The fox that was Miss Raposa inspects her tail while a large limestone geode forms around her like a protective den. She takes a seat inside right before the boulder rises to hover a few feet above the ground.

She breaks off a stalactite of white crystal from the geode's low ceiling and, with the glittering rock wedged between her paws, begins gnawing on it like a bone.

"You. Boy." The sandy-colored fox pauses in her chewing to openly glare at Wade. "I'd say you did a good job luring them here, but it's obvious that their arrival happened despite your best efforts to prevent it."

Wade, who'd been standing off to the side throughout our capture, steps forward.

The fox that once was Miss Raposa sighs. "If only you'd brought them here as instructed. Then I could give credit to your cunning, rather than admit that one of mine is no more useful than smelly bait."

Without hesitation, Bear's brother bows in response.

"I'm sorry, Caliza," he says, still looking at the ground. "If I'd known it would be this easy to bring them, I wouldn't have hesitated from fear of being discovered."

My eyes go wide.

"No," I breathe.

"Ha!" The fox, apparently named Caliza, throws the crystal in her hands at Wade, which hits him squarely on top of his head. "Don't lie to me, mongrel! I'm tempted to take back your stone and donate your body to the cause. Would you like that?"

Wade shakes his head.

"Wade! What are you doing?" Bear suddenly yells, fighting against his restraints. "Run away! Go get help!"

The reptilian man restraining Bear laughs at the outburst and cuffs him on the side of his head. I watch as Bear's face shifts from shock and denial to silent, burning understanding and fury at his brother—who, for whatever reason, has pledged loyalty to a group of monsters over his family and friends.

Though, other than Bear, we're all a bit monstrous these days.

"Enough of this." Caliza curls up in her floating den and closes her eyes, apparently ready for a nap. "Tie them up in the courtyard. Oh, and," the sandy-colored fox opens an eye in my direction, before adding, "be sure to use chains."

Chapter Fifteen

Dani

Ynez is still crying.

She's not the first to cry. In the hours since those monsters locked us in this moldy, spider-infested cellar, with little food and only one candle for light, we've been taking turns with who gets to cry and who has to sit and listen to it. Nadia, who was sobbing just an hour or two ago, now alternates between total silence and quietly crying to herself, so that no one can judge her for carrying on during Ynez's turn.

And really, Ynez had been almost optimistic until an hour ago. Despite the dingy reality of our capture, she'd been manically determined to find a way out, creating half-cocked plans and floating ideas that no one was willing to support. But when she saw a broken shard of glass on the ground and excitedly moved toward it, thinking that we could use it to cut the zip ties from our wrists, that's when futility set in. Because what she saw shining on the floor was not glass, but a piece of clear packing tape.

That's when she started wailing.

I have no issue with her crying, but I wish she'd pick a better time to do it. I haven't slept at all since we got here, and in the brief silence between Nadia's and Ynez's tears, I'd finally dozed off.

Maybe I should try to sleep through it. Might be a handy trick to learn for however long we're going to be down here.

The only ones who haven't cried yet, aside from me, are the Clark sisters: Sasha and Imani. Quiet and cautious, the two sisters have been sitting in the back corner of this cellar since before we got here. Neither has said much, but Sasha, the younger sister, was willing to exchange names and stories when we first arrived. She's only fourteen, but she and her sister Imani, who's eighteen, were cornered and picked off in the woods near their family farm when they were out looking for a runaway calf.

It's been weeks since they last saw their family.

Sasha also mentioned that before we got here, there were others—more kidnapped teenagers stored in the cellar, until they were taken out one day and never brought back.

There wasn't time for her to tell us more. Not long after we arrived, that vampire came down to feed on Sasha, which put her right to sleep. She's been napping since then, resting her head in her older sister's lap.

Imani hasn't said a word to any of us. She just watches the shadows cast on the opposite wall as they dance along with the flickering candle.

Based on the number of bite marks on Imani's neck, she and her sister have probably been feeding that vampire for a while.

So, what were the other students for?

What are we for?

Ynez wipes her runny nose against the back of her hand with a loud snort. She moves to wipe her hand against her pant leg, only to find it caked in dried mud from last night's kidnapping, and begins crying all over again.

"Ynez," I mutter, eyes still closed, "crying isn't going to help."

"I can't help it!" she snaps at me. "We're never getting out of here!"

"Probably not."

"Well then, I'm allowed to be upset! You saw what that thing did to Sara!"

She's right. I was inches away from Sara before that thing—that monster—ate her.

I wince, fighting to block out the memories as they play across my mind. I don't want to keep reliving Sara's death, but it's all I see when I close my eyes.

Back on the bus, my plan to open the emergency exit and escape was a complete failure. The giant clawed thing had already moved to bite down on my shoulder when Sara jumped into the aisle, her arms raised between me and the monster.

It bit into her arm instead of my shoulder, and in that moment of confusion, the sight of her blood was enough to send the creature into a frenzy.

She died quickly, but it was horrible to watch.

What Ynez doesn't understand is that my ability to cry died the moment Sara did. I can't allow myself to feel sorrow or fear right now. Not with these monsters still circling.

I just have to get out of here, somehow.

I won't let Sara's death be for nothing.

Lifting my eyes from the floor, I watch the rusted washing machine thump and gurgle as it spins wet sheets and dirty clothes at an awkward pace. A plastic sink for rinsing laundry sits next to it, silently standing guard.

The appliances cast weird, tall shadows on the wall that shift like towering, paper-thin skyscrapers. Illuminated by the candle behind us, the shadows' shapes are easily scattered by any passing draft, but rooted to where they stand, unable to topple completely.

My eyes blink between the shadowy illusions and the permanence of the laundry sink, stained with blood, and I wonder which one of us will disappear next.

The pounding in my head thumps in time with the sink's leaky faucet, building to a feverish, blood-curdling rhythm until the cellar door opens at the top of the stairs. Light pours into the cellar from the outside world, which draws new, sharpened shadows onto the wall to our right and lets me know that more than one monster is descending to greet us.

Flanked by two lackeys—the woman with short blue hair and the lizard man—the vampire they call DeLucia opens his arms to address us.

"Behold! Human beings living in an underground den, which has a mouth open towards the light."

The blue-haired woman snickers in recognition and replies, almost as if she's reciting a line from a play. "You have shown me a strange image, and they are strange prisoners."

"Like ourselves." The vampire nods approvingly. Then, gesturing to the man with scaly features, he commands: "Mishal, get them up."

The brutal man corners us with reptilian speed, grabbing me and my peers by the arm and pulling us to our feet. In an instant, the remaining members of Errolton High School's girls' track team are lined up, ready to be paraded like cattle in front of hungry restaurant patrons who wish to inspect each cow before ordering the best steak.

When the blue-haired woman moves to grab the two sisters in the back corner, the vampire shakes his head. "Not those two. They're too important to risk for Caliza's experiments."

The word "experiments" sends a jolt of adrenaline up my spine. Against my better judgment, I find an opening between the lizard man and my classmates and bolt for the stairs.

They can experiment on my dead body if they want. I won't be taken alive.

"Get her," the vampire says in a bored tone.

I get halfway up the stairs before I'm tackled by the blue-haired woman. She slams my face and chest into the wooden staircase, cracking the bones in my nose and chest. Blood gushes down my face like a faucet, and as my mouth fills with the taste of copper, I can't catch my breath.

"Gotcha." The blue-haired woman growls over me.

Twisting in pain, I cough as new injuries inflame across my temple, forearms, and ribcage. I try to push away my captor, but her grip on my arm bends it unnaturally, keeping me pinned.

The vampire drags Ynez by the collar to the bottom of the stairs. She whimpers, and he bares his fangs.

"That's quite enough, human. Cooperate, or another one of your friends will die at your expense."

I can't hold it in any longer. I laugh at him.

"What's the point? In here or out there, you're going to kill us anyway."

In response, the vampire curls his lip into an unnatural smile.

"To you, the truth is nothing but the shadows of the images."

Chapter Sixteen

Saphir

Following their pathetic escape attempt, DeLucia, Mishal, and I push the meatbags—I mean, human teenagers—into the yard with little issue. After all, this is not our first time dealing with prisoners.

Breaking the bones of one dissenter is usually enough to silence the rest.

Once we exit the cellar, I notice that the boy, Wade, has found use for two of the metal troughs abandoned in the yard. After filling them with dark, shimmering oil, he lowers a torch to light them. Large walls of flame erupt on opposite sides of the clearing.

The warm glow of the troughs and the growing threat of wildfire ignites a giddiness in my chest.

Nothing compares to playing with fire.

We guide the teenagers onto the porch and begin tying their wrists to the railing just as the boy retrieves three sets of metal chains from a basket—one for each unexpected trespasser. He clearly wants to get back in Caliza's good graces, but I doubt his cooperation during tonight's rituals will be enough to convince her. Putting the lives of humans above our goals is unforgivable, and he knows it.

At the west end of the yard, Caliza lounges in her throne of jagged rock. She lifts her head to inspect Wade's movements as he locks up his brother and friends, confident that he will follow orders without further attempts to deceive her, like pretending to lock them up while leaving the cuffs open.

Loosening their bonds won't help them, anyway. They can't outrun us, and they can't fight us.

Still, Caliza's tasked the boy with this as a test of his loyalty. If he can't be trusted with something as menial as locking up prisoners, then he has outlived his usefulness.

After attaching each chain to a sewage grate in the center of the clearing, Wade walks over to the trespassers with a sunken expression. He's weighed down by the length of chain and metal cuffs.

His brother, named Bear for some reason, stares in disbelief as the cuffs lock around his wrists. The orange-haired girl next to him silently glares, daring the turncoat to look up. Once Wade clicks the lock of her cuffs, she spits on him.

I let out a cackle.

"Show them how we treat their kind!" Mishal yells, laughing along with me.

The boy doesn't bother to wipe the spit from his face. He gathers the final set of cuffs and shuffles up to a girl with wild black hair and quiet eyes, actively avoiding her gaze.

"So." The girl with black hair speaks loud enough for us to hear. "You found these chains pretty fast. Doing a lot of ritual sacrifice out here in your spare time, are you?"

I chuckle. This one is funny.

Then the girl whispers to Wade in a concerned tone. He pauses to listen but makes no move to reply.

Caliza lets out a loud yawn. "Boy, are you done?"

Wade turns to her and bows formally. "Yes, Caliza."

"Good. Now stand to the side before I chain you up as well."

As he backs away like a wounded dog, all eyes move from him to Caliza, pacing in her floating den.

"Human teenagers," she begins. "How do you like being caught in a snare? Did you really think a solitary axe was enough to fight a forest full of monsters?"

Our fearless leader steps further into the limestone geode, wraps her black-tipped tail around the girl's axe, and tosses it to the ground.

"Your frontal lobes must be especially underdeveloped."

Caliza hops down from her seat and stalks past each of them, sniffing their coats for clues. Eventually, she turns to the black-haired girl with a glare.

"Though, you're no ordinary teenager. Are you, Striga?"

The girl's eyes lock on Caliza. "What did you call me?"

Back on the porch, Mishal nudges me. "Saphir, what does she mean by that?"

My head tilts to one side as I consider their words. If this girl is the striga, then our night just got interesting.

The fox Caliza preens her sandy-colored coat as she continues. "Oh yes, I know all about your troubling situation, Ellie. Sealed by paladin and fairy magic?" Caliza purrs. "We had to go to ridiculous lengths to remove your grandfather's protection. Up until this week, it was the only thing keeping your more beastly personality traits at bay."

I watch as the girl called Ellie twists her neck in a jagged, unnatural path, fighting to extinguish her burning rage. Through clenched teeth, she asks, "What do you mean, fairy magic?

But her words are quickly ignored in favor of Caliza's continued monologue.

"Thankfully, once your house burned down, all of that protection vanished. And now that you have tapped into your true nature as an abomination—a malformed ghoul—a *striga*," Caliza says the last word with hatred in her narrowed eyes, "we can strip you of all that raw magical potential and use it for more . . . exciting projects. Which reminds me . . . "

The swift fox, Caliza opens her jaw mere inches from the girl's face before snapping it down on her frail, human neck.

Or, more accurately, on the human's woven necklace.

Caliza tears at the threads of the necklace until a black stone bounces to the ground, landing dangerously close to the grate. Then, with a growl, our leader scoops the stone up into her mouth before adding:

"I believe you have something of mine."

Mishal nudges me again, this time more violently. He points to Caliza in excitement.

"Look! Look! This means—"

He is interrupted by the firm grip of DeLucia, squeezing the back of Mishal's neck.

"Yes, you idiot. We all saw her pick it up. Now shut your mouth before she comes over here."

But Mishal's outburst is enough to pull Caliza's focus away from the humans and onto the three of us.

Overgrown lizard. I will make you suffer for this.

Thankfully, Caliza doesn't appear too upset at the interruption. I mean, she reclaimed Mishal's stone and captured the striga without even trying, and this isn't even the event she planned for tonight. Hopefully, the stroke of good luck encourages her to be patient with us.

Rather than lashing out at Mishal, the sandy-colored fox nods graciously in our direction. "Good timing. I need to look over the prisoners before we begin."

Caliza climbs back into her limestone geode and flies her throne over to the porch. As she gets close to us, DeLucia is the first to bow his head.

"Apologies for the outburst, Caliza. We didn't mean to take away from your moment of victory."

She waves a dismissive paw to the vampire. "Never mind that. I only see eleven humans out here, DeLucia. This isn't all of them, is it?"

The marquess keeps his eyes lowered. "No, Caliza. There are two others still in the cellar—the children you permitted me to keep for blood."

Our leader's floating den moves slowly as she inspects the humans chained to the porch railing. "Even so, I thought we had five spares just last week. Have you three . . . " Her eyes narrow on Mishal as the question looms in her mind. "No one has been snacking when I'm not around, have they?"

The three of us shake our heads in violent denial. I don't know about my compatriots, but I am not stupid enough to eat the power supply.

To direct her focus back to the prisoners, DeLucia speaks again. "If you recall, the five you speak of perished the other day, during that failed ritual with the lemming and the porcupine."

"Ah yes. What a waste." Caliza peers over her fox snout at the humans. "These new ones are greasy and tired, but otherwise healthy. They're not nearly malnourished or beaten enough for what we need, so we can't use them at all tonight. Saphir, I trust you can fix this mistake before tomorrow?"

"Yes, Caliza," I answer, eyes downcast. I don't love the idea of torturing humans, even if I consider them lower on the food chain than myself, but it is not my place to question Caliza's methods.

I am but a fist for the cause.

"Good." She turns to watch the boy, Wade, push a wheelbarrow of meteorite stone to the center of the clearing with newfound excitement. "Then we can start with the striga."

Chapter Seventeen

Ellie

Once she's finished checking in with her underlings, the swift fox Caliza—previously known as my biology teacher, Miss Raposa—turns away from the porch and directs her floating den back toward Cyndi, Bear, and me.

The three of us are still chained to the sewage grate, so I'm not sure why I'm more concerned now than I was earlier.

Since she took away the salamander stone, I'm not as nervous as I should be, but more on edge, sharply aware of each living thing that moves, like that spider spinning a web in the patch of grass to my right, or the earthworms digging into the soil beneath my feet, or the magical talking fox seated inside a floating rock as it hurtles toward me with an air of oncoming violence.

Caliza hovers right above us, flanked by her henchmen. I'm not sure when or how the bloodshed will start, but since the sandy-colored fox who used to be my biology teacher has already shared some of her obligatory "bad guy" speech, there's a good chance it'll be soon.

There's also a good chance I'm the first in line to die.

What was she trying to get at earlier? Calling me a striga—a malformed ghoul? Is a striga some sort of special type of ghoul? But then I'd have to be dead, or undead, for that to be the case. And I'd be craving human flesh . . .

Well, some of that description fits already.

I stretch my shoulders and yawn to feign apathy at my impending demise, while covertly nudging against my jacket pocket with my arm. Sure enough, Caliza and the gang neglected to check my pockets, which means I still have Grandpa's knife.

If I can get out of these cuffs, I might be okay.

With her floating den back on the ground, Caliza begins to rummage through some items hidden at the back of her giant geode. The sandy-colored fox searches for a minute before locating a gold satin pouch and bringing it to the mouth of the cave. She delicately unties the knot of the pouch with her teeth and lays its contents carefully at the edge of her stone seat.

There, on the outer rim of her limestone geode den, sits four colorful stones.

The two stones on the left are the same size and shape: smooth, perfectly round, and about the size of a quarter. The first stone is a glittering, deep blue sapphire, while the second is matte black.

I immediately recognize the second one as the salamander stone.

Has it really been hers all along?

The stones to the right are irregularly shaped and a bit larger than the first two. The one beside the salamander stone is purple, with the pigment fading from deep violet to light gray. The stone next to it is also black—but unlike the salamander stone, it's glossy with white veins running through it.

Then, in true shape-shifting-fox fashion, Caliza opens her mouth to drop a final stone between the others. It's gray, smooth, and similar in shape to the first two, with flecks of ivory and pearl shimmering beneath its polished surface.

Once all five stones are in place, they give off a faint glow, and the courtyard begins to hum with energy.

I glance at Cyndi, hoping to ask a question about magical stone power mechanics, but her eyes are glued to Caliza in horrified awe.

Quietly, Cyndi whispers to herself. "There's no way . . . "

The sandy-colored fox chuckles and places the now-glowing gray stone back into her cheek. She sits reverently behind the remaining line of gems.

"Aren't they beautiful?" Her tail points to the smooth stones. "These two were collected from powerful foxes, now since departed, and given to creatures worthy of ascension."

Caliza scoops up the blue stone in her tail before tossing it to Saphir, the woman with dusty blue hair.

Immediately upon catching the stone, Saphir transforms into a small, gray fox with sharp fangs and fierce eyes. Her tail lights up with crackling sparks of blue and white electricity.

"Whoa," I breathe.

With the gray fox fully shifted, Caliza throws the salamander stone to Mishal, her reptilian lackey, who catches it hungrily.

He swiftly transforms into a large salamander of magma and stone and flame, nearly the size of a horse. As his tail coils possessively around the stone, Mishal's ashen scales leap to life with gleaming, fiery power.

Cyndi, Bear, and I, gape at each other, stunned.

What I would give for a quart of ice cream right now.

As Caliza gives her lackeys approving nods, I notice Marquess DeLucia hanging back for the first time all evening. Perhaps he's been instructed to stay out of the fighting, but an old-school vampire like him might be more interested in self-preservation than . . . whatever it is the fox is up to. I can see the vampire is torn; sure, he might want to fight, but he's hesitant to get involved when he hasn't seen his opponent's hand.

I can't imagine myself, a sixteen-year-old locked in chains, being much of a threat to him, but then it's been a few hours since I saw the photo of "Monster Ellie" eating that moose.

The stony fox gestures to the wheelbarrow of dark gray rock nearby. "What I'm most proud of, however, is our work with the meteorite stone. The meteorites that landed here are so transformative. They can be made into powerful totems when paired with the right host. For example . . . "

Caliza tosses the veined black stone to Wade.

Immediately after catching it, he begins to transform.

An inky black goo spills from Wade's stone, traveling up his arms, across his torso, down his legs, and finally over his head. The slimy, opaque liquid molds him like pottery, and before our eyes he changes from a teenage boy with floppy hair to an enormous black dog.

No, not a dog. A wolfhound. A dire wolf. Cerberus with one head.

And bright, glowing eyes.

"The barguest is the newest of our recruits," Caliza announces with a satisfied grin.

The same eyes I saw in the woods the night we met.

"Are you kidding me?!" I yell.

The lumbering dog, wreathed in shadow, lowers his head in response. The edges of his fur seem to pull away from his body and float upward into small blobs of what looks like goo before vanishing from sight, as if he's being slowly absorbed by the air. Wade the Barguest certainly appears solid as he stands in front of us, but I wonder if he's wholly made of flesh and bone.

"Oh, you're 'with them' with them, huh?" Cyndi barks at Wade. "So, what, you've been on team cannibalism and human sacrifice since the beginning?"

Bear's expression burns with shaking anger as he looks between his brother and Caliza.

"What have you done to him?"

"Hm?" Caliza sits proudly above Bear, preening the tip of her tail. "Nothing too dramatic. All we did was save his life."

She offers a menacing smile. "Imagine my surprise when I, while wandering down Mount Washington in search of meteor stones, found your brother, lying dead in a ravine."

Bear narrows his eyes. Then something clicks in his mind.

"The ski trip? Wade, you . . . " He studies the black dog—his brother, transformed—awkwardly pawing at the ground. "You came back all beaten up, but I didn't think . . . "

Caliza nods at Bear with mock sympathy. "Yes, it's all quite tragic. We revived him the best we could and offered him a choice: join us or die. Of course, he's not an idiot, so he chose to live, though his recent behavior has me wondering if I shouldn't have just left him where I found him."

I hate myself for the tears welling in my eyes.

"Was any of it real?" I ask the barguest.

The large dog doesn't look up, but Wade's voice, an echo of its normal pitch, replies:

"I wanted it to be."

I unclench my jaw, realize that I've been gnawing on the inside of my cheek, and spit some blood on the ground at my feet.

"Enough about this." Caliza's voice tumbles hard as stone. "Mishal, Saphir," she pauses, then points at me with a malicious snarl, "and Barguest, you, too. Kill the striga."

Wade barks at her, fuming. "That's not what we agreed to!"

"I said she'd be useful to us, dog. I never promised to keep her alive. Now," Caliza pulls on an invisible tether between herself and those with stones, and cackles, "do it!"

"No!" Bear yells.

"Leave her alone!"

Everyone turns to Cyndi, the source of the second outburst, as she thrashes against her chains. "Ellie, we can fight this!"

Caliza holds up a hand to her henchmen, preventing them from jumping me at once. "And who are you, pathetic human, to try to stop us?"

In an impressive feat of strength, Cyndi plants her feet, rolls her shoulders forward, and breaks her chain free from the grate.

"I am Cyndi Lauper's biggest fan, and Ellie's best friend, you murderous butt!"

Chains dangling, Cyndi quickly sheds her human persona and becomes a massive red fox, larger than ever before, until she's the size of a small car. Even the flame salamander looks intimidated by her snarl.

Caliza stares at Cyndi, stunned. She lets out an irritated breath.

"So, the Carnelian stone found a competent host in one of our own, only to side with humans. Is that it?" The sandy-colored fox clicks her tongue once. "No wonder you've been so guarded. Were you able to hide your true nature by manipulating my senses? If so, then I'm impressed."

Cyndi the human, Carnelian the fox, merely growls in response. Then she bites through Bear's chains and tells him, "Bear, get behind me so that Ellie—"

But as Cyndi turns to me, I feel a cold grip on my arm and throat.

"You'll do nothing, oversized fox," the cool voice of Marquess DeLucia threatens. "Or else I will destroy this one in front of your very eyes."

Bear, Cyndi, and I stand frozen in place, while Caliza laughs. "A dramatic display, for sure. But unhelpful. You're disturbingly attached to humanity, Carnelian."

"And why shouldn't I be?" Cyndi glares. "At least humans are trying to make things better!"

"Only at the expense of others!" Caliza snaps back. Her tail and feet begin to harden with limestone. "Have you lived among them for so long that you've forgotten who you are? You know the carnage they create for sport, drunkenly hunting us with dogs and wearing our fur as trophies." The stony fox points to the huddled teenagers to the side. "Why shouldn't I treat them the same way?"

"Because it's not like that anymore! It was, a long time ago, but—"

"Only because it fell out of fashion. And now that they're better equipped to fight us, it's bound to start again. It already has, hasn't it?"

Caliza looks at me suddenly, as the limestone climbs across her torso.

"The Beowulf Brigade uses dogs to track down missing humans, but they also use them to circle and trap creatures they need to 'relocate,' don't they?"

I open my mouth, only to close it without answering.

She's not wrong.

"Carnelian, we now have the opportunity to strike back. Making new stones, recruiting new shapeshifters—all of these efforts will help me to build an army that can fight against our enemies. Why is that idea so offensive to you?"

"Because humans can change!" Cyndi argues. "They just need to learn the truth of what they're doing wrong. They can adapt their behavior to be better!"

In response to Cyndi's words, the gray fox, Saphir, shoots a thick spike of blue and white lightning into the sky.

"Are you that naïve, red fox? Humans love to claim ignorance, but the truth is that they don't care," Saphir snarls. "They're only out for themselves, and as they scramble for power, they're ripe to be picked off."

Caliza nods. "Well said. Why fight for those who are actively fighting against your existence? Fight for your way of life, Carnelian. Your powers are awesome, but without a family, you are weak."

"Humanity does not deserve your kindness," Marquess DeLucia adds.

Saphir, the gray fox, nods in agreement. "At best, they're a renewable resource. At worst, they're an infestation."

"And they're tasty!" Mishal, the flame salamander, chimes in.

Cyndi's eyes burn, flickering between each of our opponents before responding.

"I don't go by Carnelian anymore, Caliza. My name is Cyndi, and I can't justify murder like this—even if it means that humans will take advantage of my good will and eventually betray me."

The limestone spreads over Caliza's head and finally encases the fox in a suit of stone armor. "I'd hate to destroy a true stonebearer," she tells Cyndi, "but if you get in our way, I will."

Cyndi steps toward her. "Come and get it, rockface."

Following Cyndi's invitation, the yard quiets, too full of ferocity to make space for words. Each beast is begging to be let loose, like a dog on a leash.

But just as Caliza rears back on her hind legs, I start to laugh.

I can't help myself. This entire scene feels like a fever dream, and with my life being held in the literal grip of a vampire, there's nothing else for me to do.

Besides, during the foxes' ethical discussion, debating whether or not humans should be exterminated, a familiar ringing started in my ears.

Hello, Striga. Took you long enough.

Growing hysterical, I continue laughing until my knees buckle beneath me, which pulls me from Marquess DeLucia's grasp.

The vampire backs away, as if he knows what's coming next.

Do I?

Caliza shouldn't have taken away the salamander stone. I'm pretty sure that was the only thing holding me back until now.

My elbows, wrists, and waist pull out of joint, bending me forward as stinging pain climbs into my limbs and chest. My vision grows darker; my muscles grow and twist in shape.

These freaks caused the fire, burned down my home, and put Grandpa in the hospital. And they did it all so they could summon this thing from the darker recesses of my soul—a side of myself that I still don't fully understand or trust—only to steal and exploit my power as a weapon.

And Wade was in on it all along.

It doesn't matter what his reasons are.

It doesn't matter what anyone's reasons are.

I take a deep breath, louder and heavier than before, and straighten my back to look at the beasts and humans around me, all staring.

The group of kidnapped students scream and huddle in the corner.

They smell like French toast.

Excited at the prospect of fresh meat, I turn toward the frightened humans until something pulls me back.

My earlier chains, tied to the grate, are still clamped around one wrist.

While I work to break free, I notice Marquess DeLucia sprawled at my feet. He stares up in horror at my transformation.

His sniveling expression makes me salivate.

Hello, dinner.

I tear the remaining chain from my wrist with the ease of a child removing an unwanted sock and lean down, closing the gap between the vampire and my sharp, hungry teeth.

Not ready to die, DeLucia quickly transforms into a bat and flies off.

Well, that's no fun.

"Coward!" Caliza yells after him. She spins on the rest of her minions. "The rest of you, don't even think of running away!"

Hunger gnaws at me—enough for me to ignore the remaining conversation in search of anything to eat. As I look around, I recognize Grandpa's double-edged axe laying at my feet, tossed aside during Caliza's earlier tantrum.

I pick up the axe, which feels like a toy in my heavy, monstrous hand, and let out a violent roar before charging forward.

Chapter Eighteen

Ellie

The mind of the beast is a strange place. It's not that transforming makes me someone new—I'm still me under all the jagged teeth, and I'm generally aware of what's happening as it happens. But instead of my rational brain directing my behavior, my instincts are driving the car.

Also, my senses are turned up too high. Unfamiliar scents and noises are attacking my brain from every direction, and I can't turn them off.

At least now, I'm able to loosely dictate the monster's movements. The other transformations felt like I was holding on for dear life while I rode on the back of a wild animal; this time, though, it's more like riding a horse for the first time, without the experience to pivot or guide the animal.

And this horse wants to buck—but it's holding back for some reason.

Maybe the striga knows that right now, I'm not afraid of what it wants to do, or what it can do.

I'm just pissed.

I glance to the left just in time to see Saphir, the electrified gray fox, run straight for me. Her wide grin betrays her excitement, as if she's been hoping to challenge a lumbering beast of my size.

All right, then. Let's dance.

I swat at the gray fox with the axe's blunt edge, only for her to dodge the blow by splitting herself into six mirror copies. The six foxes alternate between biting my ankles and zapping me with electricity, which doesn't hurt enough to be concerning, but certainly stops me in my tracks.

Blue jagged lines of lightning climb up my legs with increased frequency, and soon my left knee grows numb from the residual sparks and stings of her attacks.

Growing bored, I toss aside the axe and grab one of the foxes at my feet. It squirms in my grasp and feels solid, but as I bite its head off, it melts into dust in my hand.

Immediately following the gray fox's demise, a duplicate takes its place at my feet. Each fox is an identical copy of another, and each moves quicker than the eye can catch, making it impossible to find the original in the cloud of dust and fur and lightning.

Tiny fox, you are annoying.

As I continue to step on, kick at, and bite into illusions of Saphir, I see Caliza and the salamander charge at Cyndi as she plants her large feet in front of Bear.

The salamander's fighting style is pure destructive force. He swipes at Cyndi with his tail, landing a burning blow on her front leg.

Enraged, Cyndi screams before lunging at the flame salamander and sinking her teeth into the meat of his hind leg.

Mishal, the flame salamander, roars in response. Twisting his neck, he tries to burn Cyndi with his fiery breath, but she relentlessly bites into his leg until he falls over and curls up in pain.

Cyndi hobbles away from the salamander just in time to catch Caliza, who's headed straight for Bear.

Caliza is fast, but Cyndi's large form can easily block her path, sending the stony fox spinning away from Bear.

Within seconds of reaching our friend, Cyndi shrinks down to the size of a normal red fox, grabs Bear's pant leg with her teeth, and closes her eyes.

Then Bear and Cyndi shimmer into invisibility and vanish from sight.

Caliza circles back to pounce on the spot where my friends stood mere seconds before, but she's too late. Furious to find nothing, she swipes at the empty air.

"Carnelian!" the stony fox yells. "Show yourself! Stop playing games and fight me!"

I nod at Cyndi's cunning and return to the frustrating problem at my feet. The gray foxes have continued multiplying, despite my occasional murder of one or two. I'm now surrounded by twelve copies of Saphir, all biting and zapping me.

Irritated, I stomp on the foxes aggressively, smash four from existence, and try to think.

Electricity. Thunder. Lightning.

Lightning happens first, right? Followed by Thunder?

My head hurts.

Fighting the urge to smash them all into powder, I close my eyes and listen.

The foxes at my feet aren't making much noise. There's just a rush of wind on my left side, followed by the sudden crackle of electricity behind me.

Gotcha.

With my eyes still closed, I reach out and pluck a gray fox from the air. My claws tighten solidly around its torso, and I open my eyes just in time to see the other foxes collapse into dust at my feet.

I come face to face with the real Saphir, growling and baring her teeth.

"You got lucky," she scowls, sending a thread of blue electricity up my arm.

I watch the electricity bounce away from my skin and shoot back up into the sky.

Pretty.

The fox thrashes against my grip. "Put me down!"

In response, I throw her small body as hard as I can into the trunk of a nearby tree.

Saphir's bones crunch upon impact. She falls to the ground in a light thud, and stays there, motionless.

Finally. Quiet.

The small gray fox is too skinny to be a full meal, but the lean meat on her bones might lessen my hunger until I can get something substantial.

I stalk over to Saphir's wheezing body and watch as she struggles to catch her breath.

Hopefully, her muscles aren't gristly.

But just as I reach for the fox, a black mass of fur barrels into my right shoulder to push me away.

The barguest previously known as Wade blocks my path.

"Don't do this, Ellie." He whines—a strange sound to come from such a menacing frame.

On all fours, the dog is nearly as tall as a horse in height—not taller than me, but certainly massive. But it's the wide paws, gleaming teeth, and noxious fumes of his green and gold aura that are the real threat. Something about the beast smells poisoned, decaying.

Smells. Wrong.

"We don't have to fight." The dog pleads.

I run at him, claws first, but the dog is quick to block. He raises his front legs high to push against my attacks, and his mass is enough to keep my claws away from his eyes.

But my goal isn't to scratch him—it's to catch him off balance.

The barguest absorbs the blows by leaning backward, placing most of his weight on his back leg. So, when I have an opening, I dive for the other leg.

The push sends him falling onto his back, exposing his underbelly.

I bite into the meat of his stomach.

The hound sends up a mournful howl, but I'm too distracted by the nuances of flavor to pay attention to his distress. Barguest meat, at least when served raw, is strangely absent of blood. It tastes and feels like soft, stinky cheese, which isn't my first choice to eat, but I'm not opposed to a second helping.

"Get off!" the dark beast yells. He rolls to push me off before biting into my neck and tossing me to one side. Once free of me, the barguest struggles to stand. "Will you listen?!"

He leans awkwardly to one side, panting. "I'm sorry for approaching you, all right? I was told to make sure that you were the monster we suspected you to be. But I didn't know Caliza meant to kill you! I mean, I suspected it, but once I got to know you, I . . . didn't want that to happen. I tried to reason with her, and I thought . . . "

His words are boring and I hate them. I dig a handful of claws into his chest to shut him up.

It works. The attack turns his words into screams, but when I pull my hand away from his chest, there's no blood—just black goo coating the tips of my claws before it evaporates into nothing.

What's more, it seems like he's already healed from my previous bite.

Strange.

I feel heat at my back and notice the large trough of fire and oil behind me.

Perhaps a barguest is best served deep-fried.

I grab his front leg, hoping to drag the dog into the trough of burning oil, but Wade digs his heels into the mud, determined to finish our conversation.

He faces me directly.

"Ellie, I was trying to figure out how to save you from them, honest. And I was going to break free from Caliza's grip, somehow, but . . . I don't think I'm the one who can fix this." The barguest pulls against me, breathing hard. "You're the only one who can."

With his front leg still pinched between my claws, I pause my attempt to burn the barguest alive.

"You're strong enough to beat Caliza on your own—I just know it. And if you take her down," he pulls again, trying to release himself from my grip, "then I'll be free from her power."

Why should I care about this? He's the one who made a deal with an evil magical fox. He got himself into this mess; I shouldn't have to clean it up for him.

Wade the dog stops fighting me and lowers his head in defeat.

"If I'm free, then we can run away from all this. We can find a place where these cursed forms won't matter. Just you and me."

Images of Wade the boy return then, filling my head with the sound of his laugh and the taste of hurried kisses. And the dream of he and I, running freely through the woods without fear or shame for these new, twisted forms, is tempting. It's more enticing than I expect, to the point that my vision clouds over and my ears start to ring.

My control of the beast starts to waver.

"Ellie, I know you have no reason to trust me, but my feelings for you were always real. They still are."

The barguest's eyes glow in a haze as he continues.

"I'm probably the only person who could ever understand what you are."

All I've ever wanted was to run away, even before becoming this monster. But leaving isn't as easy as he promises. My mother doesn't deserve to be abandoned without an explanation. Not when Grandpa is . . .

I take a deep breath. Grandpa's not gone. Not yet.

And this past week has shown me the truth of other things, too. Relationships that I assumed would fall apart if I was ever too honest have held on despite my best effort to push them away.

I can't leave them. Not like this.

Regaining control, I focus on my breath, counting the low thump of each monstrous heartbeat until the injured chuckle of Saphir pulls me back to the present.

The gray fox lies still in a crumpled heap, her eyes flitting between me and the barguest.

And she's laughing.

"Was this your plan all along, dog? Get the toughest brawler to fight for you and escape? Can't say I blame you, though I doubt the striga will be all that understanding when she learns that you're manipulating her."

The gray fox pauses to spit blood. "Or did you tell her already? That you're the one who bit her grandfather?"

The ringing in my ears stops instantly, and despite my beastly form, I find the gravelly rumble of my voice:

"Grr . . . and . . . pa?"

"Right, right. Your grandfather." Wade glares at the gray fox. "I was going to tell you about that, eventually . . . "

He avoids my eyes.

"The night of the fire, Saphir and I were told to go and check on things at your house, to make sure the fire had spread. When I got there first, I found your grandfather outside, wrapped in a blanket, and since meeting you just hours before . . . I didn't want to hurt him. I only had a few seconds to hide him from Saphir, so . . . I dragged your grandfather into the bushes by his pant leg, and I might have left a, ahem, mark on his leg."

The poison that has my grandfather in a coma—that was from the bite of a barguest?

My claws push into the earth with growing ferocity.

"When are you going to be honest, dog?" the gray fox croaks, still in pain. "You keep abstaining from fresh meat like you're better than the rest of us, but that just sends you into a frenzy when you finally get a bite. That's why you killed that girl on the bus last night, when we were supposed to bring all of the students back here alive."

He . . . killed someone?

"Shut up, Saphir." Wade's eyes darken.

But Saphir is unfazed by his threats. "And that's why you bit her grandfather, too. You would've killed and eaten him right then if the fire department hadn't shown up when they did."

My vision narrows.

The barguest looks up at me pathetically. "Ellie—hey. If anyone could understand what I'm going through, you do. Right? I mean, you've probably killed someone by now?"

In response, I pull hard on the dog's ankle, breaking a few bones.

He cries out, but I'm not listening.

No more.

I sink deeper into the beast and in seconds, I've pinned the barguest's front leg up behind his back. His heartbeat bursts into a fluttering panic, but I don't stop. The world is blood red as I hold the leg in place and push it up, up, up.

His shoulder begins tearing at the socket, and as he howls in agony, begging me to stop, I remind myself that the few cherished people and items I can call my own have all been hurt by his choices.

No more.

The tendons and ligaments in the barguest's shoulder pop and dislocate, leaving his front leg to hang limp in my grip. Then, with one final tug, I rip the leg free from the dog's body and toss it into the trough of burning oil.

No more.

His leg burns up in an instant, and as I turn back to the barguest, I see blood trickle from the open wound.

Chapter Nineteen

Ellie

"Ellie!"

Cyndi's cry for help invades my darker thoughts and allows me to regain control of the beast. I turn away from the broken, bleeding barguest to find my friend pinned flat by the flame salamander. Her tail is partially burned, and since she's still in the form of a regular fox, it's clear that she's too worn out to grow in size right now.

A few feet from Cyndi, Bear nervously lifts his arms out in front of himself, hoping to keep the swift fox Caliza, now armored in limestone, at arm's length.

"Stay back!" he yells.

But without Cyndi's protection, he's a much easier target.

The swift fox closes the distance between herself and Bear in seconds, shoving him to the ground. She places a victorious paw on his chest, but right when she does, a faded purple stone falls from her mouth and lands inches away from Bear's hand.

That purple stone is the last of Caliza's magical rocks, and based on how she's handed things out, this stone is apparently without an owner.

Cyndi, still a red-orange fox, glances between Bear and the stone. "Hey, pal," she says, hesitating, "I wouldn't—"

She's interrupted by Caliza's roar.

"Don't even think about it!"

But it's too late. Before Caliza can stop him, Bear closes his fist around the purple stone. It glows instantly, sizzling with sudden heat.

Screaming in pain, Bear throws the shocked Caliza aside and runs to the center of the courtyard. He collapses atop the grate, scratching at his burned palm, but the stone only burrows deeper. It glows brightly in his hand before radiating incandescent, blistering light through his body.

Despite being trapped and terrified, the kidnapped students watch Bear with rapt awe as he shapeshifts from a teen boy to a beacon of light to a fluffy, white bear.

Theodore "Teddy" Bear Drummond stands before us, newly transformed into the body of an actual bear, and examines his paws carefully.

"Am I . . . a bear?" he asks.

After a long pause, the flame salamander Mishal is the one to answer him. "Yep."

Bear reaches up to touch his ears, now covered with fur and placed atop his head. Then he looks down at his feet. "It figures."

Furious, Caliza lunges at him again. This time, Bear absorbs the blow of her body into a bear hug and, after spinning the fox in a circle, sits on top of her.

"Bad fox," says Bear, the fluffy bear. "Stay."

Caliza growls with impatience. "Mishal, what are you waiting for? Kill the red fox!"

"Hey!" Bear yells back at her.

"No, wait!" I shout.

The flame salamander opens his jaws above Cyndi, readying himself to set her aflame.

I look down at my body, and only then do I see that the monster is gone.

When I'm the monster, there's no room for fear and doubt. There's a thirst for blood, which isn't great, but at least it keeps my mind away from scarier thoughts, like the fear of being killed by a flame salamander.

But now the striga's gone, and I have no immediate way of bringing it back. All I have to offer is Ellie, a sixteen-year-old girl who is currently very cold and nearly naked.

I whip my head around, searching for anything to fight with, but there's only a random assortment of lawn furniture and a double-edged axe.

I blink again, thankful to see my grandfather's axe so close by. I'd casually discarded it earlier due to my striga-brain considering it ineffective and not as fun as claws, but now it will do just fine.

My gaze switches back to Cyndi, fighting to get free from the salamander, and Bear, fighting to keep Caliza trapped, before meeting the eyes of one of the kidnapped students.

She's visibly shaking with fear.

So am I.

Then I grab the axe with both hands and run as fast as I can toward the salamander, whose mouth is now engulfed in flames.

Seconds before the beast roasts Cyndi alive, I raise my axe high above his tail and smash it into his crackling flesh.

The salamander rears back in pain, shooting a swirling tower of fire into the sky.

I lift the axe again, and the blade strikes home, deepening my first cut.

Mishal, the salamander, twists around in pain. He bites at me, and I'm forced to roll and crawl to avoid his teeth. I finally rest behind his injured back leg, which I hope is a blind spot.

After more unsuccessful bites, the salamander gathers a mouthful of lava in his cheeks and prepares to melt me from this plane of existence.

But he's not quick enough.

I lift my grandfather's axe in a wider, faster arc than before, and slice right through the remaining muscle and skin of the salamander's tail.

Mishal shrieks. Without a tail for balance, he falls forward and curls into a ball. As he investigates the extent of his wound, his body shrinks down to the size of a normal salamander—minus a tail. Then, finding no fatal injuries, the tiny flame salamander scurries into the underbrush, never to be seen again.

I walk over to the severed salamander tail, holding my breath, and—thankfully—my instincts are right. The tip of the salamander's tail is wrapped around a small, matte black stone.

My stone.

Once in my palm, the salamander stone sends a rush of heat through my body. The dull, achy exhaustion of my muscles recedes, and my chest feels lighter, allowing me to breathe freely.

I'm thankful for the stone's warmth, but it does little to cover my nudity. I search the grounds for my shredded jacket, pull it on, and place the stone in the jacket's inside pocket.

I turn back to Cyndi, Bear, Caliza, and the group of students, all of whom are stunned.

"Hey guys." I wave. "Sorry you had to see . . . " I gesture to Wade and Saphir, or rather, the previous location of Wade and Saphir's bodies, as the two have vanished, and add, "all of that."

Cyndi and Bear wave back, hesitantly.

Still pinned beneath Bear's butt, Caliza screams at me, enraged.

"How dare you destroy all I've worked for!"

She bites into Bear's leg until he bends his knee upward, leaving just enough room for her to escape. Once free, the furious fox runs to the closest trough of hot, burning oil and kicks it over.

"None of you are getting out of here alive!"

The back porch instantly catches fire, and with the amount of oil feeding the flames, the house—and Errolton High School's girl's track team—will burn with it.

Chapter Twenty

Dani

Ynez is the first one to start screaming.

The rest of us are quick to follow her lead, though I'm not sure why we're screaming. It's not like any of these shapeshifting freaks are going to save us from the flames.

I guess screaming is just a required part of situations like this, being an instinctual response to imminent death, or whatever.

The red-orange fox, who I recognized earlier as the ever-absent Cyndi Renard from my Spanish class, suddenly grows to the size of a school bus and runs over to us.

"Don't panic. I'm here to help." The oversized red fox bites through the porch's wooden railing, allowing each of us to slide our cuffs off in a line. "Once you get your hands free, climb onto my back," she says to reassure us. "We're all getting out of here alive."

"How can we trust you?"

The accusing question leaves my mouth before I can hold it back, but I stand by it. Just because she's offering a way out doesn't make her any better than the freaks who kidnapped us. Sure, maybe she'll take us home to our parents tonight, but she'll probably eat us next week if we're out past curfew.

Cyndi the fox turns to me with a wink.

"Oh, you don't need to worry about me. I stopped eating humans a century ago."

My peers climb one by one onto the large fox's back, chatting excitedly, but I'm still not convinced.

Before I can reply, Nadia stands beside me with a tired smile.

"You act like we don't know about the Gingerbread Man." Nadia sighs, playfully. "He trusted a fox to bring him to safety, too, and it didn't work out so well for him in the end."

"Well, that doesn't really apply to this situation, since you're not made of gingerbread. Besides," the red fox nods to the growing flames behind us, "I'd say you don't have much of a choice right now."

She's right. One look at the fire and it's clear that we're out of options. Add to that the fighting shapeshifters below us—the limestone fox, the white fluffy bear, and that terrifying striga thing, now in the shape of a normal human girl—and I'm willing to take a chance on Big Red.

I don't want to wait around to see who wins.

Following Nadia, I climb onto the fox's back and find a spot behind her right ear.

"Hey! Before you leave," I yell, tugging on the fox's ear. "There are two girls still locked in the cellar. Someone's got to get them out."

Big Red furrows her brow, but instead of answering me, she shouts back to the rest of us:

"Everyone back there?"

When the crowd of high schoolers yells back affirmatively, Cyndi turns to the remaining shapeshifters.

"Bear! Ellie! Two girls are still in the cellar. Can one of you grab them?"

The big, fluffy bear who used to be Bear Drummond, the top student in my calculus class, is too busy defending against the evil fox's attacks to hear Cyndi's question.

Meanwhile Ellie, the girl who transformed into that huge, creepy monster, keeps her eyes forward and her axe raised while yelling back, "We'll do it! Just get them out of here!"

Cyndi the fox nods and turns away from the house. "Ready, everyone? Hold on!"

Then Big Red takes off with us on her back. She's huge and fast, which is terrifying as we race deeper into the woods, where moonlight is blotted out by wild, overgrown branches. But even the icy wind, whipping against my cheeks, is a welcome change from the cellar's stale air.

I turn to watch the shack's fiery blaze as it fades behind the welcoming arms of green pines. Once the abandoned house is out of sight, something loosens in my chest.

I can't stop thinking of the look on Sarah's face as she died.

And I cry. Loud, ugly tears that I refused to let free in the cellar are back with a vengeance, pushing out of me in hiccough-y sobs.

I'm sorry I couldn't save you, Sarah. I'm sorry that all I could do was watch in horror as that thing killed you.

After that striga thing ripped the dog's arm off, I thought she'd finish the job right there—in fact, I was hoping for it. But then she just turned away from his mangled body, distracted by other concerns, and he was allowed to crawl off.

What if that dog finds out where I live? What if he crawls in through my bedroom window to finish the job?

I mean, sure, the beast was bleeding out when he crawled into the woods, but I doubt a thing like that can die of something like blood loss.

No, that monster is still out there, living while Sarah is dead dead dead.

I wipe away the tears with a shaking hand.

The foxes, the vampire, the striga—they're all the problem. That dog is just part of it.

What is it that the gray fox said back there?

"Humans love to claim ignorance, but the truth is that they don't care. They're only out for themselves, and as they scramble for power, they're ripe to be picked off."

The Beowulf Brigade wants everyone to think that these attacks are from supernatural creatures with sharp spikes and fiery breath, but limited intelligence. Do the authorities know that some of these monsters are smart and hidden in plain sight? Are they clueless, or are they just keeping it to themselves?

Is Big Red, Cyndi the fox, working for them?

I remember Caliza, that wretched fox, also saying something about humans—back when she was trying to recruit Cyndi to her cause.

"Why fight for those who are actively fighting against your existence?"

New Hampshire is one of the first states trying to pass laws to help vampires and other intelligent supernatural creatures join society, rather than being hunted for what they really are.

Antagonists to human existence.

If I can just show the world what these things are capable of, then maybe we can start passing laws that will protect us, rather than making us more vulnerable.

We shouldn't be defending monsters that can so easily destroy us when the impulse strikes.

We need to fight for our way of life.

Chapter Twenty-One

Ellie

Fire climbs into the creaky old house, burning hotter and faster with each breath.

We have minutes before it spreads into the trees.

Caliza's speed makes it difficult for Bear, still the white, fluffy bear, to subdue her. He's done well to block her attacks this long, but it's clear—he's getting tired.

The limestone-encased swift fox, on the other hand, doesn't seem tired at all. Her rage-induced spike in adrenaline has only made her fiercer and more unhinged than before.

"Give me the striga!" she bellows at Bear, shaking with fury. "I need her blood!"

And those girls in the cellar are running out of time.

"Bear!" I yell, "Get into the cellar before the whole place collapses! I'll hold her off until you get back!"

He looks back, unsure. "Maybe you should be the one—"

But before he finishes the thought, Caliza leaps into the air and shoves into his shoulder. Upon impact, she grabs hold of his ear and bites down, drawing blood.

"Ow! Get—" Bear tears the fox free from his ear and throws her against the ground, yelling, "Off!"

Caliza laughs, leaning to one side before returning to attack position. "Enjoying the show, Striga?"

I watch as blood from Bear's ear collects in the corner of her mouth, staining the limestone that covers her face.

"Is it fun to watch your friends sacrifice themselves for you?"

The stone is more fragmented around certain joints, like Caliza's jaw and shoulders, but there's no clear break in her armor. Every inch of the fox is covered in rock.

"Ellie," Bear starts, pressing a paw against his bloody ear, which is slowly staining his otherwise pristine white fur, "I don't feel right leaving you here with her. What if she . . . "

With no time left to discuss it, I rush toward Caliza and smack the cheek of my grandfather's double-edged axe across her temple. The fox's limestone armor stays in place, but the blow disorients her long enough for me to run deeper into the yard.

"Bear! Just go! Those girls will die if I . . . I'm not strong enough to carry them out myself!"

The white bear nods and runs over to the cellar doors, briefly fumbling with the lock before tearing into the rotting wood of the door's handle and breaking it free. Once open, he yells down inside and enters the cellar.

Good. Now all I have to do is stay alive until he can come back and rescue me. And then . . .

Well, I'm not sure what happens after that.

Caliza shakes her head and blinks to find me again. Discouraged by the distance between us, she growls.

"What, is that all you've got?" I shout, taunting her.

I should have kept running.

The swift fox catapults toward me, and despite my attempts to twist and dodge her attacks, she anticipates each move. It's not long before she collides with my chest and pushes Grandpa's axe from my hand.

The blow knocks me to the ground, slamming my head into the cold dirt. And as I look up, or at least try to see which way is up with blurry, unfocused vision, Caliza's claws dig into my chest with sharp pressure, trapping me under the weight of her stone armor.

"Is that all you've got, Striga?" she asks, mocking my earlier comment. "You got lucky with Mishal and the axe earlier—I'll give you that. But as a human, you're pathetic. Just like the rest of them."

"Oh yeah? How's your head feeling?" I glare up at the tiny fox.

Ignoring my reply, Caliza closes her eyes in concentration.

Three crystal spikes emerge from the limestone covering her front leg. She's clearly exhausted with the use of this much magic, but the gleam in her eyes tells me that she's more determined than ever to achieve her goal of killing me, so she can use my blood for . . . whatever she wants it for, I guess.

"It's best for you to die at my hands, anyway," Caliza gloats, biting into my shoulder. She swallows a bit of blood before spitting it back into my face. "Now that the beast is awake, it's only a matter of time before you start killing everyone around you. Sure, in the beginning, it might just be livestock that goes missing. But what happens when animal meat isn't enough?

"You might try starving the hunger for a while, to see if it goes away, but it won't. And then one day, you'll find someone alone in the woods, far from the hiking trail. And they won't make it back to camp."

I grind my teeth. "You don't know that."

"Oh, don't I? I saw what you did to the barguest." She laughs, pressing a crystal spike into my open wound.

I scream. I have to. The pain blisters and blooms throughout my arm.

"And you're going to keep doing things like that until you," she twists the spike, "are," another sharp twist, "dead!"

Make it stop! Make her stop!

The striga beats against the bars of my mind, roaring for me to let it out.

But this is a fight I need to win on my own.

More teeth and spikes press into my arm, and as the pain becomes excruciating, I struggle not to pass out.

Instead, I pull my left arm free from Caliza's grip, grab the hunting knife from my jacket pocket, and stab it into the stone armor's gap between her neck and shoulder.

Caliza rears back at the puncture, but I tackle the swift fox, cutting deeper into the meat of her neck while her crystal knives dig into my upper arm.

For a moment, we're frozen in combat. Both bleeding, both daring the other to die first.

It's Caliza who breaks the silence with a raspy chuckle.

"Ah. So you've found the point."

Despite the crystal spikes shooting through my arm and chest, I tighten my grip on the knife.

"The . . . point? What point?" I grimace, leaning my body weight into the fox's neck.

"The point of your knife." She lets out a rough cough. "Striking the fatal wound first . . . before your opponent can."

I look down at the knife, its polished, wooden handle newly splattered with blood.

"I . . . I didn't—"

"You did." She pauses to spit some blood into the grass. "Just acting on instinct. Any cornered animal would do the same."

My fingers twitch, wanting to leap from the blade—to wash my hands of this bloody business.

But I can't. I'm a cornered animal, fighting to survive.

Is that all I'll ever be?

I glance at the ground where she spat and recognize the small, gray stone peeking out from the grass.

Her stone.

The fox's eyes follow mine, only to widen at the same discovery.

"N . . . no . . . "

Caliza makes a desperate attempt to grab it, but the crystal spikes from her arm limit her movement just enough for me to reach across and snatch the stone myself.

The flickering light of the house fire dances across the polished surface of Caliza's stone, flecked with ivory and pearl. As it rests in my hand, I can sense a network of other interconnected stones—their names, their strengths, and their stories.

The salamander stone in my pocket lights up, and I hear the words: *Volcan. Stone of the Forge.*

Following another thread, I see the stone inside of Bear's arm light up.

Amethystos. Stone of Mental Acuity.

Further out, I sense Cyndi's stone. She's stopped running to let the kidnapped students climb down from her back.

Carnelian. Stone of Perception.

Then, off to my left, I see two more stones resting deep in the woods.

Saphir. Stone of Energy.

Onyx. Stone of the Void.

Finally, my eyes settle back on the stone in my hand. I look up to find Caliza the fox staring murderous daggers in my direction. A cold voice thunders in my ears.

Caliza. Stone of Compulsion.

I place the stone between my thumb and forefinger and look down at the fox, still pinned by my knife.

"Why . . . " I start, unsure of where I'm going. "Why do you keep calling me a striga? Don't I have to be dead for that to be the case?"

The bleeding fox lets out a vicious laugh. "Aren't you?"

Her words rattle around in my head, clanging in an angry chorus, but I hold my ground.

"I'm . . . not dead," I say, steadying my breath. "I would know."

The swift fox cackles again as blood pools behind her teeth. "My, you are a broken thing, aren't you?"

I shake the stone above her face. "What does that mean?!"

But by now, she's lost the will to fight. The fox glances upward to watch the house fire's smoke pirouette into the dark sky, before answering in a tired whistle:

"Only that your kind is a virus—one that splinters and spreads and could end it all."

Her left leg twitches, an involuntary motion.

"And that's why you're his favorite."

Then her eyes glaze over, and she's gone.

Empty, haunted, and exhausted, I untangle myself from the fox's crystal spikes and sit up, only for the wounds in my arm to bleed out faster than I can stop.

I'm too preoccupied with Caliza's stone to even notice.

The gray stone glows brighter than before. It fills my chest with light and heat, drawing energy from the other stones

And for a moment, I'm tempted to keep it.

But this kind of power demands blood, and I have enough of that on my hands already.

I glance back at the silent body of Caliza, who just hours before was assigning homework as my biology teacher.

"Hey, Miss Raposa," I wince, delirious and achy from blood loss, and laugh, "flunk this."

Then I let out a roar and crush Caliza's stone to powder in my hand.

A rush of compressed magical energy expels into the air, instantly severing the network of connections in my mind. Seconds later, the swift fox's eyes darken and close, and her stone body breaks into pieces of well sculpted, but empty, stone.

The surge of energy throws me across the yard, and as my vision grows blurry and dark, the last thing I see is a white horse covered in dirt and blood.

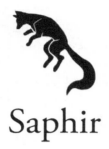

Chapter Twenty-Two

Saphir

"Just kill me now," the dog barks in a hollow whine.

"As tempting as that is, Barguest, I will pass."

Comfortably seated on a log—and still in my preferred form as a fox—I return to cauterizing the dog's wound with a sustained spark of electricity from my tail.

The barguest's whimpering almost makes me lower the voltage in my tail, to make the process less painful. Not because I want him to be comfortable, or anything. I just want him to stop crying about it.

When the whimpering continues, I reach for a conversation topic that might distract him from the pain.

"This wound is your fault, you know. I told you over and over again that humans are the worst, but did you listen? No, of course not." I mock him in a pitch meant to imitate his own voice, "Oh Saphir, you don't understand. You are just a wizened magical fox who impersonates humans for fun; you can't possibly understand the intricacies of a high school relationship."

Annoyed, the barguest bites down on a strip of tree bark as I continue closing the wound.

A minute of blissful silence passes between us—one that ends when his teeth cut deeper into the wood and it snaps, splitting to pieces.

The dog spits the broken bark onto the forest floor, furious.

"I just don't get it," he grumbles. "It seemed like she didn't know what was going on at first—I mean, she was attacking me out of nowhere. But then, it was almost like . . . "

The black dog cocks his head to one side, thinking. "And with my leg, throwing it into the fire . . . " He chuckles bitterly. "But there's no way she'd do that if she understood what I was saying, right?"

"If that is true, then how do you explain," I pause before releasing my best striga voice, "GR . . . AND . . . PA?!"

"Uh-huh." His eyes narrow. "Thanks for telling her about that, by the way."

I shrug. "The girl deserved to know. Also, I may have wanted to see what she would do after learning the truth. And boy, she did not disappoint."

My tail twitches as I talk, singeing a piece of the barguest's unmarred skin. He growls in pain.

"Quit whining," I say, cutting off the power to my tail. "I'm done. Anyway, the arm will probably grow back within a week."

"Yeah," he replies. "Maybe."

The barguest stands on his remaining three legs, testing how his weight and balance have changed with the loss of his front leg. After a few beats, he arches his back and shifts slowly into his human form. Howls of pain escape his throat throughout the change.

Once again human, Wade the boy wobbles on two legs after the difficult shift, only to see that his human body is also missing an arm. The missing limb has been replaced by a burnt stump—an unexpected result of the striga's rage.

At the sight of his missing arm, I shift cleanly into my human form to further inspect it.

"Wow," I breathe, reaching toward him. "That girl did a number on you, didn't she?"

The boy lets out a furious roar and pushes me away.

"You've done your part, Saphir." He spits my name like venom. "Now leave me alone."

With a shrug, I walk back to the duffle bags I retrieved from the house before fleeing. "Fine, if that is what you want. But we have a better chance of surviving if we stick together."

Unzipping my bag reveals bundles of rolled clothing. I retrieve a black sweatshirt, denim pants, and hiking boots before turning back to the boy.

"Now that Caliza's lost control of our stones, we can go wherever we want." I make a kissy face, quoting his earlier words, "We can find a place where these cursed forms won't matter."

His glare darkens.

"Maybe I'd rather try to do this on my own than have to deal with you. Besides," he looks down at his missing arm, "how can you be sure that Caliza's gone?"

Caliza's stone never actually controlled our powers. She was able to pull on our stones and compel us to do her bidding, but the stones' power always remained with us, whether or not they were physically in our hands. That's the benefit of becoming a stonebearer—until the stone's mantel passes to someone else, a stonebearer can tap into their magic for as long they live.

Which makes that striga girl all the more impressive. Defeating a stonebearer in combat offers her the option to possess their mantel. Tonight, she could have taken my stone, as well as the barguest's, if she knew.

She did take Mishal's stone, though, so he is no longer of any use to us.

"Don't be so sensitive, Barguest." I toss the second duffle bag to him. "You and I both felt that slackening of Caliza's leash before it snapped. She's gone."

"I did feel something happen. I just don't want to get my hopes up."

"Well, this is what it feels like when she's not trying to control you. You just don't trust it because, by the time you joined us, she was heavily relying on her powers of compulsion."

"She wasn't always like that?"

I shake my head. "Not even close."

Caliza's face is intertwined with my earliest memories. I don't recall anything of my family—I think I was taken from them well before I developed conscious thought. But I will never forget the sight of Caliza's snout against the bars of my cage at that fox farm, telling me about a life beyond being skinned for human consumption. She'd waved that sapphire under my nose with promises of freedom and magic, so long as I would always serve her.

My tongue presses against the sapphire in my cheek, confirming its location.

Working for Caliza has always been the repayment of a life debt, one I was happy to live out—at least, until she met DeLucia. That's when her mild distaste for humans solidified into brutal hatred.

It was hard to disagree with her, of course. If humans are up to something, it's usually bad for the world. But we always found ways to live beyond humanity's reach, using our wits to undermine their goals without mass bloodshed.

Not that I object to blood being shed in the name of the cause. It's often necessary. But amassing an army? Kidnapping large groups? Attacking children? It seemed too complicated, too messy, and too much work for not enough reward.

After all, it's not like we can exterminate them.

Caliza used to feel the same way, until she got caught up in this blood sacrifice business. And sure, the process was interesting, especially in those rare moments of magical transference. But once it became about power and fighting, it ended the way those things usually do.

Two sticks of beef jerky peek out from a pocket of my pack. I reach down and toss one to the boy, who catches it with a surprised expression.

He bites into the snackable stick of dried meat before pulling his head through the neck hole of a clean shirt. "Where do you think DeLucia scurried off to?"

I grin. "What a weakling. Gets one look at the striga and wets himself. Still," I bite into my stick of beef jerky, musing, "he joined Caliza as a free agent, because working with her allowed him to eat some humans, harvest some blood for later, and—if things got messy—blame the kidnappings on us. But I'm sure a guy like him doesn't stay bored for long. DeLucia probably has something else going that we could jump into, if he needs the extra muscle."

"So, wait. Your idea of total freedom and opportunity is to immediately enlist as a paid thug for someone else?"

"As opposed to what? Killing people for free?"

"Who says we have to kill anyone?"

I laugh in his face. "You must be joking."

"And what if I'm not? We can do things differently now."

"What would that even look like?"

"I don't know, I . . . " The boy trails off, frustrated. "I'm just sick of this constant cycle of hunger and killing. I don't want to do it anymore."

Once I zip up my duffle bag, I throw it at Wade—this time hitting him in the face—and take advantage of the split-second distraction to sprint until I'm right in front of him.

His eyes are brown and gold, not unlike the dirty-blond hair that hangs down against his temple. Standing this close, I notice a black line running through his irises.

It looks like it's spreading.

I blink, remember my original purpose, and grab the boy by his hooded collar. "I don't know what's worse, Barguest—your never-ending pungent odor, or the fact that, with all the time you've spent with humans recently, you think you can become one again."

His eyebrows twitch with silenced anger. "My name is Wade. Not Barguest."

"Maybe it used to be, dog." I bare my teeth. "But not anymore. I mean, can't you hear it?"

He breaks my gaze, confirming that I'm not the only one with voices in my head:

"The stones are getting louder."

I let go of his shirt and take a step back. "They are restless—probably because Caliza's not keeping them in line anymore. So sure, we can try things your way for a few days if you want, but 'being a good guy' usually leads to 'being hungry all the time.'

"Meanwhile, if we link up with DeLucia, he can help us get fresh meat when we need it. Maybe even something 'ethically sourced,' just for you."

Wade the boy pinches the bridge of his nose. He's clearly frustrated at his lack of options, but instead of arguing further, he just nods.

"Good." I grab both duffle bags and drape one from each shoulder. "I'm glad you came around to my suggestion. As a show of gratitude, I will carry your bag for a bit."

He nods again, more tired than annoyed. "Do you know where to find him?"

I laugh at his inexperience.

"Vampires are easy to track, Barguest. You just follow the scent of fresh blood."

Chapter Twenty-Three

Ellie

I wake up to the smell of burnt coffee and dusty file cabinets.

Sitting up, I recognize the faded green wallpaper of the Beowulf Brigade's central office. It looks like I've been sleeping on the spare cot kept in the back office for medical emergencies and the occasional late night of paperwork.

I glance at the cot's mattress, estimate the number of bloodstains I'll find if I remove the fitted sheet, and choose not to investigate.

When I stand, I notice four things. First, I'm wearing a pair of black joggers and a gray t-shirt with the words "Beowulf Brigade" and "Support Your Local Monster-Hunting Militia" printed across the front. Since I haven't seen either item of clothing before, it looks like I have Cyndi or the Colonel to thank for this outfit.

Second, my shoulder is aching. Really, my entire body aches, but the pain in my shoulder amplifies once I'm upright.

I pull aside my sleeve to inspect what should be a grotesque shoulder wound, but my skin is unmarked. The spots where Caliza stabbed me are sore, but otherwise healed.

Strange.

The third thing I notice is how long I've been asleep. Considering that our fight with Caliza and the gang happened around midnight, and it's still dark outside, I doubt it's been more than a few hours since I passed out. The wall clock above me corroborates the theory as it clicks steadily forward, reporting the time to be 4:31 a.m.

Finally, I recognize Cyndi and Bear standing by the window at the front of the office. Cyndi is back in her everyday attire of red-orange lipstick, bright green windbreaker, and electric blue combat boots—a feat she can easily achieve with illusion magic, though something tells me that the jacket is real. I've seen her wear it more than once, and she's the type to be sentimental about an item she actually owns.

Bear, on the other hand, is still a bear. His lumbering frame is seated on the ground next to Cyndi, comfortably insulated by his coat of white and tan fur while he munches happily on the pack of cheese crackers pinched between his claws.

The two stare wordlessly through the office's large picture window.

I hobble over to them, my muscles spasming from overuse, and take a spot beside Cyndi. Through the window, the flashing lights of squad cars and ambulances illuminate the parking lot in alternating streaks of red and blue and white. Colonel Adams stands with other members of the Beowulf Brigade, taking statements from the small gathering of kidnapped high school students, while local police officers record details for their reports and EMTs and paramedics inspect the wounded.

"Wow. That's a lot of people."

My voice comes out in a broken whisper, either from smoke inhalation or general vocal strain. It's probably the latter, after a night of growling as the striga.

Finally aware of my presence, Cyndi and Bear look over at me. Their expressions switch from surprise to relief.

"You're awake!" Cyndi yells, crunching my battered body into a hug.

Bear bites into another cracker with his oversized bear teeth. "Feeling better?"

"Yes. Sort of." I furrow my brow. "Why are you still a bear?"

Bear shrugs. "Not sure. Everyone else with a stone seems able to switch back and forth pretty easily, but I've been stuck like this since it happened. Cyndi thinks it's because I absorbed the stone, rather than just holding onto it, but that doesn't explain why the stone reacted to me that way."

"Well, why did you grab it in the first place?" I ask.

"Would you believe I was acting on instinct?"

Cyndi snorts, "I didn't think that was possible for you."

He lets out a rumbling laugh—an unexpected sound. "I didn't know what I was doing. I just remember watching Cyndi run herself ragged as she fought them off, and I wanted to help. It seemed like using the stone to our advantage was the only way to even the playing field, but I had no plan going into it. I just remember thinking, 'With this, maybe I can help,' before grabbing it. And now I'm stuck this way."

I nod, understanding.

"It's not so bad." He continues, "Being a bear is strangely relaxing, compared to being a human. Maybe once the initial transformation's effects wear off, I'll be more concerned. Still don't know how I'll explain this to my parents, though." He wrings his paws together, suddenly nervous. "Or how I'll get into college now." His eyes go wide as he looks at me and Cyndi. "Wait, do you think I'll have to quit the ice cream store?"

Cyndi laughs at him. "Oh, he's still the same old Teddy."

Bear glares at her. "No, no. We talked about this."

"But it's the most perfect name for anything that's ever existed!" she says in a singsong tone. "Theo the Teddy! The Bear who was a boy and became a bear! You're a real, living Teddy Bear!"

"I am not a Teddy Bear!" He lets out a roar, which stuns Cyndi into momentary silence.

After a beat, she crosses her arms and pouts in response. "You're no fun. And here I was, about to use my powers of perception to help you look the part of a real boy while you talk to your parents."

Bear's eyes narrow at her response. He pauses, thinking.

"Fine. You can call me Ted, if you wish. But don't call me Teddy Bear. I am not a plushie."

She bows to him. "Sir Ted, I'd be honored to help you speak to your folks about your predicament, if you require my assistance."

I shake my head at them and glance back at the crowd outside. When I do, I notice one of the girls speaking to Colonel Adams is pointing at me through the window. She looks particularly upset, waving her arms around in erratic lines.

My eyes meet Colonel Adams' through the glass, and I give her a slight wave. She responds with a concerned nod and makes a shooing motion, instructing me to stay away from the window and out of sight.

Following the colonel's order, the three of us leave the window and find seats where we can. Cyndi sits atop a desk, I fall into a rolling desk chair, and Bear finds a new spot on the floor, cheese crackers still in hand.

"So," I say, finally, "dare I ask what's happened since I passed out?"

"You do have a thing for falling asleep in the worst places," Cyndi laughs. "When I got back to the shack, the house was about to collapse from the fire, while you and Bear were just sitting there. Well, he was sitting there. You were unconscious."

"The fire!" My hands rub at my temples, overwhelmed. "How did that even . . . "

"Oh, they're still putting it out."

I blink at her. "What?"

"Yeah, a few trees caught on fire, and the U.S. Forest Service had to be called. The national guard might be coming out, too." Cyndi tugs on her ear, recollecting.

"I'm not surprised," Bear adds. "With how much oil they were burning, the fire had a lot of fuel."

I let out a breath. "Shouldn't we be back out there? Helping to put it out?"

Cyndi laughs and pats me on the back. "Maybe after a real night of sleep, but I doubt they'll let us. Besides, it's not like we started the fire. That was all Miss Raposa—er, Caliza."

"Yeah, but if we hadn't been there, then the fire wouldn't have started."

"If we hadn't been there, more people would have been hurt," Cyndi replies.

"Yeah, but Caliza is—"

"Gone." Bear interrupts, rubbing his paw with a grimace. As he touches it, his palm emits a faint purple glow. "Thanks to you."

The three of us sit quietly after that, considering the weight of our evening.

"Was Caliza right?" I ask, looking down at the carpet.

Cyndi shakes her head. "No."

"You don't even know what I'm going to say."

"I don't need to. Caliza—Miss Raposa—was objectively bad. I wouldn't trust anything she said. The world is better off without her."

"Okay, but," I chew on my cheek, still not looking at her, "I'm not sure if that makes it okay that I . . . "

Killed her.

I want to say the words, but I can't. I was there when the light faded from Caliza's eyes. As much as I want to blame her death on the striga, I took Caliza's life as Ellie.

"It just feels convenient to draw lines between ourselves, when we have more in common with her than the kids we rescued," I finally say. "Caliza kills some of ours, we kill some of hers. When does it end?"

Cyndi frowns. "What other option did we have? Should we have let her kill us?"

"No, but . . . "

"But nothing, Ellie." My friend, the fox, stands up. "Defending yourself is not a crime. Being a shapeshifter doesn't mean that you're evil or cursed." She balls her hands into fists and sits back down. "And punishing yourself for stopping that fox—an active threat to innocent people—doesn't help anything. And it's not going to make you feel any better."

"Fine." I sigh, too tired to argue. Cyndi can't understand how I feel about this. She wasn't there. She doesn't know how small Caliza looked when she died.

Satisfied with my answer, Cyndi asks, "Anyway, do you think Miss Raposa was ever a real person?"

Bear smiles. "You haven't figured it out yet?"

"Um," I glance at Bear, the bear, "and you have?"

He puts on his best, "Well, actually," expression, which, when seen on the face of a giant white bear, is rather silly.

"I started putting two and two together once I knew that Cyndi was a fox. Cyndi's last name is Renard, after all."

"And that is significant because . . . ?"

He turns to Cyndi. "Cyndi, why did you pick Renard as your last name?"

She perks up. "It's the French word for fox!"

Bear turns back to me. "You see?"

"All I see is Cyndi being way too obvious."

"Hey!" Cyndi crosses her arms to pout.

Bear laughs. "True. But also, Raposa is the Portuguese word for fox. And the first name Catherine can be shortened to Kit, which is another word for fox, so Catherine Raposa's real name was . . . "

"Wait." I hold up a hand. "Are you saying that her name was Miss 'Fox Fox' this whole time? Who does that?!"

Bear and I burst out laughing, while Cyndi watches us, confused.

"What's so funny? Calling herself Miss 'Fox Fox' makes sense, because she was a fox. I think it's clever."

Cyndi's comments just make us laugh harder, causing her to squint at us, still pouting. "You guys are being dumb. It's not that funny. And anyway, your name is Teddy Bear."

"Yes, but I didn't name myself, and I didn't know I'd ever turn into a Bear. Is it a point of pride for foxes to do this?"

"We just don't care about keeping secrets! I mean, I don't know about other foxes, but I like that other people know about my identity. I'm sure Miss Raposa enjoyed hiding in plain sight with her name like that."

As they bicker, I'm hit with a flash of warbled memories. They cross my mind with seconds of sharp clarity, but the order's all wrong.

"Maybe, but Caliza needed to hide her true identity so that she couldn't get caught."

I hold up a hand to interrupt. "Did I . . . earlier, before the shack caught fire. I think I know what happened, but it's . . . fuzzy."

Cyndi grins at me. "Watching you take them down was insane. In fact, Bear and I came up with a new name for you. Henceforth, you're to be known as," she lifts her hands above her head, displaying an imaginary banner, "Ellie, the Cleaver."

I roll my eyes. "Awesome."

Returning to her seat on the empty desk, Cyndi starts rooting around in its drawers. "No, really! Don't get me wrong, I've seen what you can do as the monster, but even in your human form, I don't want to get on your bad side." She winks. "You just have to get a handle on the monster stuff. It'll take time, but you'll get there."

She finds a permanent marker hidden beneath a stack of rubber bands and tosses the marker's cap aside before drawing a trail of dots up her forearm.

"I don't know if this is something I should be getting used to," I reply, looking down. "What if this striga-monster-thing isn't something I should be letting out at all?" I gesture to the white and tan bear sitting in front of us. "I mean, look at Bear. It's his first transformation and he's fine, not mauling us or causing property damage. He didn't seem to have any issue taking control, and neither did . . . "

I stop, biting back the name.

"Wade?" Bear offers.

"Um, yeah." I press against the mountain of emotions looking to surface. Anger, shame, sorrow—they line up, waiting for their turn to speak. "Speaking of which . . . "

I silence them all. I'm not ready to talk about Wade. Not with Bear, and maybe not ever.

"I'm sorry about . . . what I did." I finally manage.

Bear shakes his fluffy head. "Don't be. My brother died on Mount Washington, before Caliza even found him. That thing might be using my brother's face, but that doesn't mean it's him. And if I ever see him—it—again? Well, I might just tear the other arm off myself."

Cyndi and I exchange looks, but neither of us contradicts him. There's a good chance Wade is the person he claims to be, but if Bear needs closure, then maybe this is for the best.

Besides, we don't even know if Wade made it out of the woods alive.

You know he did.

Be quiet, whoever you are.

"And by the way," Bear bites into a new cheese cracker, "I don't have total control over my animal instincts yet. Though snacks have been helping." He smiles, gloating.

Cyndi throws her marker at Bear, hitting him in the cheek. "Speaking of snacks, I'm hungry. Let's go get some breakfast. Oh, and Ellie?" She shoots a pair of finger guns my way. "You're paying, since you still owe me."

I stand up, notice my lack of shoes, and sigh. "For what?"

"For rescuing those students from burning to death, for one."

The answer comes from a voice behind us, which turning reveals to be Colonel Adams. She smiles approvingly at Cyndi, my friend, the shapeshifting fox.

"You did good work today. You all did," she adds, nodding to me and Bear. "Cyndi, those kids would not be alive right now if you hadn't helped them to escape. Everyone is very thankful for what you did."

Colonel Adams opens her palm to reveal a silver plastic badge with the word "Deputy" written across it.

"This is the best I was able to find on such short notice, but the team wanted you to have it."

She clips the plastic badge to the front pocket of Cyndi's windbreaker. "I'm not sure how long you'll be sticking around town, but the Beowulf Brigade would love to have you as part of the team, giant fox or not."

Speechless for maybe the first time ever, Cyndi nods in response and looks away, overwhelmed at the gesture.

The colonel turns to Bear, who is still in his form as a bear. She sighs.

"Do I want to know?"

He shakes his head. "It's been a weird night."

"So it has." She lifts a second badge. "I have one for you, too, though I'm not sure where to clip it."

The white, fluffy bear opens his paw for Colonel Adams to place the toy badge, which looks like a coin atop his wide, leathery palm.

"Running into that burning house, even as a bear, could have killed you," she says. "But you risked your life for Mr. Clark's daughters, and though they were gone before you went into the cellar, their father is incredibly grateful—we all are. After interviewing a few members of the track team, it's likely that the girls were taken by Marquess DeLucia as thralls, which is the best lead we've had in a long, long time."

Bear looks away. "I'm glad that I could help, Ma'am. Are, um, my parents here?"

"They're outside, waiting for you. I mentioned your . . . new look. They're also looking for your brother, Wade. He wasn't in the group that came with Cyndi. Do you know where he is?"

We all shake our heads. Bear's eyes cloud over at the mention of his brother's name.

"All right. Well, tell your parents to call me if he doesn't show up in twenty-four hours."

Then the colonel turns to me, clicking her tongue.

"You just couldn't go on a normal ride-along with us, could you, Ellie?"

I offer her a half-hearted smile. "I wanted to. But things—"

"Happened," she finishes for me. "I can tell. Well, to honor your acts of bravery, I've also got one of these for you."

She gives me the final plastic badge in her hand, which is identical to the first two except for one detail. Beneath the word, "Deputy," someone's added two words with the help of a label maker: "The Cleaver."

Cyndi bursts out laughing. "I guess . . . word travels fast?"

I grimace at the moniker.

Is this the legacy I want?

"So it seems." Colonel Adams suppresses a smile, returning to her professional persona. "Ellie, you and I will have to talk more after this, but right now, I have two pieces of important news to share. One is good, the other . . . not so much."

"Okay . . . what's the bad news?"

"Bad news is that about a dozen witnesses reported that you are the giant monster we saw on my lawn the other night. A few of them confirmed your identity, and many more will testify that you're a threat to the community. And if what they're saying is true, then it's hard to argue the point."

Growing frustrated, I look down at my bare feet, still covered in mud from the night's conflict. Of course, Cyndi and Bear's shapeshifting would be accepted easily by the town. They turn into cute, recognizable creatures—the kind that people pay to visit in the zoo.

But what I become isn't cute. It's meant to destroy, or be destroyed.

I figured something like this would happen, but hearing it straight from the colonel hurts more than I expected.

I have no control over what happens to me now. Those with more power and influence than I get to make choices about my future, and there's nothing I can say or do to change that decision.

Is this how my mother felt when she was institutionalized?

The thought elicits a jarring laugh, which I let escape without thinking. Cyndi, Bear, and the colonel watch me with carefully controlled expressions.

Well, if my options are to be locked up or put down, I choose the latter.

I've seen what a cage can do to the human spirit.

Without meeting her gaze, I ask the colonel, "What could possibly be the good news?"

She softens, thankful to hear my voice instead of the monster's growl, and replies, "Your grandfather's awake."

Chapter Twenty-Four

Ellie

Hours later, I'm once again sitting in a waiting room at North Bern General Hospital with the colonel. Unlike our first visit, she's here on official Beowulf Brigade business. We had to request permission from the sheriff, the mayor, and the majority of town council members for me to see my grandfather, and this visit was only granted with the understanding that I'd attend a hearing immediately after.

I sigh impatiently, tapping my foot in time with the second hand of the waiting room's wall clock. According to my phone, the clock is seven minutes slow.

As if my frustration summoned her, a nurse suddenly peeks into the waiting room.

"Karlsen?"

The sound of Grandpa's last name makes me bolt upright, nearly running to the door. It hasn't even been a week since he and I last spoke, but between the house burning down, the murderous cult of shapeshifters, and my transformations, it feels like it's been weeks.

I follow the nurse at an aggressive pace, while Colonel Adams trails behind. She won't need to be in the room when I speak with Grandpa, but she is required to stand watch at the door. It's hard to find a loophole that lets me roam without a chaperone when the council members say things like, "Don't let her out of your sight, Colonel."

The nurse raps on my grandfather's door three times. Thankfully, we hear a grumbling voice yell from behind the door.

"Yes? Well, come in already!"

The nurse signals for me to wait for a minute and enters first. "I'm here to check on your pain, sir. How are you doing?"

"I'd be better if you gave me some more pills, already! The ones from this morning wore off hours ago!"

"I'm sorry to hear that, Mr. Karlsen. We can only administer this medicine every six to eight hours, but I can give you your next dose in about forty-five minutes." She leaves a cup of water on the table next to his hospital bed. "The doctor should be in to see you in a bit, so be sure to mention your pain levels to her, too. Oh, and," the nurse adds on her way out, "by the way, there's someone here to see you."

"Well, and who is it? Can't they see I'm a very busy man?" my grandfather gripes, leaning over to grab the water cup. He chugs the water, crushes the paper cup with one hand, and drops it into the waste bin.

With the nurse now gone, I hover in the open doorway.

"Grandpa?"

He meets my eyes, and immediately my grandfather's gruff exterior softens. "Ellie! Come over here!"

I run to him, instantly throwing my arms around his neck, and burst into tears.

"I'm sorry," I say, sniffling. "I just didn't think I'd ever talk to you again."

"Well, thanks for the vote of confidence, granddaughter." His chest rumbles with laughter. "But I wouldn't let something as simple as a house fire take me out. No ma'am."

"Everyone kept telling me that you weren't doing well, and that something poisonous bit you. I was so scared."

Grandpa pats me on the head and shushes me until I quiet down, like a child seeking comfort after a fall.

Then he settles back against the pillows propping him up. "All right, Ellie. Let's talk for a minute. The colonel called earlier and shared some information with me, but I want to hear it all from you."

I nod and push a chair closer to his hospital bed. Its armrests and seat cushion are covered in a tessellating pattern of blue and pink honeycomb, printed on gray polyester—a fabric that presses into my wrists with scratchy persistence.

Once I'm seated, I tell Grandpa about everything: my monster transformations, the salamander stone, the house fire, the conversations with my mother and Lord Vance, and anything related to Caliza and the stones that I can remember.

The only thing I omit from our talk is Wade. That string is too knotted to untangle with him.

Grandpa listens carefully, and despite his lack of immediate context and proof, he seems to believe me. When I'm finished, he steeples a pair of fingers in front of his mouth, drumming them against one another.

"So. You think I know something because your mother claims that you're cursed, and an evil fox confirmed a lot of the same details?" he asks.

I respond without hesitation. "Yes."

He avoids my gaze. "I don't know how digging into this will help anything."

"Please, Grandpa." I press. "If you know something, you have to tell me."

Letting out a tired sigh, he stares out of the window in his room before speaking.

"What you have to understand here is that I've held onto this since before you were born, to the point that your grandmother never even knew. I had to swear not to tell anyone, so that you wouldn't become . . . well, whatever it is you are, now."

My eyes widen. "What?"

A coughing fit erupts from Grandpa's chest, and it takes nearly a minute for him to steady his breathing. He wheezes slowly before speaking again. "I always hoped that the whole thing was a strange hallucination, but once you were born and your mother went off the rails, I had to stop lying to myself."

My grandfather looks directly into my eyes, then, and asks, "You know your father's car accident? The one that killed him?"

"Yes," I breathe, terrified of the answer I've waited sixteen years to hear.

But I have to know.

"He wasn't the only one in the car."

Wait, what?

"It was . . . your mother. She was in the passenger seat."

My eyes fill with tears again, overwhelmed at how close I'd come to learning anything about my father's disappearance, only to find what I'd already expected: this curse, like everything else, is about my mother and her unwavering cloud of confusion.

Grandpa continues, "I was the first one to arrive at the scene, and when I got there, your mother was in the front seat. She was six months pregnant then, so you were there, too, in a way."

The question leaves my mouth before I have time to think.

"Was she . . . were we okay?"

Shaking his head miserably, Grandpa opens his mouth but remains silent, unable to say more.

Lord Vance's description of the striga returns to me in an instant: "Born with two souls . . . when one dies, the other brings the body back to life and begins hunting animals or people for nourishment."

At the time, I'd corrected the vampire lord, saying that I wasn't dead, so I couldn't be a striga.

The vampire had asked, "Are you sure?" with a curious expression, hinting that I should know more.

It was the same, knowing expression that crossed Caliza's face as she taunted me:

"My, you are a broken thing, aren't you?"

My ears begin to ring, and the beast growls against the bars of its cage.

Let me out, Ellie.

Rather than allowing the striga to rampage, I grab the salamander stone from my pocket and let its residual heat radiate up my arm and into my chest. It blisters my palm, but I'm grateful for the pain as it quiets the monster's roar like a brand on fresh skin.

"All right," I say, finally. "So, we died. Then what?"

Grandpa reaches for his water cup with a shaky hand. When he finds it gone, he returns the seeking hand to his lap, unsure.

"I . . . pulled off to the side of the road and found your mother in the car. But not your father. He was gone, just gone." He blinks for a moment, reliving the scene. "And then, before I could dial 911, a boy stepped out from behind a tree."

"A boy?"

He nods.

"His skin looked blue, or maybe gray." Grandpa rubs his temples. "I remember his clothes were bright white, and his hair was long and dark."

I lean forward, tense. "Was he holding a violin?"

He shoots me a look of surprise.

"How could you . . . "

"I've met him, Grandpa. At least, I think so. The night of the house fire, there was someone like that in the woods, though I wouldn't call him a boy. He looked older, but he had a violin, and I was going to . . . " I hesitate, retracing the monster's memory of wanting to lunge forward and devour the man for dinner, and shudder. "I was going to hurt him. But I stopped when he started playing music. It," I pause, thinking, "it made me human, again."

Grandpa listens with a stunned expression, processing my words until he can recover his voice.

"Well, the boy I met brought you and your mother back to life."

I stop breathing.

"He . . . how?"

"It doesn't make sense to me, either. All I had to do was promise to protect you once you were born. If I failed in protecting you, the blue boy said that you would transform into an uncontrollable monster, because fairy magic requires a balancing of scales. So I made the deal."

I grip the scratchy armrests. I've seen insane, unimaginable things in the last few days, but even with all the evidence telling me not to discredit Grandpa's story, I don't want to believe him.

Resurrection from the dead . . . what kind of powers are we playing with?

"Anyway," Grandpa speaks again, unaware of the potential property damage, "once I shook hands with the boy in white, he played a song on his violin. That's when your mother, pregnant belly and all, was lifted from the wreckage and placed ten feet behind the broken car. All her wounds were healed, and she looked fine, physically. Completely whole again."

"And then he vanished?" I ask.

"And then he vanished."

The chair's wooden frame cracks beneath my grip, forcing me to pry my hand from the armrest. My fingers are gnarled and raw from the patterned upholstery.

"Grandpa, I don't . . . what do I . . . "

He places a hand on my shoulder. "Ellie. I never considered that my getting hurt would affect you so much. At the time, I didn't know that pledging to protect you for the rest of my life meant that once my life was over—or once I failed to protect you—you'd be stuck with this curse regardless. If I'd known all this then . . . " Grandpa sighs. "I don't know what the right choice was that day. I never imagined that saving my daughter's life would do this. I'm so, so sorry."

I stare out the window, not wanting to reply. But one thought hounds me.

"Does my mother remember the accident?"

"As much as she can remember anything."

"Do you think . . . "

He nods, sadly. "Even though she was brought back, she was never the same."

Minutes of tense silence pass between us. When I make no move to break it, Grandpa turns to the door.

"You can come in, Colonel, instead of hovering over there."

Colonel Simone Adams walks into the hospital room with a strained smile.

"Hello, sir," she says, trying to remain professional as my escort. "I just wanted you to have enough time to talk in private, but it's good to see you awake. Do you think you'll be back in fighting shape anytime soon?"

The colonel's question pulls Grandpa away from our tense conversation, and he chuckles.

"Hard to tell. Most likely, my fighting days are over."

"What will you do instead?" the colonel asks.

"Probably collect insurance money from the fire, to start. Speaking of which, tell me about the house. Is there anything left?"

I exhale a frustrated breath and step into the hallway. It's nice to know we're done discussing my existential crisis, so that we can get back to business as usual.

Grandpa's always been like this, though. He'd allocate a section of time to discuss emotional burdens, but once that time elapsed, there was to be no more wallowing or picking at the issue.

"You can't live in despair, Ellie," he'd say. "Sorrow shouldn't be anything more than a temporary holding place. You just have to find your way out."

A glance down the hallway reveals what I've suspected since we entered the hospital: we're being followed by two police officers. They're leaning casually over the nurse's circulation desk a few rooms down, sipping coffee from paper cups as if this is a routine visit. But their occasional looks my way confirms their real assignment.

Either Errolton's council members don't trust Colonel Adams to escort me back, or they expect me to cause a scene—one that might require more bullets than the colonel brought in her concealed weapon.

How do I find a way out of this, Grandpa? I'm not just surrounded by enemies on all sides. I'm being forced to fight while carrying the weight of all this new baggage.

What other choice do I have but to hulk out and destroy everything in my path?

Leaning against the doorframe, I review the details of Grandpa's story.

So, my mother and I aren't supposed to still be alive, but we are anyway. Only neither of our lives are free. She's stuck in her head, and I'm stuck in this body.

Is there any way to reverse the fiddler's magic? Is it possible to change these unpleasant side effects?

I bend over to stretch the growing cramp in my thigh, hoping the new point of view provides clarity, when I spot something silver on the ground near my foot.

It's . . . a pen?

I don't want to pick it up. The pen's owner will likely be back to claim it in a few minutes, and I've got to stop collecting things I find on the ground.

But I've seen this pen before.

A closer inspection confirms that the silver pen's repeating pattern of engraved violins, spiraling around its barrel, is identical to the one I'd borrowed from that nurse the last time I was here.

What was his name again?

I squint at the memory, hoping to visualize his nametag.

"Hal?" I whisper, curiously.

Maybe it's a sign, or maybe it's just a coincidence, but the pen offers me something I haven't had in a long time:

A possible way out.

I pocket the pen—remembering to place it somewhere separate from the salamander stone—and look back at the officers drinking coffee. Thankfully, their backs have been turned to me since the nurse asked them to sign in, so it's unlikely they saw me pick it up.

I walk back into Grandpa's room with a renewed sense of purpose.

Grandpa sighs at the colonel's report. "It's a shame to lose the house that way, but selling the land might help me to buy a place closer to North Bern, or to rent something small near the mental hospital. Gotta keep a close eye on Roen, after all."

"You could always live with Bingo, sir," Colonel Adams offers. "I hear he's looking for a roommate."

My grandfather lets out a loud guffaw before grabbing his side in pain.

"Oof. You couldn't pay me enough to live with that idiot." He glances back at me before asking, "Now, about that town hall meeting in twenty minutes. That's about Ellie, right?"

The colonel lowers her head.

"Unfortunately, sir."

"Well, I guess you should start walking over there now if you're going to make it in time."

"I guess so." Colonel Adams sighs regretfully. She looks at me, then, and says, "Ready, kid?"

"Oh," Grandpa interrupts her, "no. Ellie won't be joining you."

I lift my head, confused.

The colonel does the same. "Sir?"

"Colonel, I need you to march over to that meeting and report that Ellie transformed into a fearsome beast before your very eyes, and that you're lucky to have escaped with your life before she took off into the woods. If anyone needs a witness to your story, they can come to me."

"Pete," Colonel Adams starts, "now, you know—"

But my grandfather cuts her off, "Simone, she's my granddaughter. I can't let them hurt her."

Head on a swivel between us, the colonel purses her lips and looks me over.

"I suppose it's not very fair that vampires and giant foxes have been approved to stay in Errolton, only for your kind to be outlawed without even a trial." She sighs, conflicted. "Maybe it is best that Ellie disappears, in case the council's decision causes more bloodshed."

She doesn't specify who would be starting the bloodshed, but I understand her meaning. If they rule to lock me up or kill me, there's a good chance I'll lose control again, and no one wants that.

Well, maybe the striga does.

I glance up at the colonel with a suppressed smile. "Does this mean . . ."

"Thank you, Colonel." My grandfather grabs a piece of paper from his nightstand and scribbles a phone number on the back of it. "Ellie, I wish I could go with you, but if you're going to leave with your life, you have to go now.

"Head west," Grandpa says sternly before handing me the phone number. "This is the number for Marquess Bayard, one of Lord Vance's men. He'll be able to find you shelter out there, but you'll have to find him on your own, and you have to be away from Errolton and North Bern by nightfall tonight. Can you do that?"

I nod. "Cyndi is out front, waiting for us. If she's willing to come with me, then we can leave right now."

The colonel clears her throat, extending a hand to me. I pause for a second before shaking it as confidently as I can.

"I'm glad to have met you, Ellie," she says. "Please never come back to our town, or else I'll have to shoot you on sight."

"Noted," I reply.

"Oh and," the colonel opens her cell phone and texts me a contact file, "this is the number for my daughter, Ayanna. She's a sophomore at Minton College, which isn't too far from Bayard's camp. When Ayanna's not trying to switch her major from business to psychology, she and her friends are volunteering with a monster-human coalition. They advocate for the acceptance of 'other-beings' into society, like vampires. Anyway, she might be someone to talk to while you figure things out."

My grandfather laughs at the colonel.

"Well, well. Simone, are you getting soft?" He winks at me. "Smart of you to get on her good side."

Colonel Adams turns to my grandfather. "Sir, I just wish to ensure that the young lady finds food and shelter, so that she doesn't come looking in other people's homes for dinner." She pauses, lowering her voice. "But are you sure this is the best way to handle this, Pete? With all due respect, you haven't seen her transform. That thing she turns into . . . "

"I trust my granddaughter," he says. Then, to me, he smiles. "I think it's time you both left, though. Before things get hairier than they already are."

"I promise to check in once we get settled." I say, hugging him goodbye.

"I'll hold you to it, kid. Please, be safe."

The colonel leaves first, and once she's able to lead the law enforcement officers toward the back entrance, I turn and slip out the front.

Then I'm on the hospital's front steps, blinking into the sunshine.

Cyndi is there, as promised, but I'm surprised to see Declan standing proudly next to her. Saddled and ready to go, the dark courser harumphs at me as I approach.

I pet Declan's dark mane and give Cyndi an incredulous look. "How did you . . . ?"

"I figured we'd need a quick getaway. What better horsepower to use than that of an actual horse?"

I scrunch my eyebrows in confusion.

"Also," she laughs, "your grandfather called me before you got here. Told me that Declan was a going-away present for you."

I inspect the saddlebag to find my hunting knife alongside the remainder of last night's supplies and a few melted chocolate bars—Cyndi's additions, no doubt. Strapped in beside the pack is my grandfather's axe, still caked with salamander blood from the night before.

"Did he mention the axe, too?" I ask her.

"Nah, but c'mon. What's he going to do with it? And how could I possibly separate you from the weapon you wield so well?" She pantomimes chopping off the salamander's tail. "Thwack! Schwam! Ellie 'The Cleaver' Adair strikes again with her Nordic axe of might! I mean, the headlines write themselves."

I grab the reigns and start walking with Cyndi. "Hey, I'm not 'The Cleaver.' Though, 'Nordic Axe of Might' has a nice ring to it."

"See? And I've got tons of ideas for branding. First, we . . . "

I shove her. "Cyndi."

She glances over at me. "Yeah?"

"You don't have to come with me if you don't want to." I shake my head. "You're not the one being hunted; you shouldn't have to give up everything just for me. Not when you've already done so much."

Cyndi crosses her arms in false annoyance. "As if I'd let you run off without me. You're about to embark on a brand new adventure!" She lifts one arm toward the nearby trees, gesturing to the great unknown. "I mean, how could I possibly say no to that? And it's not like we're saying goodbye to Errolton forever. We're just saying yes to something else for a while, until it's safe to come back."

I blink back a few surprised tears. "Well then, thank you. I mean it. I wouldn't have gotten through this week without you."

Cyndi places a hand to her chest, pretending to be overwhelmed by my proclamation.

"A rare sighting of 'The Cleaver' expressing emotional vulnerability? I may swoon!"

I karate chop the air between us. "Hey. Don't test me."

"Ha!" Cyndi pops a piece of chewing gum into her mouth. "So, rogue wanderer. Where to?"

I take out my phone to check the compass, turn until we're heading west, and point "That way. But first," I pause, staring at the phone in my hand. "I think I need to make a call."

My friend the fox cocks her head to one side. "Right now? Do we have time for that?"

"I'll be quick," I reassure her, taking five quick steps away while I scroll through my phone, searching for the number I need. Once found, I dial the number.

The line rings three times before a woman answers.

"North Bern Community Mental Health. How can I help you?"

"Hi." My voice puffs into vapor, warning me of the cold night ahead. "I'd like to leave a message for Roen Adair."

I've always known that it's wrong to blame my mother for her mental illness, but there's a difference between knowing something and feeling it. It's impossible not to take it personally when she pushes me away, scared of the monster I'm becoming. And even if my mother couldn't control what happened to her any more than I can control what's happening to me, it still doesn't remove the anger and loneliness I've carried since I was a child.

"Sure thing. Can I have your name?"

"No, I . . . " I pause, working to organize my thoughts. "Just tell Roen that her daughter will be gone for a while. I don't know when I'll—when she'll be back."

For now, my pain is staying put, ready to be misplaced on the next person who breaks my heart—as if it's their fault I'm so desperate for love that I'll take the first hand offered to me.

I guess we have more in common than I thought, Wade. It's too bad the traits we share are linked to mortal decay and unresolved angst.

I clear my throat. "Tell her that . . . her daughter is going to get help. She's going to try, anyway. She's going to try to get better."

I don't know what "better" means, of course. There's no guarantee that chasing after a musical fairy in the woods is going to heal us or make us whole again. In fact, reversing his magic might cost us our lives.

But the lives we currently have are borrowed, cracked, and cursed. We've lost years to a freak accident and a magical promise, and I'd rather take a chance on something better than stay as we are.

Tears sting my eyes, and my throat grows tight as I speak into the receiver.

"And if her daughter, Ellie, can get better, then maybe Roen can, too. Anyway, tell her that."

Then, before the lady on the other end can ask me any follow-up questions, I hang up.

Wade's acceptance of Caliza's offer—his choice to become a barguest—meant that he was more willing to live a life of corruption and cruelty than to not live at all.

A week ago, I wouldn't have taken that deal. Not because of my superior morals or anything. I just wouldn't have fought that hard to stay alive, because I've never seen life as valuable or precious.

Living was just something to do, until I wasn't meant to anymore.

But now, I want to live. Looking death in the face has straightened my spine; it's made me want to fight against apathy and engage with the world, even if that world brings me nothing but more pain.

If this curse has shown me anything, it's that I've been pushing others away for too long. Sure, I've only attacked animals thus far, but it won't stay like that if I continue to see human life—mine and others—as disposable.

My actions are one of the few things I can control, monstrous curse or not. And if that means I'm meant to use the time and abilities I have to fight evil vampires or bring victims to safety or try to undo my family's curse, then I will.

I wipe the remaining tears from my eyes while I walk back to Cyndi and hope she can't see that I've been crying. She's too busy chatting with Declan to notice.

"As if humans taste anywhere near as good as gingerbread!" Cyndi snorts, patting the horse on his shoulder. "It's not even close, Dec. Gingerbread wins, hands down."

Declan neighs in response, though he's more interested in the sugar cube she's holding than the topic of conversation. When Cyndi realizes this, she rolls her eyes and feeds it to him.

"He's a snob," I say, smiling as I hop into Declan's saddle. "Only likes to talk about horse things."

"Well, that's got to change!" Following my lead, Cyndi begins shifting from the girl with red-orange hair to an oversized fox with red-orange fur. "Any idea when we'll have time to stop for a bite?" The fox grins.

"I wouldn't mind stopping at a Denny's on the way. Apparently, their chicken-fried steak is terrible."

Her grin widens. "Let's order two."

Epilogue

Roen

Let's do Chinese History for 400, Alex."

"All right." The host of Jeopardy, Alex Trebek reads the prompt in precise, dulcet tones. "Begun in 486 B.C., China's 'Grand,' this is the world's longest manmade waterway."

I tug at the loose strands of my hospital blanket and answer without looking up at the television. "What is the Grand Canal?"

Gretchen, an adjunct professor from Wisconsin, rings in nervously.

"What is . . . " Gretchen pauses before answering, "the Great Wall?"

Alex Trebek shakes his head. "No."

Another contestant rings in. Her name is Ara, and she's a caretaker from Mississippi.

"What is the Grand Canal?"

"And that is correct. Ara, you're in control of the board."

"I'll take Rhyme Time for 800."

It's not Gretchen's fault that I'm smarter than her. I've watched this same episode of Jeopardy four times today. It ran first at 3 a.m., then again at 11 a.m. and 2 p.m. before finally playing now, at 7 p.m. I've memorized enough answers to win the whole thing.

"A yearly instruction book." That's the next clue from Alex Trebek.

I speak at the same time as Ara, the contestant. "What is an annual manual?"

"800 points to Ara. Pick again."

There's a blue thread woven into the hem of my white blanket, but the color is fading at the corners. Probably from how many times it's been bleached. That's the nice thing about white bedding—no matter how many times someone pees or pukes in their bed, a little bleach should make things good as new.

Well, almost good as new. The blue dye in the hem only appears on one edge of this blanket now, so it's probably seen its fair share of bodily fluids.

"The Author Writes for 2000, Alex."

"And here is the clue: Stephen Dedalus is my name, Ireland is my nation. Clongowes is my dwelling place and heaven my expectation."

Gretchen, the adjunct professor trailing in third place, rings in quickly. "What is *Ulysses*?"

"No. We're looking for an author."

"Oh!" Gretchen nods. "Who is James Joyce?"

"Thank you, but too late. Sorry."

While 2000 points are subtracted from Gretchen's score, Ara rings in.

"Who is James Joyce?"

"Correct. Go again."

I lift my eyes just in time to see Alex Trebek award the points to Ara. In response, Gretchen's face pulses with fury right before she lunges at the podium to her left, which contains Ara, the one who stole her answer.

The adjunct professor tackles her opponent to the ground and viciously bites into her shoulder, all while flashing a pair of bloody vampire fangs to the camera.

The cameras pan away from the gore just in time to show Alex Trebek lifting a wooden stake from behind his podium. Weapon in hand, he looks straight at the camera with the grace of a professional.

"We'll be right back after a word from our sponsors."

I laugh to myself, sure that this is just another stunt being pulled to improve their ratings. The same thing happened on The Price is Right last week, when a werewolf got angry during a game of Plinko and attacked three audience members. Allegedly, anyway. I'm pretty sure that was just a regular guy in a wolf costume.

Still, watching a vampire get angry because of a game show, to the point of savagely attacking another contestant, bugs me. It's reminding me of something, though I don't know what.

I tug at my eyelashes in frustration. Why can't I remember?

Tossing the blanket aside, I walk over to the bathroom mirror. My eyes are red and irritated, and my face looks gaunt—worse than it was last week, though I guess I stopped eating most of my meals a few days ago.

That's when I notice the three sticky notes stuck to the mirror.

The first one reads:

But Jonah had gone down into the lowest parts of the ship,
had lain down, and was fast asleep.

Right. Jonah. That's me.

Jonah ran away and now she's lost in the belly of the whale while Elijah's busy pouring water on the altar because she's so sure fire will come down without a match.

Elijah, Elijah, your father loved us. Until we were corrupted by the stench of death, anyway.

Please, find the words I'm hiding from you.

The next note reads:

Pick me up and throw me into the sea;
then the sea will become calm for you.
For I know that this great tempest is because of me.

You should have been brought to heaven in a chariot of fire but they wouldn't take you like they won't take me. I tried to fix it, tried to jump into the sea for you, but now I'm trapped and I can't do anything from in here.

I don't know why, but you're the one meant to fix things.

Only you can bring us back from the dead, so bring us back bring us back bring us back

The final note says:

THERE'S A MAN OUTSIDE

Oh no no no no no

Not again.

My hands begin to shake as gray and purple smoke billows into my room through an open window. The windows lock from the inside, and the attendants are the only ones with keys, but that never seems to matter.

He always gets in.

Acknowledgments

This book—like countless others—was born from the isolation of 2020's COVID-19 pandemic. It is this author's best attempt to wrestle grief and depression to the ground and declare, "No more."

Ellie's story would not exist without the love and support of my husband Jon, who makes space for me to write when the world becomes too much, as well as family and friends who are willing to listen to half-baked plot lines and character descriptions while I brainstorm.

Special thanks to my editor Julie Hutchings and beta readers D. M. Domosea and Robin McDonough, for their invaluable insight and feedback. Also thanks to Io Nomycin for the amazing illustrations and to Cortney Donelson, Amber Parrott, Gayle West, and the team at Morgan James Publishing for believing in this story.

Finally, thank you Drew Cochran, for creating *The Epic of Dreams: Unbound Fantasy Roleplay*, with pages of bestiary entries that inspired many of the monsters Ellie meets on her journey.

About the Author

Heidi Nickerson is a speculative fiction writer who strives to tell irreverent stories with introspection, humor, and action-packed pacing. When not writing about monsters, Heidi creates, reviews, and edits marketing material for Morgan James Publishing. She currently resides in Richmond, VA, with her husband, young children, and grumpy cats.

About the Illustrator

Io Nomycin is a freelance illustrator focusing specifically on visual storytelling and environmental art. She has a bachelor's degree in interactive media and mostly works on video games, RPGs, and book illustrations. She currently resides in Germany, but her art is mostly inspired by the nature and culture of Finland, where she was born and lived for most of her life.

CPSIA information can be obtained
at www.ICGtesting.com
Printed in the USA
JSHW081937150323
38990JS00002B/337

9 781631 959967